SHANNA SWENDSON

NLA Digital, LLC
1732 Wazee Street, Suite 207
Denver, CO 80202

This book is a work of fiction. The characters, incidents, and dialogue are drawn from the author's imagination and are not to be construed as real. Any resemblance to actual events or persons, living or dead, is entirely coincidental.

Production Manager: Lori Bennett
Cover art and book design: Angie Hodapp

ISBN 978-1-62051-248-7

To all the librarians who fell in love with *Rebel Mechanics*
and shared it with readers.

CONTENTS

AUTHOR'S NOTE

This novel is a work of alternate history. Adding magic to the mix meant that events didn't play out the way they appear in history books. Some things are entirely different, and some things are happening at different times or in different places. Figuring out where the real history might fit in is part of the fun.

NEW YORK CITY
1888

REBELS FLEE CITY, ESCAPE MAGISTER PERSECUTION

BY LIBERTY JONES

THE REBEL MECHANICS MADE A DARING LAST-minute escape from a magister sweep, safely removing all their machines from the city, one step ahead of the redcoats.

Acting on a tip from a well-placed source, the rebels vanished as if by magic, leaving the authorities baffled. Imperial soldiers made a house-by-house search of the entire neighborhood surrounding the Mechanics' alleged headquarters in an attempt to round up the rebel leadership and their machines, but the wily Mechanics outwitted them yet again.

WHERE ARE THE REBEL MECHANICS? LEADERS VOW TO CONTINUE FIGHT

BY ELIZABETH SMITH

IN THE WEEKS SINCE THEIR DRAMATIC ESCAPE, the Rebel Mechanics have set up headquarters in an undisclosed location outside the city, out of reach of the British authorities.

The leaders say that while the rebels and their astonishing machines may be out of sight, they are even more focused on the cause of liberty. "The revolution is coming, you can count on that," said one rebel leader, who must remain anonymous for his own safety. "We just believe we can prepare better without having to watch our backs all the time. When it starts, you'll know it."

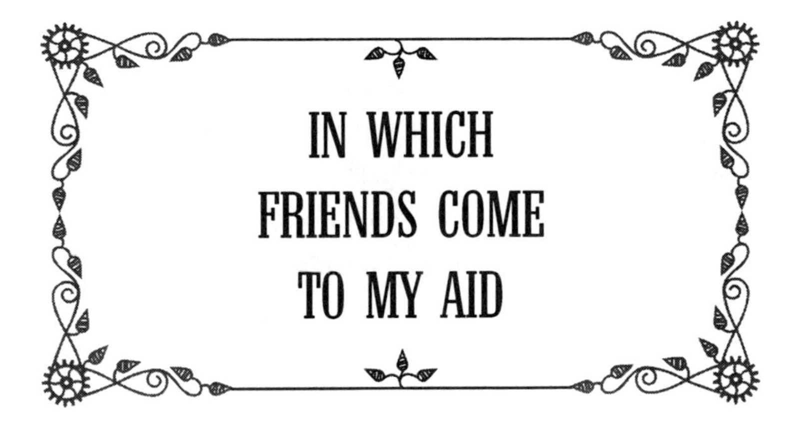

IN WHICH FRIENDS COME TO MY AID

I made my way through the greenmarket, pausing from time to time to examine a shiny gourd or plump pumpkin. After chatting with a farmer, I purchased some apples and tucked them into my basket. I hadn't noticed anyone watching me, but it never hurt to be cautious and act as normal as possible, these days. Finally, I reached the stall that was my true destination.

"How are you this morning, miss?" the young Indian woman working at the stall said in her musical accent as I approached. Someone would have had to be watching us very closely, indeed, to catch her minute flicker of a wink.

"Very well, thank you," I replied with a polite nod as I moved past the stall.

She jumped out in front of me, impeding my progress. "I have many very fine vegetables and exotic fruits to offer you today, miss," she said. "My biggest customer is not buying nearly the same amount. And you benefit."

"How fortunate for me," I said with a weary sigh, giving in and stopping at her stall.

As we bent together over the bins of fruit so she could help me make my selection, she whispered, "The military has dramatically reduced next week's order. Unless they've found a different supplier, it looks as though they might be moving out."

"Thank you," I whispered. We completed our transaction, and I visited a few more stalls before leaving the market to head farther downtown, toward Chinatown. There I went to a particular laundry and made sure the right person was behind the counter before I took the paper-wrapped bundle out of my basket.

The girl working there was about my age, with a sleek, fat braid hanging over her shoulder, tied with a red ribbon that was the only spot of color on her otherwise gray outfit. She saw me and smiled, but her smile faded instantly when the door opened behind me and another patron entered—a military officer in uniform.

Disregarding me entirely, he advanced straight to the counter and demanded, "Is my order ready?"

"Your name, please?" she said meekly, exaggerating a Chinese accent I knew she didn't normally have. He handed her a ticket, and she scurried to the back room. Only then did he appear to notice my presence. I gave him a half smile of acknowledgment that didn't invite further interaction, to which he responded with a cursory nod.

The girl returned with a bundle and gave it to him, bowing deferentially. He went to the end of the counter to open the bundle and inspect its contents.

It looked as though he would be there for a while, and if I tarried longer without conducting any business, I would raise suspicions, so I approached the counter with my bundle.

"So sorry," the girl said. "It will take one week. Very busy right now. Officers choose us to do their laundry." She flashed a brief smile at her other customer as she said it and squared her shoulders proudly.

"I suppose that will be all right," I said. "I know the military must take precedence."

She took my bundle and made a show of filling out a ticket for me, even though we both knew that the "laundry" consisted of a stack of banknotes that would be passed on to the underground rebel movement. I put the ticket in my purse, and the soldier managed to get to the door just in time to open it for me. I nodded a thanks and went on my way.

That had been a close call, but I had to grin at the thrill of passing money from the Masked Bandits to the Rebel Mechanics right under the nose of a British officer without him having the slightest idea of what was happening. Now, in the aftermath, my heart started racing. If I'd followed Henry's instructions, I would have left rather than take the risk, but I thought it would have looked even more suspicious if I'd entered a laundry without handing over or retrieving anything.

Now, though, my thoughts were on the intelligence I'd

gathered. If the officers were suddenly sending out a lot of laundry that they needed done immediately and if the army wasn't ordering as much food, that surely meant they were removing some of the troops from the city. Perhaps since the departure of the Rebel Mechanics and their machines the authorities had decided that the rebellion had been quashed.

That sounded like a story to me, so I went straight to a coffee shop on Greenwich Square. It was a popular gathering place for the students at the nearby university, but in recent weeks it had been filled with soldiers who were being quartered in the university halls. Today, though, it was much quieter. The waitress who met me at the door gave me a knowing nod before escorting me to a table.

"It seems so quiet in here today," I said. "What happened, did you drive away all your customers?"

"It sure seems like it," she said. "Maybe all the soldiers wanted tea."

To be perfectly honest, what I wanted was a nice cup of tea, but thanks to taxes on tea, that was something the rebels never drank, out of protest. I supposed it would have been a good cover to order it, but I might have lost the loyalty of the waitress if I'd done so. As deep as I was in the rebel movement, there were nuances I still struggled to grasp.

Instead, I ordered lemonade and a slice of cake. While I waited for the waitress to return with my food and drink, I took a couple of sheets of paper and a pencil out of my basket and went to work. I doubted that any of the other patrons were watching me, but if they were, I thought I must look for all the world like a young woman writing a letter.

What I wrote was a short news article speculating on the departure of the British troops and what it meant for the rebel movement. It was close to the deadline for the next day's edition, but I thought I could make it if I hurried. I finished the article while absently sipping lemonade and nibbling cake, gave it one last read, and folded it up, placing it against my palm as I put my gloves back on.

Now all I needed to do was drop it off and then I could return home before the girls were through with their art and music lessons. I left the café and turned toward the hat shop that was the nearest drop-off point for the rebels.

Before I reached the end of the block, I had the strongest feeling that I wasn't alone. Although I had that itchy sensation between my shoulder blades that told me someone was watching me, I didn't dare turn around to look. It was absolutely imperative that I gave no one any reason to suspect me. I was merely an anonymous young woman, out running errands. Now I regretted my impatience to write the article. If I'd waited until I was home and left it at the nearest drop, the article might have been delayed a day, but I wouldn't have had anything incriminating on me.

I stopped at a street corner and waited to cross to the opposite side. Looking both ways for oncoming traffic allowed me to see whatever—or whomever—was behind me. The sidewalk wasn't so crowded that any one person could blend into the background, and there was one person who didn't quite fit in this part of town, which was mostly populated by students, and lately by soldiers. He had the look of a government functionary: gray suit, bowler hat, nondescript face. I thought he might have been in the café, but he was so unremarkable that I couldn't truly be sure. He stood nonchalantly against a lamppost, but I'd have bet he was the one watching me.

But why would he follow me? I hadn't done anything suspicious. All I could think was that one of my contacts was being watched, and therefore anyone else who dealt with her would also be watched, at least for a little while. Had he followed me to the café, or had I only come to his attention there? My real worry was that he had followed me from the laundry. If he knew what was in that bundle, I couldn't let him connect me with my employer.

To throw him off my trail, I darted across the street at the first sign of a clear path and entered the first shop I encountered. It was a candy store, which seemed innocuous enough, and the shopgirl wasn't part of my network. I bought a couple of pennies' worth of candy for the children and left the store. Out of the corner of my eye, I noted that the man in gray was still there.

There was a ribbon shop nearby, but I was known there, for my employer rather than my covert activities. I passed the shop, going instead to a different one that the Lyndon family didn't patronize. There I bought a yard of blue ribbon I thought might look nice with my hair, if I ever wore it down rather than in a no-nonsense bun.

As I came out of the shop, before I could look for the gray man, I thought I saw another familiar face—or, rather, familiar hair, a shock of bright red curling out from under a shabby top hat. *Colin?* I wondered. But he was out of town with the rest of the Rebel Mechanics. I walked right past him without a second glance, hoping that if it was, indeed, Colin, he would get the message and not speak to me.

At the next intersection, I found that the gray man was still there. I didn't dare drop off my article or go home while I was being watched. Ahead of me I saw a shop that I thought might do the trick. No gentleman would follow a lady into a lingerie shop. To be honest, I was a little bashful about entering such a place.

The air in the establishment was lightly scented with lavender, which calmed my nerves somewhat. All around me were concoctions of lace and silk. There were corsets and petticoats, as well as nightgowns that made my serviceable muslin gown look rather dowdy in comparison.

The shopgirl approached me with a grin. "Let me guess, you've got a man problem, and you want something to make you feel better."

She was one of ours, so I said, "It's more like I want to get rid of one."

"He won't dare come in here, so have a seat, and let me show you our latest range of silk stockings."

I wasn't sure how much time I spent looking at stockings

I would never buy, but I thought that anyone waiting for me would be bored by the time I decided on a new pair of wool stockings. When I left the shop with a ribbon-wrapped parcel, the gray man was nowhere to be seen.

I made haste for the hat shop, where I slid the article out of my glove and passed it to the milliner. "I suppose I'd better buy something for show. I've been followed," I said. "I think I lost him, but I'm not sure."

"I'll fix that right up for you," she said, removing my hat. She put a new ribbon on it, with a curling bow to the side. "There, that should be an obvious enough difference that even a man will notice it."

There were more soldiers outside when I left than there had been before, but they didn't seem to pay any attention to me. I passed the gray man on the next corner. I was a little safer now that I had nothing incriminating on me, but I still preferred to get away without being questioned. If they got my identity, that would lead them to Henry, and his clandestine activities were far more dangerous than mine.

Then I noticed that there were a lot of other young women on the street, all dressed similarly to me. They came from every angle, shopping baskets like mine over their arms. There weren't so many that it looked like an organized meeting, but as I moved toward a more crowded neighborhood, it became slightly more difficult for anyone to tell exactly which soberly dressed young woman was which.

I heard a loud, "Oh! Excuse me, sir! Oh dear, I seem to

have spilled it on you. I'm so very, very sorry," behind me and resisted the temptation to look back. A moment later, there was a shrill scream and a cry of, "Help! Police!" from a side street. Several soldiers went running.

I took advantage of the distraction to duck into a bookshop, where I told the yellow-haired man at the counter, "I need a getaway."

A man lurking in the shop came forward and unlocked a door that led to steep stairs into a basement. This time, I wasn't blindfolded. As many times as I'd used the secret subway, there was no longer any point in hiding its location from me. I felt my way through the darkness to the station.

The station was nearly empty, just a few people keeping the system running. A car waited at the platform. "Only a couple of stations uptown, please," I said as the operator helped me board. "I need to look like I'm getting home a normal way."

The car shot forward, and in no time at all it stopped. I felt my way through a dark passage from the station to a staircase, where I rapped on the door at the top in a certain pattern. The door opened, and I found myself in a florist shop. "It looks like it's clear here," the florist said, handing me a bouquet to add to my basket.

I strode confidently out of the shop and hailed a magical horseless cab. Only when I was inside and on my way home did I let myself relax at all. There was still a chance that the authorities could be waiting for me at home, but they would have no evidence against me unless that soldier at the laundry had confiscated the bundle I'd dropped off there. Otherwise, it appeared that my growing network had done its job.

Six weeks ago, I'd never have imagined I'd have so many friends who would jump into action to aid me. I'd had no one, not even family. My network of friends was rather odd in that I knew none of their names, and few of them knew mine. It was safer that way. But we could count on each other, and we all usually went unnoticed because we were the invisible people: the shopgirls, laundresses, governesses, maids, and others whom society relied upon but otherwise didn't notice.

The cab stopped in front of the Lyndon mansion across from Central Park, and Mr. Chastain, the butler, was immediately there to pay the fare and help me down from the carriage. I barely made it into the house before Lord Henry Lyndon, my employer, accosted me in the foyer and pulled me into the drawing room.

"Where have you been?" he demanded, gripping my shoulders tightly. "I was expecting you an hour ago. Did something go wrong? I knew I shouldn't have sent you."

"I was a little worried about someone who might have been following me, but I seem to have successfully eluded him," I said.

Henry went pale, and his grip on my shoulders tightened. "You were followed?"

"Briefly. But my behavior while he followed me was above reproach, and with some help I was able to get away.

It would be impossible for him to have tailed me home, and by the time my friends were through with him, he would have no way of knowing which girl he was watching." I was nearly as nondescript as my follower had been, so I was sure the other girls with baskets had thrown him off the trail.

He released his hold on my shoulders, but he still stood very close. "Why would you be followed?"

"It's the café," I guessed. "It's a known meeting place, and I was perhaps too familiar with the waitress. I'll have to avoid it in the future."

"The café?"

"I stopped to write an article. It seems that at least some of the troops quartered in that area will be leaving soon."

For a moment, I was afraid that Henry's worry would turn to anger. My errand had been to deliver the money for him. Everything else I'd done had been on my own. He knew about my other activities and generally endorsed them, but perhaps I shouldn't have jeopardized his mission.

"You weren't followed from the laundry?"

"If I was, there was no evidence whatsoever of any other ill-advised behavior," I assured him.

"I'm going to quit using you as a courier like that," he said as the color gradually returned to his face. "It's too dangerous, and I can't ask you to take that risk for me."

"Well, since you've stopped pulling off armed robberies for the time being, you shouldn't have much need of a courier for awhile," I shot back.

He grinned. "Touché, Miss Newton. But really, Verity, we must be careful."

"I'm always careful. And as I said, I have friends looking out for me."

I thought for a moment that he might say something more—he always seemed to be on the verge of saying more to me when we talked like this—but a small figure flew into the room. "Miss Newton! Did you bring me anything?" Olive cried out as she threw her arms around me.

"Olive, Miss Newton is under no obligation to bring you anything when she runs errands," Henry said, scolding his niece.

"No, I am not," I said, unable to restrain a smile. "But on this one occasion, I did happen to pass a candy store." I took the bag of candy out of my basket and handed it to her. "But you must share with your brother and sister."

"Flora won't want any. She's watching her figure," Olive said with all the disdain a six-year-old could muster for a teenage sister.

Before she could run off with her treasure, Henry cleared his throat. She stopped, her eyes widening in horror. "Oh! Miss Newton, I'm so sorry I forgot to thank you. Thank you so much. You are so kind." She opened the bag and held it toward me. "Would you like one?"

"No, thank you, Olive. But it was very polite of you to offer, and you are quite welcome for the treat."

She ran off, shouting, "Rollo! Miss Newton brought us candy!"

"I'm afraid some refresher lessons in deportment are in order," I said.

"You didn't have to do that," Henry said. "I don't expect you to purchase treats for the children."

"I went into the candy shop to distract my follower," I said. "It's one that has no rebel ties that I know of, so I knew it wouldn't be suspicious, and if I went into the shop, I had to purchase something. You give me more than enough money for these errands."

"I couldn't possibly pay you what these errands are worth to me. But this is the last one."

"You know that won't stop my actions for the cause," I said, perhaps a bit too defiantly, considering he was my employer.

"Yes, but then it's not on my head if something awful happens to you."

"I know what I'm doing, and I know full well the danger I face."

"You didn't at first. I should never have sent you on those errands without warning you."

"I already knew—or guessed."

"But *I* didn't know that, which means I sent a girl unknowingly into danger on my behalf."

It was an argument we'd had a few times since all our secrets had come out. I'd suspected he was the leader of the Masked Bandits, but had learned it for certain at the same time he'd learned I was spying for the Rebel Mechanics. Later, he'd learned I wrote for the unauthorized rebel newspaper under the name Liberty Jones. As he'd joked, the foundation of our friendship was the fact that we had enough information to utterly destroy each other.

It was only later that evening at dinner that I realized I'd forgotten to tell him about my possible sighting of Colin, but since I wasn't sure I'd actually seen Colin, I decided I didn't need to tell him, and I didn't get an opportunity to speak privately with him after dinner.

The following day was more routine for me: Olive and I walked Rollo to school, then spent the morning doing lessons. In the afternoon, Flora joined us for some supervised reading mandated by Henry, who wasn't content with letting his oldest niece be little more than a pretty face. Olive and I retrieved Rollo from school, and after going over his homework with him, I got a free hour while the children had art and music lessons.

As I usually did, I headed into the park across the street. It was a fine, crisp autumn day, and I reveled in my momentary freedom. My job was so much easier and more pleasant than those worked by most of the other members of my network, and I got to live in a mansion, but there were times when working with the children strained my patience. I knew I was a good teacher, and I was qualified, but it wasn't quite the profession I would have chosen if I'd had any options.

Not that I had any intention of leaving. I loved the children and felt like a part of the family. And then there was Henry…

I was lost in thought, musing over my employer and his unique temperament, his lovely blue eyes, and the way he was so different when he was alone with me, when I heard a familiar voice call out in a hiss just above a whisper, "Verity!"

I whirled and saw a man lurking under a tree a few feet from the footpath. He wore a somber dark suit and a bowler hat, but I recognized Alec Emfinger, the man who'd recruited me into the Rebel Mechanics under the guise of a suitor.

So, the rebels really were back in town. But why?

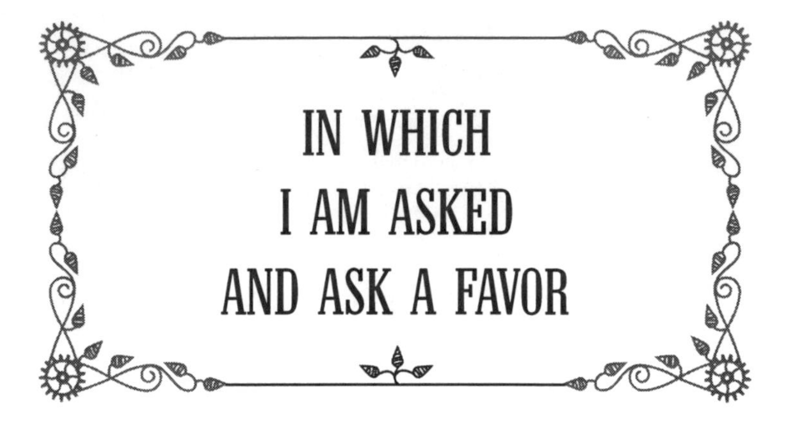

IN WHICH I AM ASKED AND ASK A FAVOR

So many emotions surged through me that I wasn't sure which one to express. I was glad to see him, even if just to know he was safe. But I also remembered my anger at him for letting me act like a lovesick schoolgirl when he was merely reeling me in to his cause. And I was curious as to what he was doing back in the city after he'd made such a narrow escape, thanks to Henry and me.

I decided it was best not to express anything at all, especially while we were in public. That required me to steady my breathing and release the fists I'd formed. "Why, Mr. Emfinger, what a surprise to see you here," I said, acting like he was any acquaintance I'd happened to encounter in the park. "I didn't realize you were back in the city."

He moved closer to me and said in a voice too low for passersby to make out his words, "It's the machines and the group they wanted. They hardly notice the individuals."

"So you've come back? I thought I saw Colin yesterday."

He smiled. "Yes, and he's rather put out that you snubbed him."

"I was in a situation in which I thought it best not to draw attention to him—or to myself."

He raised an eyebrow and smiled. "So he gathered. Otherwise, you know him. He'd have made a scene."

I couldn't help but smile in response at the mental image, but then I remembered what I'd asked. "You didn't answer my question about being back in town."

"I make frequent visits."

I gave my best impression of the kind of trilling, lighthearted laugh Flora and her friends used when they attempted to sound witty at parties. "And you just *happened* to run into me in the park when I was taking an afternoon walk. What an extraordinary coincidence!" More seriously, and with an edge to my voice, I said, "What is it you need, Alec? I thought you'd learned that it's best to be straightforward with me. We're long past the point of playing coy games with each other."

He offered his arm to me. "Would you care to join me for a turn around the park, Miss Newton?" In a whisper, he added, "For appearances."

I stared at his arm for a long moment, as one might contemplate a potentially venomous snake, before I took it, and we began strolling. "We're doing quite well," he said, speaking softly and tilting his head toward mine in the manner of a young man courting his girl. "I won't tell you exactly where we are, but we're out of reach of the British government. We're still working on our machines, and we believe we've proved that they might help equalize us against the magisters, so the revolution stands a chance of succeeding, but it will take far more than one or two steam engines and an airship. What we have are merely prototypes. We need to produce dozens—even hundreds—of them in order to make a difference."

"You'd need a factory," I said.

"Yes, and raw materials. Lots of steel. Coal for furnaces. People to do the work. All that requires funding. Since we're doing this in secret as part of a revolution, we can hardly go to the bank for a loan, and we won't be selling anything we make, so there will be no profits for investors, until perhaps after we win and we turn these machines to civilian uses. We'll need them then for power other than magic once we kick the magisters out."

"Wars are rather expensive. That's part of why taxes are so high. Just maintaining a military presence throughout the Empire must take tremendous amounts of money."

"Exactly. What we want to do will take almost as much money as running a small country, but we can't collect taxes to pay for it. We're all poor—part of the reason we're rebelling—so we can't fund ourselves. Which is why I wanted to talk to you."

I was afraid I knew what he would ask of me, but I pretended I didn't and said, "You think an article in the newspaper might help?"

"Not to the extent we need. I thought you might talk

to your employer. The Masked Bandits might be the only ones who could raise that kind of capital, and they've already been helping fund our activities."

I stopped abruptly and faced him. "Absolutely not." I surprised even myself with how vehement my protest was. "Do you realize the amount of money you're asking for? Robbing a train a day wouldn't be enough, and that would be far too dangerous. They'd surely be caught. As a matter of fact, the Bandits are taking some time off because one of them did get caught. They need to throw off suspicion. I can't possibly ask Lord Henry to take that kind of risk."

"I think he should get the chance to say no for himself, don't you?"

I had protested when Henry didn't want me running errands for him because he wanted to keep me safe. Was my refusal to even ask him if he was willing or interested the same thing? "I'll talk to him," I said, grudgingly. "He may have other ideas. I know he's as committed to revolution as you are, and he'd be pleased that you're finally being practical about it instead of just making a lot of noise."

"That's all I want, for you to ask. Even if he has nothing to offer but advice, we'd be grateful. It would be that much more we owe him."

"It is interesting how much more you like the magisters when they have something to offer you," I remarked dryly.

"Well, maybe if more of them were as generous as your Lord Henry, we wouldn't be plotting revolution. And maybe there are a few who aren't bad sorts."

"Didn't you once say something about how magic corrupts people?"

"Maybe not everyone, but look at the evidence all around us." His gesture encompassed the mansions nearby and the magical roadsters humming down the park paths with little regard for pedestrians.

I bit my lip to keep myself from saying anything as we resumed strolling. He still didn't know about my magical heritage, and I wondered what he would think about it. He was willing to ask Henry for help, but I doubted he'd ever see Henry as a friend. If he cared at all for me now, I wasn't sure that esteem would continue if he knew my secret.

"I'm sure you'll manage to find me to learn what Lord Henry has to say," I said, my voice sounding stiff and a little frosty.

"And you know where to go so I can find you. Failing that, you know the usual places to leave word."

"Do you want the article, as well? I know most of your followers are poor, but pennies can add up."

"Write something and we'll see." He turned to face me, looking earnestly at me in the way that used to set my heart aflutter—which had been carefully calculated to achieve that effect, I reminded myself. There was still a tiny involuntary reaction, because few girls are entirely immune to being looked at that way, but it wasn't the same. "I do appreciate this, Verity."

"Yes, I'm very useful."

He groaned. "I know how it sounds. But you really

were heaven-sent. More than that, though, you're a truly amazing girl who can make the most of your opportunities. I feel lucky to know you."

I knew he meant well, but he was incapable of expressing affection for me without mentioning my use to the cause. There wasn't much point in pushing to get more from him, not if I wanted him to be honest. "And I am glad I met you because you opened my eyes," I admitted. I deliberately removed my hand from his arm. "I must be going. We'll talk again."

It was probably just my imagination, but it seemed to have grown chillier since I entered the park. Had an autumn wind blown through, or was it merely my nerves giving me chills? I pulled the collar of my coat closer around my neck and hurried my pace.

As much as I wanted to leave Henry out of it, I felt honor-bound to at least pass on what Alec had said. It would be wrong to withhold the information. But would Henry be sensible? He wouldn't have done things like rob trains and government offices in the first place if he hadn't been somewhat predisposed to taking risks.

I already had an appointment with Henry that evening. We met regularly after the younger children had gone to bed, supposedly to discuss the children's academic progress. The truth was, ever since he'd learned about my magical heritage, he'd been teaching me magic.

I wasn't sure what good it would do. My powers must

have come from an illicit liaison between my mother and a magister, since no one else in my family had magic. My very existence as a half-breed was illegal, and I wasn't sure what would happen if anyone found out about me, but it likely wasn't good. I didn't dare use magic in public because another magister could detect when magic was being used nearby. Henry was the only person who knew, and he believed that anyone who had a gift needed to develop it. Given the nature of our activities, he thought I should know how to fully use my powers.

After dinner, I helped Olive get ready for bed and read her a story. As I left her room, I ran into Henry in the hallway. In a whisper designed to be heard by any eavesdroppers, he said, "May I have a word with you, Miss Newton? I would like to discuss Rollo's latest report from school."

"Of course," I replied, matching his tone. He escorted me into his study and closed the door. I had to move a pile of books in order to sit. Henry's study was a carefully cultivated image of chaos, with enough bugs pinned to cards on the wall and spiders in jars to keep the housemaids out of the room if they dared disobey orders to stay out. This was the nerve center of the Masked Bandits and the place where Henry hid his most incriminating secrets. It was also the one place at home where he dared drop his guard and his pretense of being an absentminded amateur scientist.

As soon as he'd closed the door, he set about activating the wards he'd built into the room, which blocked anyone outside the study from being able to detect magic being used within or hearing anything we said. Then, without warning, the lights in the room went out.

I knew what that meant. I held my hand out in front of me and tried to sense the ether swirling around me. It took some concentration, but I managed to pull energy from the ether into the palm of my hand to create a light. More concentration magnified it to illuminate the room. Once I'd created the light, it took little attention to maintain it, though Henry put me to the test by picking up a butterfly net and waving it around. My light flickered as I giggled and went out entirely when he threw the net at me.

The room's lights came back on, and he said, "Better. But you need to be able to form the light instantly and maintain it when distracted."

"Even when someone's throwing something at me?"

"*Especially* when someone's throwing something at you. And it's not just about the light. Learning to control the light is learning to control power, and that applies to any magic you perform. Now, let's work on physical manipulation." He dumped a dish of paper clips on the floor and handed me the dish. This was a little easier for me, as it was a use of magic I'd taught myself when I'd discovered my powers. After the third paper clip, however, the task became more difficult, as I found myself battling with Henry. He moved them so that I had to redirect the ether, and we had a tug of war with each other over the last clip. It was fortunate that the wards muted sound in the room because I couldn't hold back a cry of victory when I wrested the clip away from him and landed it in the dish.

"Excellent! This may prove to be your area of expertise," he said, sitting in his desk chair and removing the spectacles I knew he didn't need. I thought for a moment that this meant he was ready to let me rest, but instead he held up the butterfly net and said, "Make it look like a fan."

I tried not to groan out loud. Illusions were the most difficult thing for me, and I'd never seen another magister other than Henry perform one. But Henry said they'd once been a staple of magic, before magisters grew lazy and complacent with their position in society, and he wanted me to have every advantage. I stared at the butterfly net for a long time, picturing the fan I would make it look like. Next came the hard part, shaping the ether around the net to give it the illusion of a fan. It flickered back and forth between the reality and the illusion for a moment before finally settling on the illusion.

"Good," Henry said. "Now, have you read any good books lately?"

"Books?" I asked, baffled by the abrupt change in topic.

Henry laughed and pointed at the net, which still looked like a fan. "Good work, Verity! You managed to maintain the illusion while you were distracted. Now let's see how long it will last. Tea?"

Breathing a little heavily from my exertions, I wiped beads of sweat off my brow and said, "Please."

"Then boil the water."

I should have known better than to expect him to give me a break so soon. This was a tricky use of magic because it required finding just the right amount of heat. I'd already broken three teapots when I got it wrong. I activated the ether around and within the teapot, fighting to keep the excitement slow and under control. When steam came out of the spout, Henry measured tea into the pot, and I slumped back in my chair. The fan was flickering, but it was still visible. I allowed myself a small smile of triumph.

"Much better," he said. "Perhaps I won't have to order another box of teapots."

When it appeared that I really was getting a break this time, I thought it might be an opportune time to bring up what Alec had asked me. "Some of the Mechanics are back in town. I ran into Alec in the park today."

He raised an eyebrow. "Oh? Even after that narrow escape?"

"They believe that was more about the machines." I tried to think of how best to phrase the next part. While I wanted to be honest with him, I preferred to steer him in the most reasonable direction. "They've taken what you said about playing at revolution to heart and are trying to plan rather than just making noise. They believe their machines really are the edge they need to defeat the magisters, but they need to make more machines, and for that they need funding. They asked me if you had any ideas." I didn't feel it too dishonest to avoid mentioning them wanting money from the Bandits. If Henry thought of that, it was up to him.

"Mass production of machines like that? Do they know how much that would cost?"

"I'm not sure."

"I suppose they could start with some existing machines and fit them for new power supplies, so they wouldn't have to start with smelting iron, but still, the materials, the facilities, and the manpower—well, they're essentially creating a new industry. They wanted my input on this? Why? Because I'm the only rich person they know?"

Now I had no choice but to tell him. "Because you lead the Masked Bandits and have already been funding the cause, to some extent." Before he could say anything, I hurried to add, "I told him that robbing trains wouldn't raise that kind of money without you taking huge risks, and you're lying low to avoid suspicion for now. He understood, but he wanted to see if you had other ideas."

He stirred the teapot, poured through a strainer into two cups, added sugar, and handed one to me before taking a sip from his own cup. "You're right, even my biggest heist ever wouldn't have been enough to raise that kind of money. What they need are investors, but that's difficult when their activities are counter to the interests of most of those who have money."

Although he'd agreed with me, I felt deflated by his pessimism. "So there's no hope?"

"I didn't say that." He rubbed his eyes and leaned back in his chair. "There have to be some people with money who are committed to—or at least interested in—the idea of revolution. It's not just my friends and me."

"Do you really think so?"

"Given the rate of taxation in the colonies, a lot of property owners might think a break with the Empire would be good for them, whether or not they also want to overthrow the class system. And there are some wealthy and influential nonmagisters who are held back by their nonmagical status. But I don't know if they'd be open to allying with the Rebel Mechanics."

"I think they'll have to," I said after mulling it over for a moment. "The only way a revolution could succeed is if there's one revolution, not a magister revolution and a Mechanics revolution. Defeating the Empire is so big a task, it will take all of us working together."

He leaned forward, resting his elbows on his knees, and looked me square in the eyes. Without his glasses blurring them, they were an intriguing mix of shades of blue, and the sight brought me back to the moment we'd first met, when he'd robbed the train I was on. I'd later recognized him by his eyes. "We need to rally the people we know are interested and get them to recruit others. It may take time to gradually grow our organization, and in the meantime, we can ask for funds even before we ask people to make public declarations." He shook his head, smiling slightly. "I wonder if there's a way to sound people out without risking my neck. Who might have rebel leanings, and how could we tell?"

I took a sip of my tea, letting the sweetness restore some

of the energy I'd spent using magic. "The military may be a fertile ground for recruiting. Consider the general—what does he think about being considered a lesser race by people who put so much responsibility on him?"

"I never thought of that."

"That's because you were brought up as a magister. You don't know what it's like for the rest of us."

He smiled ruefully. "I suppose I've been too busy thinking about how limited my options were to consider that there were those who had even fewer choices in life, regardless of their abilities."

"That's why we're doing this, isn't it? So everyone can make the most of themselves without artificial limits."

He looked at me in a way that made me feel quite naked, in spite of the many layers of clothing I wore. "And how must you feel, having to hide what you are when you have so much power? It's not just us, is it? You can't tell your Mechanic friends, either."

"They're coming to accept you—or at least your help—so perhaps one day they'll look beyond their view that power is inevitably a corrupting force. For now, though, I'm afraid you're right. They wouldn't look kindly upon me if they knew I was even a half-magister."

"Then if I need to remember why I'm doing this, why our cause is just and important, I'll think of you, Verity."

The intensity of his gaze might have burned away at least one layer of clothing if it had been sustained for long. I got to my feet so hastily that I wobbled slightly. I hurried to steady myself before he noticed and offered me any assistance. I was afraid that his touch would be more than I could bear at the moment. "I—I really should be—" I stammered.

"Yes, quite," he said as he jumped to his feet. He stumbled as he took a step forward, barely catching himself on the corner of his desk. "Good evening, Miss Newton. Pleasant dreams."

"And you, too, Lord Henry." I placed my tea cup on his desk rather than hand it to him and risk any accidental touch between us.

I forced myself to walk serenely to my room rather than running headlong down the hall the way I wanted to. What had just happened? He'd acted nearly as flustered as I'd felt. For a moment, I let myself revel in the warm glow that thought engendered, but I reminded myself that it hardly mattered. The world really would have to change for it to be even remotely possible.

It occurred to me as I took down my hair and brushed it out that I somehow seemed to have become a rallying figure for two different rebel movements. My status caught between worlds was motivating Henry's fight for freedom, and as my newspaper alter ego, Liberty Jones, I was such a symbol of the Rebel Mechanics that there was an airship named after me—well, sort of. That was rather astonishing for a mousy, bookish governess.

Instead of going to bed, I wrote an article on the plan to produce more machines and the need for funding, proposing that patriotic citizens collect pennies in a Liberty Jar for the cause. I feared that would raise morale more than it did money, but I thought it might be easier to get wealthy magisters to contribute if they thought the Mechanics were doing their part, as well.

The only way we had a prayer of winning our freedom was if both sides could overcome their prejudices and work as one. It was a nice thing to envision, but was it remotely possible?

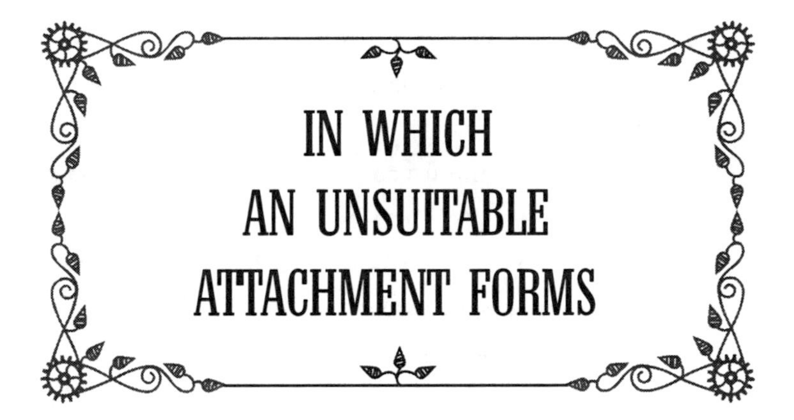

IN WHICH AN UNSUITABLE ATTACHMENT FORMS

The next afternoon, I was leaving my room to accompany Flora on a round of social calls when Henry approached me. "Could you do me a favor, Miss Newton? I'd like you to leave these for me on your calls," he said, handing me several calling cards and a list. I felt the tingle of magic in the cards and imagined they contained more information than his name, title, and address.

"Your messages to potential investors?" I concluded.

We went down the stairs, speaking softly. "Some of them. If we're ever to reach our maximum impact, we'll need to start quietly enough that it goes unnoticed, and working in these circles will require us to be very careful. One false step, and word may get to the wrong people at the highest levels." His eyes glittered, and I knew he'd found a new dare to replace train robbery. "You dropping off calling cards for me shouldn't look at all suspicious."

"Don't you have magical means of communicating?"

"None that are truly secure. It goes to the home rather than to an individual."

Flora joined us in the foyer. She swept down the front steps toward the waiting carriage with me in her wake. Although we were nearly the same age, I felt worlds apart from her. She was bright and glittering, the kind of girl everyone noticed, while I was the sort of girl no one noticed. We had very little in common for conversation, as she talked of little but dresses and balls, and my circumstances didn't lead to those things being important parts of my life. I had attended one ball, and only as a chaperone. I doubted Flora would much care for talk of revolution, and I knew she disliked discussing books.

She took the forward-facing seat in the carriage, and I sat across from her, where even though she looked directly at me she pretended not to see me. I tried not to react to her obvious snobbishness. If Henry had seen it, he would have scolded her, and that would only have made her dislike me more.

When the carriage stopped at our first destination, she finally acknowledged my presence. "You are merely here for propriety, remember," she snapped. "Do not embarrass me. Henry may be casual with you, but I remember your real place."

"Yes, Lady Flora," I said as meekly as I could bear to.

The footman handed her down and earned a scowl from her by also helping me. He ignored her scowl, probably because he remembered who his employer was and what he would want. I gave him a nod of thanks before following Flora up the steps to a grand mansion just a few blocks down Fifth Avenue from our home.

We'd barely made it into the parlor before we were assailed by a cloud of lace. Lady Charity Spencer made Flora look somber and serious in comparison. "Oh, Flora!" she cried, grabbing Flora's hands in greeting. "How good of you to come! And such good timing, too! I was just saying I wanted to take a turn around the park! We can all go together! Your governess can chaperone us!" Everything she said came out as an exclamation of utmost importance.

"A turn around the park?" Flora said, with some dismay. If Flora had thought she could get away with it, she would have had litter bearers carry her across the room.

"Oh, please, please say yes!"

Even Flora was helpless against Lady Charity. "I suppose so," she said weakly.

"Oh! You are the dearest friend! Let me get my hat and gloves!" A maid materialized at her side with hat, gloves, and coat, and soon had her ready to go out. I followed dutifully.

Once we were in the park, Lady Charity appeared to go on high alert, darting her eyes back and forth and sometimes straining her neck as though trying to see into the distance. At the same time, she kept up a rather loud chatter to Flora, twirled her parasol, and walked with dainty, mincing steps. I had to fall back to trail the girls so I could muffle my snickers. I knew exactly what was happening here. Lady Charity's behavior was a slightly more ostentatious version of the way I used to act when I hoped to encounter Alec in the park.

Flora arrived at the same conclusion. "You're hoping to meet a boy, aren't you?" she said.

Lady Charity swatted her lightly on the arm and gave a trill of shrill laughter. "Whatever gives you that impression?"

"You're acting like a silly goose. You might get his attention, but you won't impress him."

"You don't even know who he is. He might be impressed."

"No, he won't. But why did you have to sneak around and drag me and my chaperone into your schemes? Charity, he isn't some entirely unsuitable boy, is he?"

I swallowed a groan of dismay. My primary duty as chaperone was making it impossible for magister children to mix with nonmagical people—they didn't want the talent extending beyond a certain class. Did that duty apply to those outside my employer's family? I was afraid it did, if my presence meant that both girls were considered properly chaperoned. But did that mean I had the authority to intervene? At least it sounded like Flora might support me if I had to.

I sincerely hoped Lady Charity didn't run into the object of her affection. Alas, a small magical roadster slowed as it approached us. "Why, Lady Charity," the driver said with a bow. "What a pleasure to see you out this fine day."

Charity glowed so brightly we could have lit the library with her. "Oh! Mr. Brightley! This is a surprise!"

I relaxed ever so slightly. If he drove a magical roadster, there was a very good chance he was a magister, himself. They could be driven by people who didn't have power, but few nonmagisters could afford such a thing.

Flora cleared her throat, and Lady Charity said, "Oh! Lady Flora Lyndon, may I introduce my friend, Mr. Brightley? Mr. Brightley, this is my friend, Lady Flora."

He tipped his hat at Flora and gave her a slight bow. "Charmed to make your acquaintance, my lady." I noticed that I apparently didn't merit an introduction.

"Whatever are you doing out today?" Lady Charity asked, giving her parasol a twirl.

He frowned slightly. "I thought I told you I'd planned to go driving this afternoon."

Lady Charity reddened. "Oh! I suppose you did."

Now I had to wonder if he esteemed her as much as she did him, or was he truly so dense that he didn't realize she'd arranged to encounter him?

Flora took her friend by the arm and addressed Mr. Brightley. "It was a pleasure to meet you, but we really must resume our walk if we're to make it home in time for tea."

He bowed and touched his hat again before driving off. As soon as his roadster had rounded a bend out of sight, and presumably out of earshot, Flora whirled on her friend. "Oh, Charity," she said, sighing rather than giving the audible exclamation point Charity gave the word "Oh." "How could you even consider him? He doesn't have a title. His father doesn't have a title. There's no chance that he'll ever inherit a title. Your father would never approve."

"Which is why I have to resort to subterfuge in order to meet him," Lady Charity said, heading down the path in a way that I might have considered "stalking off" if she hadn't been taking such dainty steps. "He's so much more interesting than any of the titled men I know. Would you have me set my cap for someone like your uncle?"

I was glad I was behind them because I stumbled at her words. I tried not to think of it often, but I knew that Henry would be limited in his choice of wife, and I would never qualify, not unless we founded a new nation with fewer restrictions. This was the kind of girl he was likely to end up with, which might explain some of his revolutionary ardor, I thought, rather uncharitably.

Before I could mire myself in self-pity, we encountered another gentleman on the path, this one on foot. He tipped his hat and bowed to us, but I was the one he addressed. "Good afternoon, Miss Newton," Colin said.

While I hadn't been sure of the etiquette regarding a magister who wasn't nobility, I knew for certain that Colin was exactly the sort of man who was entirely unsuitable for interaction with these girls. Not only was he not a magister, but he was an immigrant from the lower echelon of society and a member of the Rebel Mechanics who would likely have had a warrant out for his arrest if the authorities knew his name and face.

Fortunately, he wasn't playing the rebel role today. While he'd never pass for a noble in his present attire, he also wasn't wearing the mixed-up rag bag assortment of clothing that was practically a uniform among the Mechanics, he didn't have brass goggles perching on his hatband, and he wasn't displaying the Mechanics' infamous red ribbon and gear insignia. Instead, he looked like a slightly shabby young working man in a secondhand suit that didn't quite fit him.

I imagined that my duty would be to throw myself in between him and the girls, but all I really had to do was prevent them from doing anything that might ruin them for a proper marriage or result in magister children of the wrong class. That seemed highly unlikely to occur in the park in broad daylight, so I decided there was no harm in being polite. "Good afternoon, Colin—Mr. Flynn," I said, barely remembering his surname.

I turned to Flora, who, as the ranking lady present, was the one to whom introductions were made. I cringed inwardly at the snobby rudeness I expected. She'd be mortified if I dared introduce her to such a person, but I considered this to be my stand for equality, and even if she reported me to Henry, Henry wouldn't care.

But instead of making every effort to pretend she didn't see Colin, Flora stared at him in something that looked suspiciously like awe. Surely she'd seen a working-class man up close before, so I couldn't understand her reaction. Was it his red hair that so startled her? I cleared my throat. "Um, Lady Flora and Lady Charity, may I present Mr. Flynn? His sister is one of my dear friends. He's an engineering student at the university. Colin, this is Lady Flora Lyndon, one of my pupils, and her friend, Lady Charity Spencer."

I was truly surprised when it took the ever-glib Colin several seconds to respond. He finally jolted himself out of a daze, swept his hat off, and executed a dramatic bow. "Your servant, ladies." The deep bow seemed to have improved the flow of blood to his brain, and soon he was more like his normal self. "Ver—Miss Newton, you never told me you had such a lovely pupil." He turned to Flora and added with a grin, "All she said was how brilliant you are."

I'd never said any such thing. Flora was actually quite resistant to being taught anything that might be useful. She thought that was beneath her, that her position in society was enough to make her worthy. I expected her to give me one of her frightful icy glares, but she turned a fetching shade of delicate pink and fluttered her eyelashes. "I'm sure she says nothing of the sort. I'm a very indifferent pupil who must sorely tax her patience. If I learn anything at all, it is due to Miss Newton's diligent efforts."

I heard a choking sound near me and turned slightly to see Lady Charity's eyes bulging in sheer shock. Perhaps Flora had become overheated, I thought. The sun was rather bright, in spite of the chilly air.

I was so surprised by Flora's reaction to Colin that it took me awhile to remember that I had a message to pass on to him, if I could think of a way to do so in front of the girls. I cleared my throat again to get his attention, and when he managed to pry his eyes off Flora, I said, "It was lovely to see you again, Mr. Flynn, but we must be going. Please give my regards to your sister. And to Mr. Emfinger. I've got a friend who would love to meet with him to discuss a possible business investment."

He was so addled, I wasn't sure if the message got through to him, but he put his hat back on his head and bowed slightly as he touched the brim. "I will be sure to let him know, and I look forward to our next chat. Ladies, have a nice afternoon."

"It was so lovely to meet you," Flora said with more enthusiasm than I'd ever heard her use for anything other than a ballgown. He gave her a cheeky grin and a wink as he passed us.

Lady Charity barely waited for him to be out of earshot before she turned on Flora. "I can't believe you! You criticize my attachment to a magister commoner, and then you go and practically throw yourself at someone like that." She hesitated and turned to me. "He's not magister, is he, Miss Newton?"

"No, he isn't," I confirmed. "And I believe we've had quite enough excitement for one walk in the park. Tea will be ready, so we should turn back."

Lady Charity had to hook her arm through Flora's to

steer her friend down the path, Flora seemed to be in such a daze. I could hardly believe it. Colin was charming, and he put a great deal of effort into being that way, but I couldn't imagine anyone swooning over him, least of all Flora.

I got the girls back to the Spencer house and turned them over to the housekeeper and maids for tea. My services as chaperone were no longer required, and I wasn't invited to join them. While they giggled and fluttered, Flora having recovered somewhat, I carried out my errand for Lord Henry.

Approaching the butler in the foyer, I said, "Lord Henry has asked me to leave his card for Mr. Philip Spencer."

"Very good, miss," the butler said. He took a silver tray from a nearby stand and held it out to me. I placed a card on the tray. The butler nodded and retreated into the house.

I wasn't sure where I was supposed to go or what I was expected to do. No one had invited me to sit down. A governess usually wasn't welcome in the servants' hall, so I couldn't go downstairs and have a cup of tea with them. I was left waiting in the foyer, which seemed the height of rudeness to me, but apparently manners only counted for the upper crust when they were dealing with each other.

A few minutes later, I heard a soft, "Psst!" coming from under the stairs. When it was repeated, I glanced around to make sure no one was watching me and edged my way toward the grand staircase. A fair-haired young man who was essentially a male version of Lady Charity lurked under the stairs, beckoning to me.

"You're Henry's gal, aren't you?" he asked in a whisper.

I wasn't quite sure what he meant by that, so I said, "I am in Lord Henry's employ, yes."

"I thought I recognized you." He looked vaguely familiar. He must have been part of the group who'd aided the Mechanics' escape. "You can tell Henry that I'm up for it. He just needs to schedule it, and I'll come up with some excuse to get away. Maybe a hunting trip? That would be jolly. We haven't had one of those in a while—not for real. Though I guess this one wouldn't be real, either, what? But we'd probably be less likely to be arrested from this one." He paused, blanching, before saying warily, "You do know about…"

"Lord Henry's unorthodox hobbies? Yes, I am fully aware of those."

"Oh, good. Thought I'd really put my foot in it. Please don't tell Henry."

"You may be assured of my discretion."

He grinned as his shoulders sagged with relief. "Right then. You can tell Henry to tell me when, and I'm game. I'd also be up to the other kind of hunting expedition"—he winked at me—"if he just says the word. It's been a bit boring lately."

"I will pass that on." I could hardly believe that the success of the revolution might rest in the hands—or bank account—of such a person. But he had to be somewhat competent to stay in Henry's band, I was sure.

Voices from the parlor above drifted down the stairs,

and Philip made shooing motions with his hands as he crept deeper into the shadows. I moved out into the foyer just as Flora and Lady Charity came around the sweeping bend of the staircase. The butler brought Flora's coat—no one had taken mine in the first place—and she kissed Lady Charity on the cheek before leaving with me.

When the carriage was on its way, Flora said, "We have two more calls to make, but they will be much shorter. I don't plan to spend more than ten minutes at each home. I would say that you could stay in the carriage, but Henry told me you had to come inside with me. I don't see why. As long as you watch me enter the house safely, that should satisfy any requirements of propriety, as I am not visiting nonmagisters."

I nodded in acknowledgment, unsure of what there was to say in response or if a response was required. Flora usually preferred me not to speak because that made it easier for her to pretend I didn't exist. She was more fidgety than usual, and she kept glancing at me rather than looking past me the way she usually did. A couple of times, she opened her mouth as though to speak, took a breath, then abruptly closed her mouth, sealing her lips tight. She got as far as saying, "Er, um, Miss Newton," before the carriage stopped.

Again, I was left in the foyer, where I handed Lord Henry's card to the butler. This time, there was no response before Flora left. She seemed somewhat distracted in the carriage, picking at the folds of her skirt, and she stopped and started an attempt to speak several more times. I was the one who was glad when we reached our destination and could get out of the carriage because I'd had to bite my tongue to keep from telling her, "Oh, come out with it."

At this home, within a minute of me handing over Henry's card there were footsteps on the stairs, and a young man came racing down. He stopped abruptly on the bottom step. "Oh, it's you," he said.

"Indeed it is," I replied, unable to suppress a smile. "We enjoyed quite the journey together." I recognized him as the passenger who'd come into my car, claiming to have fled another car with a noisy baby on it, after the train robbery during which I'd first met Henry. This validated my suspicion that the robbers had never left the train but had rather disguised themselves and blended in among the passengers.

"You didn't give me away," he said.

"I wasn't sure about you at the time."

"I'm assuming you're sure now, if you're working for Henry and carrying his messages."

"You can rely on my loyalty and discretion."

"Then you can tell him I'm up for it."

Girls' voices drifted down from the upper floor, and he glanced upward before saying, "I'd better run. Wouldn't do to be caught chatting with a chaperone. But I hope we can talk later." He sounded rather serious, not at all flirtatious, like he was treating me as an equal member of the group. He ran up the stairs and ducked into a doorway before

Flora and her friend emerged from the parlor. I noticed him darting down a hallway behind them and had to turn away so Flora wouldn't notice me smiling.

Back in the carriage, Flora spent only a minute or so fidgeting before she blurted, "You seem to know such interesting people, Miss Newton."

"I do, but which one do you mean? Mr. Flynn?"

"Oh, yes, that was his name." She smoothed an imaginary wrinkle in her skirt. "Is he from Ireland?"

"I believe so, but he and his sister came over when they were children."

"His sister is your good friend?"

"Perhaps my closest in this city." Or she had been, once. Lizzie and I weren't on such good terms anymore, after I'd learned she'd been part of the plot to recruit me through deception, but we'd remained civil.

"You said he was an engineering student?"

"Yes." At least, I thought he was. He and Alec had been introduced to me that way, but I wasn't sure what Colin's technical expertise was. He mostly seemed to serve as the group's spokesman and carnival barker. I'd never seen him work directly with a machine, and I couldn't remember ever hearing a mention of him attending a class.

"I don't believe I've ever met anyone like him." I recognized the dreamy look in her eyes. I'd seen it in my own mirror during the days when Alec had been wooing me.

"That's probably for the best," I said in my most prim chaperone voice. "Your uncle would most certainly not approve." I realized a moment later that I'd only made Colin sound even more appealing. The best way to handle this was to make her think with her head and possibly bypass her heart. "What was it about Colin that you found so compelling?" I asked.

After a deep, wistful sigh, she said, "He made me feel like I was the only woman in the world, and that there were endless possibilities available to me."

"That's just Colin," I said gently. "He's like that with everyone. He'd flirt with a lamppost, and I'd swear it would light up brighter for him."

She lost the dreamy look and narrowed her eyes shrewdly at me. "He's not your beau, is he, Miss Newton?"

"Nothing of the sort. He really is just a friend, almost like a brother." In her relief, she went back to gazing dreamily into the middle distance.

When the carriage stopped, before the driver opened the door, she reached across and grabbed my wrist. "You won't tell Henry, will you?"

"I don't see why I should. There's nothing to tell."

"Right. Nothing to tell. Good." She seemed almost back to her old self as she alighted from the carriage and made her way up the front steps to the house.

With a sigh, I realized that the last thing this household needed was yet another secret. I didn't think any harm would actually come of this one, as I knew Colin well enough to know that he was seldom sincere and had probably already forgotten the encounter.

Flora went to her room to rest before dinner, and I went to the library, where I wasn't at all surprised to be joined by Henry a few minutes later. "I hope today wasn't too painful for you," he said, leaning against the bookcase next to where I stood. "I know Flora can be a snob, and she's even worse when she's with her friends. Paying calls with her must be sheer torture."

"I did spend a fair amount of time standing in the foyer," I admitted.

"What? They didn't offer you a seat or a cup of tea?"

"On the other hand, I didn't have to listen to their conversation."

He laughed. "Yes, I suppose that's a kindness, even if it was unintentional. I'll have a word with Flora, though."

"No, don't," I urged. "Then she'll know I said something to you. And how will I carry out your missions if I'm stuck in the parlor? While I stood in the foyer, I had some very interesting conversations with your friends."

"You have responses already?"

"I do. Philip Spencer is quite keen, though I get the impression that he's quite keen on just about everything."

"He is. The banditry was largely his idea, though his suggestion was somewhat lacking in detail and logistics."

"Lord Julian didn't respond at all. I don't know if he was even at home. I left the card, but he didn't come out. Viscount Hayes was also interested. So it seems I should set up a meeting with the Mechanics for them."

"And for me, as well. I have a little money of my own."

I was sure that his definition of "a little money" was very different than mine—yet another reminder of the gulf between us.

The library door opened, and both of us jumped guiltily, although we'd been doing nothing untoward—aside from plotting revolution. Mr. Chastain stood in the doorway. "My lord, the duke is here and wishes to meet with you and the children."

Henry and I exchanged a glance. The Duke of New York, governor of the American colonies, was the children's maternal grandfather. When he called, it was usually bad news.

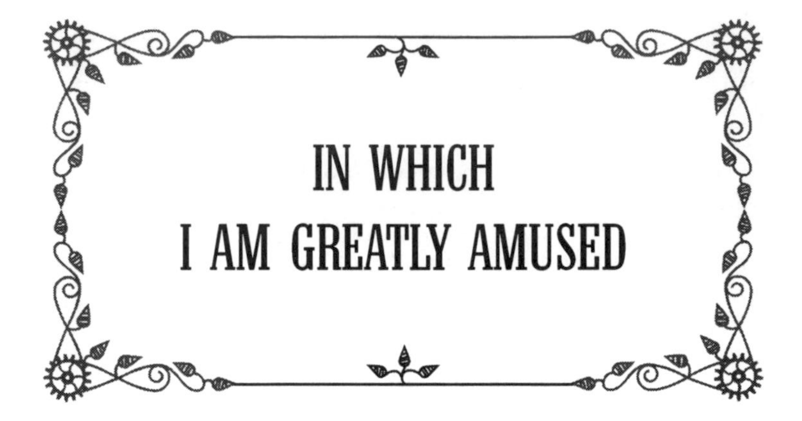

IN WHICH I AM GREATLY AMUSED

"Take him to the family parlor," Henry said. "And send the children to join him."

"Very good, sir," Mr. Chastain said, nodding before backing out of the room and shutting the door.

Henry groaned. "I wonder what he wants now."

"Does he have to want anything?" I asked. "He *is* the children's grandfather."

"I know you haven't been with us long, but have you ever known him to come just to visit his grandchildren? He only comes when he has bad news."

Although he'd echoed my own thought about bad news, I said, "Nothing much has happened in weeks, so I can't imagine what bad news he might have today."

"Well, whatever it is, I suppose I'd better face it." Henry took a couple of deep breaths, straightened his necktie, smoothed his lapels, and headed for the door. I went back to browsing the bookshelves, and a moment later I heard Henry clearing his throat. "Aren't you coming?" he asked when I looked up to see him still standing in the doorway.

"This sounds like a family affair."

He shook his head. "Oh no. If I have to face him, I want you there. He likes you."

"But there's no reason for the governess to be present."

"Go intercept the children and bring them in. I know it will have taken Chastain this long to pry Olive and Flora out of their rooms."

His tone suggested that while he wasn't making it an order, he considered it to be one, so I didn't argue further. Besides, I was curious about the governor's visit.

I hurried upstairs to the bedrooms, meeting Flora and Olive on the stairs. "There you are," I said. "I was just coming to get you."

"Chastain already sent my maid," Flora said with a yawn.

"And your uncle sent me. Come on. We don't want to keep your grandfather waiting."

Henry must have taken his time heading to the parlor because he was barely ahead of us when we reached the room. Rollo was already in there doing his homework, and he was in the process of describing some airship he'd either seen or wanted to see. The governor seemed quite glad at our arrival, but whether that was because of seeing his granddaughters or getting a reprieve from Rollo's technical discourse was uncertain.

Samuel DeLancey was a large man who appeared as though he could be quite jovial under the right circumstances. I'd never seen him in those circumstances. He always struck me as intimidating, and Henry didn't have to work to fake his bumbling young nobleman persona in his presence.

"Your Grace, this is a surprise," Henry said, stumbling slightly when he caught his toe on the edge of the carpet as he moved to greet the guest.

Instead of giving his usual disapproving sneer at Henry's ineptitude, the governor beamed at him. Whatever he was going to say was interrupted by Olive throwing her arms around him and crying out, "Grandfather! Did you bring me anything?"

"Only good news, my dear," the governor said, patting her on the back. I resisted the urge to glance at Henry and bit my lip so I wouldn't smile inappropriately. "Good news for all of us. We're going on a trip!"

Olive squealed and clapped her hands, and Henry cleared his throat. "A—a trip, Your Grace?"

"I have to go meet with the administrators of the colonies to take care of some business matters, and I thought this would be an excellent opportunity for the children to see the land. We'll take a private airship. What do you say, children?"

Rollo, of course, was overjoyed at the prospect of a trip on an airship, especially if it meant he got out of school. "Outstanding!" he cried out. Olive jumped up and down and clapped her hands.

Henry opened his mouth to respond, but before he could say anything, Flora gave a dramatic gasp and said, "Oh no! I can't go out of the city now!"

Everyone turned to stare at her. I suspected I knew why she objected. "Why ever not, my dear?" her grandfather asked.

Realizing that everyone was staring at her, she flushed a lovely shade of pink—no blotchy redness for her—and said, "Well, um, you see, I have a friend who needs me. Her health, you see, it requires frequent turns around the park, and I feel it is my duty to join her. I don't know what she'll do without me, and I'd never forgive myself if I left town and her health took a turn for the worse."

"Flora! I had no idea a friend was ill. You should have said something," Henry said, sounding truly concerned. "Who is it? I should probably call on the family."

Flora froze. After a moment's thought she said, "Charity Spencer. But please don't mention it. I shouldn't have said anything. She swore me to secrecy."

Henry turned to the governor. "Aside from Flora's obligation, I really must object, sir. We can't interrupt the children's studies, and Rollo has school."

"I planned for Miss Newton to join us. The girls won't miss a thing, and Miss Newton can keep Rollo up on his classwork."

Flora gazed at Henry with beseeching eyes, silently begging him to say no, while the other two silently pleaded for him to say yes. "I'll have to speak with the headmaster and see if it is acceptable for Rollo to be out of school," Henry said. Rollo groaned out loud in response. "And I will have to consider it."

There was a momentary staredown between Henry and the governor. Henry was as tall as the duke, but much slighter, which made him look inconsequential beside the great man. The comparison between the two also brought home just how young Henry was, barely out of his teens. If the governor wanted to use his power, I wasn't sure Henry would be able to deny him, even if he was the children's legal guardian as their father's brother.

"Very well, I will await your answer," the governor said at last, his voice tight. "I will see you later, children." With a slight—and unexpected—nod to me, he turned to go.

"Won't you stay for dinner?" Henry asked, his face suggesting that he was only issuing the invitation out of obligation.

"Not today, thank you. I'll show myself out. I don't want to interrupt your evening."

He was barely out of the room before Rollo said, "Please, Uncle Henry! You have to let us go. I'm sure it would be very educational, right Miss Newton?"

"You just want to get out of school," Flora said.

"And you don't want to be away from whichever boy it is you like this week. You're afraid he'll forget about you while you're gone."

"He would not!"

"Ha! I knew it was about a boy!"

"I didn't say that. Henry, surely the children could go without me."

"Yes! We could go without her," Rollo said. "She isn't any fun."

"I want to ride in an airship," Olive piped up. "I'm not scared of crashing." She squared her jaw defiantly even as her voice quavered slightly, and I recalled that her father had died in an airship accident.

"I said I would think about it," Henry said, sounding uncharacteristically harsh and stern. "Enough arguing. As I told your grandfather, I need to make sure Rollo's schoolwork won't be interrupted. This trip would also disrupt Miss Newton's life. Have you considered that there might be other things she wants or needs to do?"

Olive and Rollo immediately looked abashed, while Flora beamed. "Yes, you haven't even thought of Miss Newton," she said smugly. "How selfish of you."

"The only reason you're not being selfish is because you don't want to be away from some boy," Rollo shot back.

"Yes, you just like a boy," Olive parroted.

"Do I need to send you to your rooms before dinner?" Henry asked.

"He started it," Flora said. "I was agreeing with you."

"I did not!" Rollo protested.

"That's enough," Henry snapped. "All of you, to your rooms until dinner." He remained stiff and upright, his hands clenched at his sides, until all three of them had hurried away. Only when the last echo of footsteps had faded did he sink onto the nearest chair. He took off his glasses and rubbed his eyes and his temples. "This is remarkably bad timing," he said.

I eased myself onto the chair across from him. I wasn't sure it was safe to talk openly here. Too many servants were about, and he suspected his housekeeper of being a spy for the governor. "I wouldn't mind going, if that eases your mind," I said.

"You're perhaps more vital to this operation than I am. All that aside, I'm a little more worried about what might happen with the children out of my sight for that long. No harm will come to them, I'm sure, but will I ever get them back?"

I didn't know what to say. A part of me wondered if it might be best for him not to have such a great responsibility. Other young men his age in his class were having fun with their friends or courting young ladies, not playing father. I didn't think the governor would be unkind to the children. On the other hand, they stood a better chance of growing up to be good, worthwhile people under their uncle's care. Their grandfather might love them, but they'd be brought up by an army of servants, and Rollo would likely be sent to England for school.

Both of us were silent for a moment, then he smiled and said, "All of us are tired. I'll think about it later."

I went up to my room and was surprised to find Flora lurking in the hallway. "You don't think he'll make me go, do you?" she asked.

"I don't think it will make much difference. Colin doesn't live in the city. He was only visiting his sister. Even if you remained in town, you likely wouldn't see him."

Her face fell, and I thought she might cry. "Oh. Really?"

"I'm afraid so."

She held her head high, fighting to appear brave even though her lower lip trembled. "Then perhaps it wasn't meant to be, and I should go to help myself forget."

I thought she was being overly dramatic about someone she'd barely even exchanged words with, but it was the first time I'd seen Flora actually seem interested in anyone other than herself. "Broken hearts do heal," I told her. At least, I hoped they did. Mine seemed to have mended, leaving anger as a kind of psychic scar tissue. I wouldn't wish that on Flora, but I didn't believe her attachment could possibly be that strong after one encounter.

The next morning I received a note in the mail from Lizzie, inviting me to join her for a gathering Saturday evening. Since we weren't quite on friendly terms these days, I interpreted the invitation to be about the magisters. That night when I joined Henry for my magic lesson, I told him, "I heard from the Mechanics. They want to meet Saturday night. I think we should all go, including your friends."

"Did they ask to meet with us?"

"Not exactly. But I think it would be much easier for us all to talk directly. It would take forever for me to carry messages back and forth, having to arrange meetings each time."

"True. This is the kind of business that needs to be done face-to-face. What kind of invitation was it?"

"A 'gathering' was all she said. They like to mix pleasure with business, so it's probably a party. She wants me to meet her at her boardinghouse."

"I'll let the others know. Now, let's see how your illusion work is going."

On Saturday night, I took a magical cab downtown and made the driver let me off a couple of blocks before the boardinghouse, where I'd arranged to meet Henry and his friends. I almost wouldn't have recognized them, they'd done such a good job of dressing down for the occasion. No one was likely to suspect they were wealthy, titled magisters. They did get quite a few looks from any girls who passed by, though, because Philip was terribly handsome, even without his fine clothes. Viscount Hayes and Henry looked more ordinary, but I was surprised by how very young they looked without the trappings of their rank.

"Do we pass muster?" Henry asked me.

"I think you'll do."

I was rather nervous as I knocked on the boardinghouse door. I wasn't sure how Lizzie would react to having three magisters on her doorstep. She seemed friendly enough when she opened the door, until she noticed the young men standing behind me. "What is this?" she asked.

"They're the people you're asking for a great deal of money," I said. "I thought it would be easier for everyone to speak directly to each other than for me to smuggle messages back and forth."

"You'd better come inside," she said, stepping back from the doorway to allow us to pass. "But the men can't go beyond the foyer."

Once we were inside, I made hasty introductions. "Lizzie, you've met Henry, and this is Philip and Viscount Hayes."

"Geoffrey," he corrected.

"And this is Lizzie. She's one of my contacts in the organization."

Before the men could greet her formally, she caught me by the arm and dragged me off toward the parlor. "If you gentlemen will excuse us for a moment, I need to talk to Verity," she said. When we were in the parlor, she hissed, "Some warning would have been nice."

"I told Colin that my friend was interested in discussing a business proposal. That generally implies that the friend will be present for the discussion."

"But three of them?"

"What you want is more than any one person, even a very wealthy person, can provide. These three helped get the machines out of the city, so they already know most of your secrets. They've seen the machines, they know about the subway, and they even know where the headquarters was. If they want to betray you, they already have everything they need. You have a lot more to gain than to lose by talking to them."

She furrowed her brow, and the spots of color on her

cheeks gradually faded, giving me hope that she was calming down as she considered. "It's not entirely up to me, but I'll take you there," she said at last. "Wait with them."

We returned to the foyer and she ran up the stairs. "What is it?" Henry asked me.

"It's not easy for them to trust magisters," I said. "But she'll take you to the others. Maybe they'll talk. I don't know." Unable to hold back a sigh, I added, "I'm sorry. I should have better prepared them or been more specific about arranging a meeting. I hope I haven't wasted your time."

Philip's gaze tracked up the stairs to where Lizzie had appeared with another girl. "It hasn't been wasted time at all," he said, grinning. The other girl was rather pretty, with dark hair, porcelain skin, and a figure to envy. She blushed prettily when she noticed Philip's gaze upon her.

"This is Emma," Lizzie announced when they reached the bottom of the stairs. She then made introductions all around. "Now, we're going to go out for a night on the town, an ordinary group of young men and their girls."

Philip wasted no time in extending his arm to Emma, who smiled shyly as she took it. Lizzie gave me a long look, her lips twitching slightly, before turning to Geoffrey and saying, "It looks like you've got me. I hope you don't have a problem with gingers."

"I'm far more interested in what lies under the hair," he said, to which she raised an eyebrow.

I got the feeling that Lizzie had chosen to leave me with Henry, but I wasn't sure of her motive. I didn't think I'd shown any particular interest in him that would have made her think I would prefer to be his partner for the evening. Perhaps she merely assumed I'd be more comfortable with him, since I knew him best.

Lizzie, on Geoffrey's arm, led us through the crowded streets full of young working people out for a Saturday night. I was rather surprised when we ended up at the old theater where the Rebel Mechanics' headquarters used to be. There were posters up for a theatrical review, and the ticket window was doing a brisk business. We bypassed the window and were waved inside by the boy who was taking tickets. I had to look twice to recognize Nat, a newsboy who sold the underground newspaper. He looked like an entirely different person with his face washed, bareheaded, and with his hair neatly combed. "Enjoy the show, Verity," he said with a grin.

As we made our way to our seats, I leaned over to Lizzie and whispered, "Just what is going on here?"

"If we're to convince the authorities that this was always nothing more than a dramatic society, then we need to put on some shows. It's all entirely above reproach." She winced slightly. "Though not very good. It is quite amusing, however. Have you considered branching out into theater criticism?"

"I thought we were here for a meeting."

"Patience. Appearances must be upheld."

We sat in chairs whose red velvet cushions had seen better days, possibly in the last century. I noticed that the lighting was no longer electric. The globes were there, but the dynamo in the basement had been moved out of the city with the other machines. Instead, there were gas sconces along the walls and a chandelier overhead.

I was surprised by how full the theater was. I recognized many of the patrons from Mechanics-related gatherings, and a few of the girls from my network of contacts were there. Most of the theatergoers seemed to be from the neighborhood—no upper-crust patrons of the arts, except for the one woman richly dressed all in black and heavily veiled. I didn't know her identity, but she appeared at many of the Mechanics' events and funded some of their inventions. She looked at us, and I had the feeling that our eyes met for a moment. She adjusted her veil, as though making sure it thoroughly covered her face.

"Do they always do this sort of thing?" Henry whispered to me.

"They do like to put on a show. It just usually isn't on a stage."

He grinned and settled back in his seat. "It's been ages since I had an evening at the theater."

Soon, the lights dimmed, somewhat unevenly. There was a halfhearted spatter of applause when Colin—who else?—appeared on the stage in front of the curtain. I smiled at the thought that Flora would be extremely jealous of me. Or perhaps might find her infatuation fading, depending on what happened.

"Ladies and gentlemen," he said, projecting his voice to the back row. "We are pleased to present the finest collection of theatrical entertainment you're likely to find tonight on this block." That got a chuckle from the audience. "And without further ado, a scene from Shakespeare himself."

He jumped off the stage to take a seat in the front row as the curtain opened. It got stuck halfway, and someone had to run out and give it a sharp yank before it revealed the entire stage.

I recognized the setup for what had to be the famous balcony scene from *Romeo and Juliet.* The balcony was made of scaffolding on which a garland of flowers had been draped. Juliet wore a wig of long braids that trailed behind her. The scene went the way I'd memorized it, until at one point Romeo abruptly said, "Juliet, Juliet, let down your hair." She dropped the braids over the side of the balcony, and he proceeded to climb up to join her, to much amusement from the audience. The scene progressed in an odd mix of *Romeo and Juliet* and the fairy tale "Rapunzel" that I had to admit was quite clever, though rather broadly acted.

The rest of the show was more of the same, with Colin entertaining the crowd during scene changes. He put his powerful tenor voice to use, singing plaintive songs about the land across the sea, and those interludes were the only times when the show could be taken at all seriously.

It was during one of his songs that a murmur came through the crowd, and I turned to see several uniformed soldiers entering the theater. I couldn't tell if this was a raid or if they were merely looking for entertainment on their night off.

"What's happening?" I whispered to Lizzie.

"Don't worry," she replied, also in a whisper. "This is what we want. They come most every night, trying to catch us doing something clandestine. Instead, all they get are Colin's bad jokes."

"Every night? But I thought he was out of town."

"Shh. We'll talk later."

I barely noticed the rest of the show as I worried about what would happen. It would be very bad if the magister men were recognized. Even if they weren't connected to revolutionary activities, they were associating with nonmagister women in a situation that looked romantic. I knew Henry didn't socialize much and was never mentioned in the society pages, but I wasn't sure how well-known the others were. I forced myself not to stare at the soldiers. They hadn't approached us and didn't seem to be paying much attention to us. Perhaps they wouldn't if I didn't draw their notice by acting nervous.

Colin closed out the night by presenting the "To be or not to be" soliloquy from *Hamlet,* and I was surprised to find that he performed it entirely straight, without the slightest hint of satire. I shouldn't have been surprised to find that he was an excellent actor, considering how much his work relied upon showmanship. The Rebel Mechanics knew how to stage a scene.

The soldiers applauded along with everyone else as the lights came up and the cast came out to take their bows. Henry, Geoffrey, and Philip cheered along with everyone else. They grinned like they'd really enjoyed the show.

We stayed as the theater slowly emptied. Much to my relief, the soldiers left without lingering. The veiled woman remained until almost everyone else was gone before slipping away after what I felt was one last long glance at us. When only the cast was left resetting the stage, Lizzie brought our group down to the front. Colin jumped off the stage to come greet us. "So, what did you think of our little show?" he asked.

"I enjoyed it a great deal," I said, quite honestly.

"It was a rather entertaining production," Henry said.

"Jolly good show," Philip added.

Colin gave a pointed look at the three magisters, then turned back to me, raising a quizzical eyebrow. I knew it would technically be proper to introduce him to the others, as they were higher in rank, but I thought this was hardly a time to stick to social rules. "Colin, you remember Henry, don't you? And these are his friends, Philip and Geoffrey. "

Philip stuck his hand out at Colin. "Delighted to meet you. You're awfully talented," he said, beaming.

After a pause that went on long enough to become rude, Colin took his hand and shook it. "Thank you. You're obviously a man of excellent taste."

Lizzie took his arm. "I need a word with you, my dear brother," she said.

To us, he said, "I'm sure she wants to critique the *Hamlet.* She's never satisfied." In spite of his jovial tone, his eyes were serious.

"I don't think he's happy to see us," Geoffrey said dryly

as we watched them go to the other side of the theater, where they had an animated discussion. All of Colin's discussions were animated, but this one seemed particularly intense. From this distance, I couldn't tell who was arguing what or which one was winning. They were both smiling when they returned to us.

"Would you like to join us for the cast party?" Colin asked. "Then we can get to know each other. If you'll follow me..." We followed him to the theater's basement. "I'm afraid we'll have to take the long way around, since you took that doorway away for us."

"We can put it back for you," Henry said.

"That should probably wait until after the soldiers leave town. We don't have the machines here anymore, but we don't want them discovering what we've done with their old subway system in case they pull another surprise inspection at the theater."

"That's probably a good idea," Henry agreed. "But when you want the door back, send a message to Verity."

Colin stopped at the end of the passage we were in. "I'm going to show great faith in you by not blindfolding you. You already know about the subway, and you know a couple of the access points, so there's not much point in confusing you about where you are now. But I will stress that this location is a secret that only the Rebel Mechanics know."

"On our honor, we will keep this secret," Geoffrey said solemnly.

"Well, good, then. Otherwise, I'd have to kill you." Colin grinned as he said it, but his eyes were unusually serious. I shuddered at the thought that he might have meant it.

IN WHICH WE MAKE GREAT PLANS

I felt like Colin was taking us on a particularly circuitous path as we spent longer than I recalled was necessary walking through tunnels. I was tempted to mark a wall so I'd know we were walking in circles if I saw the mark again. Finally, we reached a large steel door.

"Wait here a moment while I prepare our hosts for your presence," Colin said. "Ladies, if you'll care to join me—other than Verity." Lizzie and Emma followed Colin through the doorway, leaving me with the magister men.

"I get the feeling we're not entirely welcome," Philip said, his tone flippant.

"But I thought they wanted money," Geoffrey said, frowning.

"I don't think they like having to ask for it," Henry said.

"What they wanted was more money from the Masked

Bandits," I explained. "They probably don't want money from magisters, unless it's stolen from them. This is...I think this is making them think about people in a different way. They hate owing you anything. Remember, you're what they're rebelling against."

"We're what we're rebelling against, too," Philip said. "We don't want to have to be what we are."

"Then you'll have to show them who you are, that you're individual people, not just magisters."

I was beginning to fear that Colin had stranded us there when he finally returned. "Come, and enjoy the party," he said, flinging the door open theatrically.

We found ourselves in the main station of the underground railway. "It's got to be the safest place in the city for us to gather, since no one knows about it," Colin said. "And you have to admit, an underground rail station is rather appropriate for our cause."

The magisters had seen the station the night we loaded the machines onto the subterranean railway to get them out of the city, but they hadn't had much time then to look at their surroundings. This station had been built when the railway was meant as a way for magisters to travel out of the weather. As a result, it looked like the first-class waiting area of a major railroad depot, with decorative tile and fine wood furnishings. By the time the station was completed and the tunnel bored, the magisters had moved uptown, and the railroad never went into service—until the Mechanics found it and fitted it out with their machines.

I was familiar with the station, but I'd never seen it quite like this before. The benches had been shoved aside to create an open dance floor on which people in colorful Mechanics garb were twirling around to the tunes provided by a small band set up in a corner. They didn't have the full-sized calliope that had been at the last Mechanics party I'd attended, but they did have a miniature model providing a breathy, hooting descant to their wild music.

I recognized the odd and overly complicated drink dispenser, but there was also a new one with an array of bottles and a mass of tubing flowing into a line of glasses. The big machines might be safely out of the city, but some of the smaller models were there. A small traction engine pulled a cargo of sandwiches across the floor, and a tiny airship drifted around the room with a basket of roasted nuts in its gondola. People grabbed handfuls as it passed them.

"You appear to incorporate your mechanical philosophy into your recreation, as well," Geoffrey remarked to Colin.

"It's a way of life," Colin said. "We think of new ways of doing things. Some of the machines are less useful than others, but they're still fun to make."

I noticed after watching the party for a minute or two that most of the attendees wore goggles pulled down over their eyes. I knew the Mechanics often wore goggles as part of their attire, sometimes even for practical purposes, but were they now using them as masks to hide their identities from the visiting magisters?

Philip was the first to make a move to join the party. He approached Emma and held out his hand in an invitation to dance. Soon, they'd blended into the swirl of color in the middle of the room. "Feel free to enjoy yourselves," Colin urged. "We'll talk later when all of us are here."

Geoffrey and Henry looked at each other and shrugged. "We may as well," Geoffrey said. "How often are we likely to get an invitation like this?"

Henry turned to me. "You've been to their parties before, haven't you? What would you recommend?"

"I think you should get a drink over there." I pointed to the drink dispenser. "You really ought to see it in action."

We skirted the dance floor to reach it, and Geoffrey went first in tossing a small gear into the tray that set the elaborate machine in motion, mixing various liquids to be poured into a tin cup. He and Henry laughed as they watched the machine in motion. Just as Henry was taking his turn, I noticed someone approaching us. He wore a hat and goggles, but my breath caught in my throat as I watched him. The first time I'd met Alec, he'd been dressed similarly. I wondered if there would ever come a time when seeing him didn't affect me so strongly. I'd seen him just days ago, so it wasn't as though this was the first time I'd encountered him after our falling-out.

When he reached us, he took off his hat, shoved the goggles up onto his forehead, and bowed slightly to me. "This is a bit of a surprise," he said.

"It shouldn't be. You were the one who approached

me to ask for help." I gestured to the magisters. "I brought them so you could ask them yourself."

Henry, having obtained his drink, turned around and saw Alec. "Oh, hello. Alec, was it?" he said. "Good to see you again. This is Geoffrey. I don't know if you remember him from the night we saved your machines. And Philip is around here somewhere." If he noticed any tension, he gave no sign of it, but he had managed to slip in a reminder of the aid they'd already provided.

Alec nodded to them. "Thank you again for your help. And for considering helping us again. There are a couple more people who aren't here yet, so enjoy yourselves in the meantime."

"It's quite a show you're putting on," Geoffrey said.

"You've seen the real machines. These are just demonstrations and class projects," Alec said.

"So you're a student?" Henry asked.

"Not on track to graduate anytime soon," Alec said with a laugh. "I keep missing classes."

"And I imagine your term was disrupted when you had to flee the city."

"The machines had to leave. The people can come and go, as long as we keep our heads down. In fact, us being in class keeps them from knowing for certain who was part of the movement they thought they drove out. If we'd vanished, it would have been like a confession." He turned to me. "Verity, would you care to dance?"

"Not really," I said.

"Then would you be willing to take a turn around the room with me?"

I suspected that meant he wanted to talk, and I wasn't sure I wanted to do so. I automatically glanced at Henry, reluctant to leave him and unable to avoid comparing the two men. Henry, whose obliviousness wasn't always an act, said, "Go on, Verity. Enjoy yourself. We'll be fine."

Declining Alec's invitation after that would only raise questions I'd rather not have to answer, so I took the arm Alec offered and walked away with him. "I really wasn't expecting you to bring the magisters to us," he said.

"You asked me to ask them for more money. I thought you should speak directly. You'd do a better job of making your case than I would, since I don't know what you need or what you have planned." I kept my tone stiff and formal, the way I might speak with Rollo's headmaster.

"You're still angry with me," he said with a rueful grin.

I started to deny it, but decided that honesty would be better. "Yes, I'm angry. How should I feel? You deceived me, and then even after you knew me better and knew where I stood, you didn't trust me enough to let me in on the truth. You'd have kept on using me if I hadn't figured it out."

"I told you, it may have started as a lie, but it came to be real. I miss you, Verity. You mean a lot to me, and I enjoyed our time together. Couldn't you try giving me a second chance? We could start over, with total honesty this time."

Could I? I forced myself to look at him, to remember

the time when the thought of him made me tremble. I remembered the kisses we'd shared, the time he held me against himself as we hid from what I'd believed were soldiers looking for us. That was the sticking point. He'd led me to believe so many things that weren't true, just to manipulate me. I wasn't sure I'd ever be able to trust him the way I needed to trust anyone I grew close to. "A lot more time would have to pass before I could even consider it," I said at last. "We have too much to do."

"You know nothing could ever happen with your magister boy."

"It's not about him," I said, willing my face not to flush and give me away. "Whether or not Henry and I have any interest in each other—which we don't—it doesn't change the fact that I can't trust you to be honest with me as long as the cause is involved, and the cause is what's most important for all of us right now."

"Then after the revolution, we'll talk."

After the revolution, perhaps I would have a chance to be with Henry, but that seemed like such a far-off dream that it was no more realistic than one of Olive's storybooks. "Perhaps," was all I said. "Now I think I should return to"—I almost said "my friends," which would likely have been interpreted badly—"the others."

We reached Henry and Geoffrey just as Colin app-roached them. "We're all here, if you can extract your friend from Emma's delightful grasp," he said.

Henry signaled to Philip, who handed Emma over to

another dance partner before joining us on one of the benches that had been pushed against a wall. Colin, Alec, and two other men I didn't know pulled up chairs to face us. The two strange men wore goggles, and they weren't introduced to us.

Colin was apparently the spokesman for the group. "You've seen our machines and what they can do," he said. "We've got the big engines that can haul just about anything, and they also make a rather formidable battering ram. The same sort of engine could be put on a railroad and haul just as much, just as quickly, as a magical engine. We've got an airship we're still improving. There's this underground railway, and we've got electric dynamos that can give us lights and communications."

"Yes, it's all very impressive," Geoffrey said. "I'd love a chance to get a better look."

"No offense to your lordships, but we figure these machines are the key to us beating the magisters," Colin continued. "You have magical power that you control, and that's been what stopped us from winning our freedom before, but now we've come up with ways to generate our own power. The problem is, it costs money to make enough of these to make any difference. A couple of steam traction engines aren't going to win a war for us. Having the technology will also allow us to maintain our independence after we kick you lot out. So, we need money."

"We've been funding you all along," Henry said.

"Yes, and that's how we've been able to develop the

prototypes," Alec said. "Production requires a different sort of financing. And since you've been funding us..."

"I'm afraid there won't be any money from the Masked Bandits for some time," Henry said. "We're on hiatus. We came too close to getting caught, so we want the authorities to think we've quit or have left town."

"There's also no way we could steal enough money to fund the kind of industry you're talking about," Philip added. "We'd have to hit every bank in the colonies. That's beyond our capability."

Geoffrey took a sheet of paper out of his breast pocket. "I ran some hypothetical numbers, based on material and labor costs. What you want to do is just about impossible. Do you realize how many factories it would require to produce enough to make a difference in a war against the Empire? How much raw material and manpower? You need an entire industry. And you'd have to do it without anyone noticing so you don't get shut down before you finish production."

"We thought we might take some existing magical equipment and retrofit it for a new power supply," Alec said.

"No one will notice you buying up surplus equipment?"

"So we're just supposed to lie down and take it? Not revolt at all?" Colin said.

"No, but I'm afraid this is beyond us," Geoffrey said. "It would take many more of us, all over the colonies, maybe even back in England, to have the resources to pull this off. I might be able to buy you a magical engine or two and the equipment you'd need to retrofit it. But you need hundreds of engines, plus the organizational infrastructure to hide what you're doing as some innocuous enterprise."

It was as though someone had dumped cold water over the party. The magisters and Mechanics alike looked crest-fallen. "So, you're not going to help us, then?" Colin said.

"We didn't say that," Henry said. "There are more of us than you might realize who are sympathetic to the cause. Many of us want revolution, too. We might be able to find investors to fund your efforts."

Alec's angry response surprised me. With a fierce glare, he crossed his arms over his chest and said, "Oh, so our overlords will deign to give us money? What will you expect in return? Are you buying us?"

Henry's eyes flashed, but he kept his tone perfectly cool as he replied, "You were willing to ask us to put our lives on the line to steal money to fund your cause. Is it so different if we offer to give you money?"

"If you give us your money, we're beholden to you. You might expect us to dance to your tune," Alec said. "Isn't that how investment usually works?"

"We would want to be equal partners in the revolution," Henry said. "We wouldn't just be funding your rebellion. We're doing this not because we like you, but because we want to be free just as much as you do."

Alec shook his head. "Then we'd just be answering to a different group of magisters. What's the point of a rebellion, then?"

"Freedom," Philip said. "We could make our own decisions instead of being ruled by people living on the other side of the ocean. We could break down the barriers between magisters and everyone else. People could decide for themselves what they want to be and do. Your machines would help level the field, as you said. We'd all be equals."

Leaning forward and looking Alec square in the eye, Henry said, "Look, we're planning a revolution with or without you. We have wealth and magic on our side, so we don't really need you. We've been sending money to your people because the nation we imagine is more equitable, and your technology helps make us equals. But if you don't want to participate, that makes equality a lot more difficult."

The men on both sides glared at each other. I worried that they'd come to blows, but Colin broke the tension. "This would all be a lot simpler if you'd just agree to rob each other and then give us the money," he quipped.

One of the Mechanic men who'd been silently listening all this time said, "We will have to think about this and discuss it with our people." He stood, and the others rose, as well. "Now, you are free to enjoy the party as our guests."

The Mechanics went back to the party, but before he left us, Colin said, "When you're ready to leave, let us know. We can either send you uptown via the subway, or I can guide you to the surface."

The magister men and I lingered on our bench. "What are you going to do?" I asked.

"I suppose that's up to them," Henry replied with a weary sigh. "But in case they do want our help, we should probably start doing more organizing on our end. We're not quite as ready to rebel as I made it sound, but we should be."

"What about Brad up in Boston?" Philip said. "He was a good chap—had the best ideas. Last time I talked to him, he made it sound like they'd put together quite a group. They've even been taking action, sabotage and that sort of thing."

"I'm sure there are others in the other colonies. I've heard rumors that there are rebel sympathizers at some rather high levels," Geoffrey said. "The trick would be finding them and finding an excuse to meet with the other groups. This lot here may be secretive and worried about being caught, but we're under a lot more scrutiny."

I had a burst of insight. Turning to Henry, I said, "You should come with us on the governor's trip."

"Me? I'm not sure I was invited."

"It didn't sound like you were being specifically excluded, and if he really wants to take the children for their benefit, as he said, he can hardly deny you."

"Then I'd have to face him in close quarters for an extended time." He shuddered at the thought.

"Think of it as a test of your acting ability and your cover identity."

"It's too bad it's the wrong time of year for peak insect activity," he said with a mischievous smile.

"What trip is this?" Philip asked.

"The governor is meeting with the local governments around the colonies, and he wants to bring the children," Henry explained.

"Oh, you should definitely go," Geoffrey said. "It's the perfect opportunity to make contact, and right under the governor's nose."

Henry clapped me on the back. "Capital idea, Verity," he said. "I knew there was a reason I hired you."

"I thought it was to keep a potential witness under your eye."

"Yes, but a witness who kept her wits in a crisis. That was also important." Still beaming, he shook his head. "I can't believe I didn't think of it. This trip should be just what we need to start building an organization."

"And think of the intelligence you might be able to pick up."

"I'm counting on you to do that for me. You'll probably have more access among the governor's people than I will. I'll just have to rearrange a few plans and then let the governor know that we're definitely going. I suppose it would help if you can talk Flora into coming along without sulking."

"I believe you'll find her resigned to it."

"You've already pulled off a miracle!"

"I merely reminded her that a prolonged absence is unlikely to change her situation."

"Oh? Is the object of her affections unavailable, or perhaps unsuitable?"

"Both, I'm afraid," I said, forcing myself not to glance at Colin, where he was energetically dancing in the middle of the room. "I suspect that what she needs most is a distraction."

"I never saw Flora setting her cap for an unsuitable type."

"Oh, but the person you can't have is a very romantic figure." I'd said it as a joke, only a second later realizing that it was true for me, as well. I thought of Flora as a child, but she wasn't quite a year younger than I was. I waited for him to respond, hoping he wouldn't notice the full implication of what I'd said, but his focus on the mission came to my rescue.

He was too busy thinking ahead. "I can't wait to see the governor's face when I tell him. And I suppose I'd better send messages to my friends."

"Meanwhile, we'll see what we can stir up here in the city," Philip said. "Some of our friends may have other friends, and so forth."

"But be careful," Geoffrey said. "We have to be absolutely certain who we can trust. One word to the authorities, and we're all doomed."

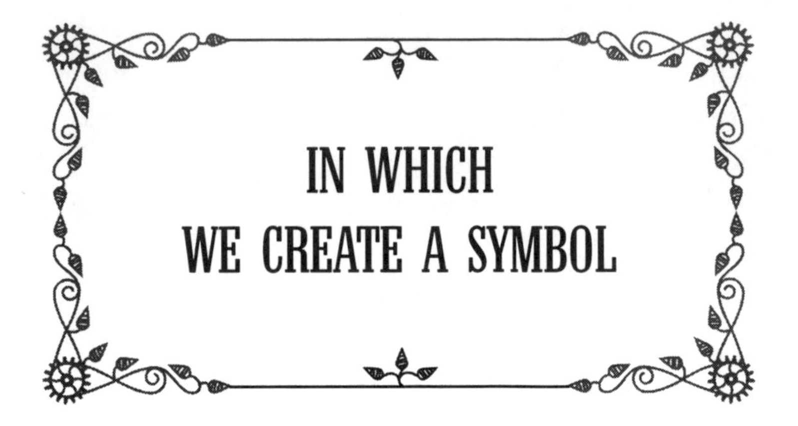

IN WHICH WE CREATE A SYMBOL

"What we need is a symbol like that red ribbon the Mechanics wear," Philip said. "Once someone's been vetted and sworn an oath, they get the insignia, and then we'll know who's truly a part of the group."

"What do you suggest?" Henry asked.

Philip fished around in his pockets and came up with a small key, the sort that might be used to open a jewelry box. "It's a symbol of how sealed our lips have to be."

"We all carry keys," Geoffrey said with a wry smile. "That doesn't narrow it down much."

"If you will forgive me, Miss Newton," Philip said, and he pulled the new blue ribbon out of my hair. With his pocket knife, he cut a small section off it and tied it to the key. "And there, we have a symbol. But I think what we should do is get multiple keys that fit a particular box, and that's the test for which keys are genuine, as a further security measure."

"I know a good locksmith who can take care of that," Geoffrey said.

Philip stuck the rest of his ribbon in his pocket. "I'll buy you a new ribbon, Miss Newton, but I like the color of this one, so if you don't mind, I'll keep it to make the first batch of keys."

"I think it's appropriate that this will have a link to her," Henry said. "Verity has been so instrumental. Now, do you want to stay for the rest of the party, or are you ready to go?"

"I need to have a word with Lizzie," I said.

"Take your time," Philip said, his gaze seeking out Emma. I wondered if I should play chaperone here, but I didn't think he was likely to do anything untoward.

I found Lizzie near the refreshment table. "I did have one other idea," I said as I approached her. I took my article out of my purse and handed it to her. "I wrote this about taking a collection to fund the cause. I know most of your members have no money, but little bits can add up, and it might make them feel less beholden to the magisters."

"I'll pass it to the editor and see if he'll consider it." She put it in her pocket, then looked up at me. "I hope you weren't offended by our response tonight. This is a whole new way of thinking for us. I know it took a lot for Alec to even consider asking for help. Bringing in magisters as partners, well, that's a big leap for an anti-magister movement."

"I'm sure they understand."

With a smile, she leaned closer to me. "Now, I need to know what you did to Colin. He's been quite addled since the last time he saw you. I mean, more addled than usual."

"Addled, how?" I asked.

"He came from meeting you in the park the other day with his head in the clouds and stars in his eyes. He was spouting terrible poetry and making up songs. He sang about golden hair, so I knew he hadn't suddenly developed an affection for you—and he wouldn't do that to Alec."

"Oh dear," I said. "It was Flora—Lady Flora, my pupil. Henry's niece. She was with me when I met him in the park, so we couldn't talk, and she's been the same way since then, only without the poetry, as far as I know. There has been a great deal of very dramatic piano playing, however."

"Are you quite sure? Colin swooning over a magister girl? That seems unlike him."

"I suppose it's possible that he encountered some other young lady, which would make all of Flora's sighing even more tragic, but I can attest that their eyes locked in a way that reminded me of the worst sort of novel."

"I won't tell him that your charge is equally enamored of him."

"I won't tell her about him, either. With any luck, it will blow over."

"He'll get over it soon enough. He always does. The next pretty face to come along will distract him. Or the next interesting machine. If not, we'll have to arrange for them to spend more time together. I'm sure that would get both of them over it."

"Very likely," I said with a laugh. "She'd bore him with talk of ballgowns, and she'd find him rather coarse."

She reached over to take my hand. "I've missed this, Verity. I know it's hard for you to believe, but I really did consider you a friend. Can we be friends again?"

I studied her for a long moment, uncertain. She'd hurt me, no doubt about it. I'd felt abused and betrayed by her deception. But at the same time, I was glad I'd become a part of her cause. Would that have happened if they hadn't lured me in the way they had? It wasn't as though I had so many friends I could afford to discard one. I had my network, but I didn't know their names and couldn't talk openly to any of them. There was Henry, but that relationship was fraught with complications. "We could try starting again," I said at last. "I don't think it will ever be the same because I'm not the same person I was then, but I would like to be friends."

Her eyes glittered, and she blinked rapidly. "I'd like that, Verity, and I mean that sincerely."

Alec joined us then, apparently not sensing that he'd interrupted a meaningful moment. "We'll be in touch to let you and the magisters know what we decide, and to find out what they can do," he said.

"I may not be in a position to communicate for a while," I said, my tone crisp and frosty.

"That sounds ominous."

"It isn't. My duties are merely taking me elsewhere. The governor is taking the children on a trip, and he's bringing me along to keep up with their studies. I know we're going to Boston and to Charleston, in the Carolinas."

"At the risk of sounding like I'm using you again, that sounds like a good opportunity for espionage or reporting. You'll try, won't you?"

"Don't worry, I'll collect all the intelligence I can, but I will have to be careful about any newspaper accounts I write. If Liberty Jones happens to report from all the places I visit, people may figure out who she really is."

"I'm sure you can compose dispatches in such a way as to hide your identity."

"And perhaps someone in New York could momentarily assume Liberty's mantle in your absence," Lizzie suggested. "If Liberty is reporting in New York, she can't possibly be traveling with the governor."

"Excellent idea!" I said. "Is there any way for me to send information from my travels, or must I wait to share it upon my return?"

"We have people throughout the colonies, and you know how to recognize them," Alec said.

"I'm not sure how much opportunity I'll have, as I'll be under the governor's eye."

"I'm sure you'll think of something, and your Lord Henry will help you get away." He still said Henry's name as though he found it distasteful. I didn't try to argue with him because I couldn't tell if it was jealousy about me or irritation that the Mechanics and the magisters hadn't been able to come to terms in the way he'd hoped.

"We may be able to get someone in contact with you," Lizzie said. "Definitely in Boston, as we have family there."

"I'll be on the lookout for allies as I travel."

"Have a safe and pleasant journey," Lizzie said.

"Thank you. Now, I think the others are ready to go, so we'll need a guide out of here."

Lizzie signaled to her brother. "Do you need to leave from this part of the city, or would you like to go uptown?" she asked while we waited for Colin to finish dancing.

"I'd better ask them," I said, nodding toward Henry. He and the others joined us, and I relayed the question to them.

"I don't think we've given anyone any reason to be watching us," Henry said, "but it's probably safest if we return home from approximately the same part of the city as we went to. You never know when a cab driver might have noticed his passengers."

"We're probably less conspicuous like this here than we would be uptown," Philip added with a gesture at his clothes.

"True," Lizzie said, nodding. "And even if someone does spot you as a magister, it's not unusual for your sort of young men to come slumming down here. There's precious little nightlife that would attract magisters near our other stations."

Colin finally came off the dance floor, red-faced and sweating. "You signaled, dearest sister?"

"If you're quite through making a spectacle of yourself,

our guests are ready to leave. Would you mind escorting them back? Or are you having too much fun?"

"I can do it. Not a problem."

"Should we perhaps escort our young lady companions back to their home?" Philip asked.

"I don't think you're being watched *that* closely," Lizzie said. "Besides, it wouldn't be that odd for us to stay out later on our own. We do it all the time."

Philip did an admirable job of keeping his disappointment from showing. "Then convey my regards to the lovely Miss Emma," he said.

Colin put on his hat and switched on the lamp in the hatband. "If you'll follow me." After a final farewell to Lizzie and Alec, we headed into the tunnels with Colin.

I'd learned my way through the underground passages well enough to get from some entrances to the station, but I wasn't familiar with the route Colin used. I was fairly certain he was deliberately trying to keep the magisters disoriented. I tried counting my steps and noticing turns, but it did no good. I was hopelessly lost. As a result, I was surprised when Colin opened a door and we arrived in the theater's basement.

"Do you think you can find your own way from here?" he asked. "The doors upstairs will lock behind you when you leave."

"I'm sure we'll manage," Geoffrey said.

"Well, then, a good evening to you, gentlemen and Verity." He vanished back into the darkness, the door closing with a clang behind him.

"So, Verity, you know the way out?" Henry said.

"Yes, the stairs are through here." I led them down the corridor toward the stairs. We were halfway up when I thought I heard something above. I froze and gestured for the others to stop.

There were definitely voices coming from the auditorium, but whose? Had some of the cast or crew stayed behind? Were Mechanics standing watch? I strained my ears, listening until I could make out words.

"I don't see anything," one of the voices said, his accent suggesting he was from England rather than a native of the colonies. "It still just looks like a theater to me."

"You know what the captain said. Search the whole place. I personally think he's got Mechanics on the brain. But we've got to be sure."

Alarmed, I motioned for the men to go back down the stairs. The voices sounded like they were moving closer. There weren't many good reasons for us to be in the theater so long after a show had ended, and even if the magisters disclosed their rank to indimidate the soldiers, it wouldn't explain what I was doing with them.

If the soldiers searched the whole theater, surely they'd look in the basement, and that meant we were trapped. I wasn't confident of being able to find our way back through the tunnels. I did know of one other way out that I'd used before. We'd been escaping from what turned out to be a fake raid, but perhaps the escape route was still valid.

I steered the men into the room near the foot of the stairs where the dynamo once stood. From there, I didn't have to tell them my plan. Geoffrey dragged over a chair and climbed up to open the window, then pulled himself up and out before turning back and leaning down. Henry helped me climb onto the chair, and Geoffrey caught my hands to pull me up. Once the other two were out, Geoffrey eased the window closed.

We were in a dark alley behind the theater. "Where do we go from here?" Philip asked.

I remembered then that Alec had blindfolded me when we'd escaped that way before. I wasn't entirely sure where to go. But I knew now exactly where we'd been, and an alley had to lead somewhere. I closed my eyes, trying to remember how it had felt, then opened my eyes and pointed. "That way."

We hurried down the alley. I had to resist the urge to look back and see if a light showed through the basement windows. I consoled myself with the thought that the searchers didn't sound like they were being particularly diligent. They were going through the motions, which made it extremely unlikely that they would go so far as to look out the windows to see if anyone had escaped into the alley.

When we saw a street ahead, I allowed myself a slight sigh of relief. I wasn't entirely sure if it was the same street where Alec and I had gone, but I was sure we could figure out where we were easily enough. Henry motioned for us to wait in the alley while he checked out the street. After barely a second, he ducked quickly back into the alley and moved his hand in a pattern that looked familiar. I felt the surge of magic as Philip and Geoffrey followed his lead. Soon, I only knew where they were because I'd seen them before. Otherwise, they seemed to have become part of the shadows.

A moment later, I understood. A group of soldiers, their weapons held ready, passed by, pausing to look into the alley. I held my breath and presumed that Henry had hidden me, as well. He'd taught me the magic he'd used, but I wasn't ready to reveal my heritage to his friends.

The soldiers lingered for what seemed like forever, but what was probably only a few seconds, before moving on. I heard relieved exhales all around me a few seconds after they left and knew that the men had been just as tense as I'd been. There really had been no logical reason to assume that the soldiers were searching for us, but it would have been hard to explain why we were in the alley. After another minute or so, the shadows melted away, and Henry checked the street once again, this time signaling that it was safe for us to leave.

We blended into the crowd very easily, but I soon saw the cause of Henry's caution. There were far more soldiers than I would have expected to be out in the street, and I wasn't sure if they were enjoying one last night out before they left the city or if they were looking for something.

"Now I think we should find a cab for Verity," Henry said.

I shook my head. "First we need to warn the Mechanics that the theater is being searched. I don't think they'll find the tunnels, and if they do they may not find the station, but the Mechanics need to know not to leave that way."

"But how can you warn them?" Geoffrey asked. "Are we going back down there?"

"We don't have to. I just need to tell someone, and they have ways to spread the word."

When we reached the next intersection, I got my bearings from the street signs. I had a contact not too far from here, and she had access to the telegraph. I led the men down the street and around the corner to a tavern.

Henry held me back on the threshold. "I'm not sure this is a suitable place for a young lady."

"I know a barmaid who works here." I pulled my hair around my shoulders. "Besides, at the moment I don't really look like a proper young lady."

Before he could object further, I entered the tavern. While the clientele was mostly male, Henry was correct that the women there wouldn't have been considered ladylike by his class. I knew some of them, and for the most part they were hardworking young women with honest jobs. I scanned the room, looking for my contact, and spotted her carrying a tray of mugs to a table. When she'd delivered her drinks, I caught her eye, and she came over to us.

"And how can I help you good people?" she said.

I leaned closer to her so our words wouldn't be overheard in the noisy tavern. "Some soldiers are searching the theater. I don't know if they'll get beyond that, but someone needs to warn the station."

"I'll take care of it," she said softly, then added more loudly, "I'll be right back with your order, if you'll have a seat."

The men all looked at me, then at each other, hesitant. Since they weren't acting, I went over to a table and sat down. They reluctantly joined me. When Henry gave me a questioning look, I leaned closer to him and said, "Well, we can't exactly walk in here, say one thing to the barmaid, and walk out. Even if that doesn't draw attention to us, it might make her look suspicious."

"Good point," he said, still looking ill at ease and out of place. Philip seemed much more at home. He leaned back in his chair and smiled at the group of girls at the next table. Geoffrey looked even stiffer than Henry did.

Then he stiffened even more. "Don't look now, but I think that's Rutledge over there," he muttered.

"Rutledge?" Philip said, starting to turn his head but quickly stopping himself. "What would he be doing in a place like this? He was always the worst snob in the school."

"He's exactly the sort who would enjoy slumming," Henry said through gritted teeth.

"True, that does make it easier to feel superior," Philip said.

"Maybe he won't notice us or recognize us," Geoffrey said, his voice sounding strained.

The barmaid returned with a tray full of glasses and set them down in front of us. She gave me a meaningful nod as she put down my drink, and I smiled in thanks. I wasn't sure what she'd brought us, as we hadn't actually ordered anything. It proved to be a sweet but potent cider. I resolved to only sip it.

Unfortunately, it seemed that the barmaid had drawn attention to our table, and soon a young man sauntered over to us. He might have been slumming in a downtown tavern, but he was dressed to show that he was above his environment, in clothes that were ostentatiously expensive. "Well, well, if it isn't my old school chums," he said in a nasal drawl. "What on earth are you lot doing here?" He brushed at Geoffrey's shoulder, like he was wiping away lint. "Whatever it is, you need to fire your tailors." He barked a laugh.

I barely stifled a yelp when Philip leaned closer to me and draped an arm around my shoulder, pulling me against him. "I'm visiting a friend," he said with a showy wink. "The others are my cover story. I'm out with friends, you know? Blending in, and all that. You won't tell the pater, will you? He'd never understand."

Rutledge eyed me, and I could feel his disapproval. "Really, Spencer, I thought you had better taste. If you want to be with a common girl, you can find them a lot prettier."

I thought Henry would come out of his chair, and he started to draw back his arm, but there was a dull thud under the table, after which Henry gasped and grimaced in pain. Breathing heavily, he stayed put.

"Not everyone is as shallow as you are, Rutledge,"

Geoffrey said. "There are so many qualities that make a woman worthy of attention, if you are worthy of perceiving them." He drained his glass, took some coins out of his pocket and threw them on the table, then pushed his chair back, forcing Rutledge to move, and stood. "Now, I'm finding the atmosphere here rather uninviting. Shall we go?"

Philip removed his arm from my shoulders, stood, and helped pull my chair away from the table. He offered me his hand to rise, and then he swept out of the tavern with me on his arm and the other two following. When we were about a block away, we stopped, and all the men doubled over in laughter. I watched them, my arms folded across my chest, unsure of what was so funny. Henry finally regained the self-control to say, "Sorry about that, Verity. You just have to know him."

"And what he must think of us," Philip said, still sputtering a little.

"I'm not sure he'd know what to think," Geoffrey added with a smirk. "Though I imagine he never thought he'd find the likes of us in a place like that. He presumes he's the only one daring enough to mix with the lower classes."

Now under more control, Philip bowed to me. "My apologies, Miss Newton, for roping you into the charade like that, but I thought it best if he didn't associate you with Henry, on the off chance that you might look familiar if he saw you again. I doubt he'll make the connection if he encounters you as Henry's governess."

"I don't think he'd recognize you if he saw you under different circumstances," Henry said, giving me an odd, appraising look.

Self-consciously, I brushed my hair back off my shoulders. I so seldom wore it loose that it felt odd to have it freed like this. I started to braid it, and Philip said, "I owe you a ribbon!" He dashed away to a sidewalk cart and returned with a ribbon that wasn't quite the same shade of blue or the same quality as the one that had become a rebel magister insignia, but I thought even the hawk-eyed housekeeper wouldn't have a reason to find my appearance suspiciously changed.

While I tied my hair back, Henry went in search of a cab. This wasn't the ideal neighborhood for hailing magical cabs, so we ended up walking several blocks before we found one. Henry handed me up into it and said, "I'll be home soon enough. We'll take the next one we find."

"I'll see you there," I said. Once the cab was moving, I leaned back in my seat with a sigh. I wasn't sure what we'd accomplished tonight, but I still felt like our circumstances had changed significantly.

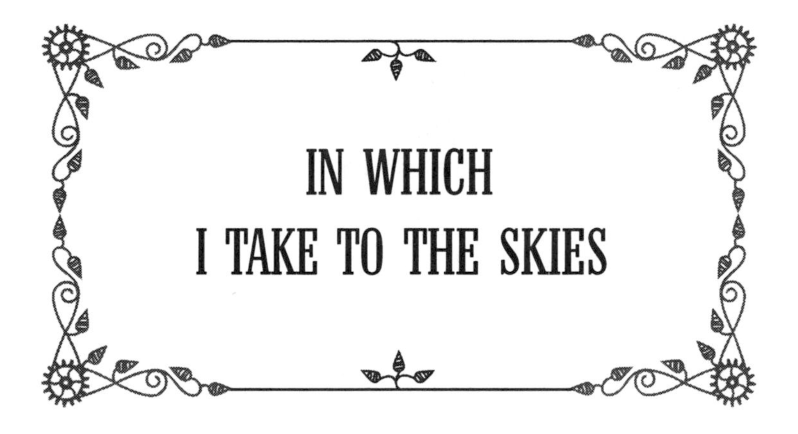

IN WHICH I TAKE TO THE SKIES

I wish I could have been there when Henry told the governor that he was not only letting the children go on the trip, he was also joining them, but Henry went to the governor's office for that conversation, and there was no reason for me to join him. Instead, I went about my usual weekday routine on Monday. Henry hadn't yet returned from his meeting with the governor when I went alone to retrieve Rollo from school while the girls began their music lessons. I was just in time to see a swarm of boys in school uniforms come rushing down the front steps of the school.

Rollo was with a group of friends, and when he glanced my way he didn't acknowledge me. I was familiar with the ritual and didn't acknowledge him, either. I began walking slowly in the direction of home, and once I'd rounded the corner, he joined me. I knew it made things easier for him at school if it wasn't obvious that the governess was walking him home, even if every other boy in the school was also chaperoned. I couldn't be quite as discreet when Olive was with me because she'd jump up and down, waving her arms and calling his name. I was never quite sure whether she was blissfully unaware of how badly that embarrassed her brother or knew exactly what she was doing and managed to look innocent.

Usually, this little game didn't bother me because I understood it. I'd been educated at home, so I'd never been in a similar situation, but I could still sympathize. Today, though, I was on edge and took it out on Rollo. "It's so nice of you to deign to join me on my afternoon walk, Rollo," I said, probably more sharply than I should have.

"Thanks so much for being understanding, Miss Newton. I don't know why Uncle Henry can't send a footman after me. That's what everyone else does. I'm too old to have a governess. Some of the other fellows tease me about having a nanny."

I immediately felt bad for my short temper. He didn't seem to have noticed my sarcasm, though, for he kept up a steady stream of chatter worthy of Olive, albeit on different subjects. Most of it washed over me while I thought about our upcoming journey, but then the words, "and since the troops are leaving, that should mean the *Hercules* will be back to get them. Do you think Grandfather can get me on board for a tour this time? I mean, if we're not off on our trip then," registered on my consciousness.

"The troops are leaving? Where did you hear that?"

"Some of the guys in my class said they saw it in the newspaper." I read the official newspaper more frequently than I did the paper I wrote for, and nothing had yet been said about troops leaving. Which meant some of his classmates were reading the underground newspaper. I couldn't think of a reason his governess would ask him precisely which classmate had mentioned the news, but I thought it might help Henry's efforts if he knew of a potential sympathizer. I made a mental note to mention it. He'd have more of a reason to sound Rollo out about his friends.

"Talk to your uncle. He might be able to persuade your grandfather," I said.

"I guess since they stopped the revolution, they don't need so many soldiers here anymore."

"Mmm hmm," I said, acknowledging him without comment, even though I wanted to say that the revolution was only just beginning.

"It's a real shame the machines disappeared, though," he continued. "I never did get to see a steam engine up close."

I had to bite the inside of my lip to keep from smiling. He would envy me if he knew how well-acquainted I was with steam engines.

"Uncle Henry will be pleased that I made the top score on my math exam. Hey, maybe he should tell Grandfather I need to tour an airship as a reward."

"That sounds perfectly reasonable to me," I said. "I will suggest it. But how is your writing coming along?"

He kicked at a rock on the sidewalk. "Maybe not as good. But I'm getting better. The teacher said I'm almost achieving coherence."

I had to laugh. Rollo wrote the way he talked, in a rush of enthusiasm, jumping from one topic to the next. We'd been working on organizing his thoughts in written communication, and I'd made him practice his penmanship. "It's good to hear my efforts are yielding some fruit."

"Yeah, I'm glad you're with us, Miss Newton."

He didn't seem to have realized how much he'd touched me, but my eyes stung slightly, and I felt a lump in my throat. I wasn't entirely sure I was qualified for the job I had. I felt like I'd bluffed my way into it. I had the knowledge, but no real experience in this kind of work, and Henry had mostly hired me because I'd challenged him during a train robbery and he wanted to keep an eye on me as a witness to his crime. So it was good to hear that I was accomplishing something aside from espionage.

When we reached the mansion, I could hear Olive carefully picking out scales on the piano. Although she was an accomplished student, she was an indifferent musician who saw it as a chore, while her sister was an accomplished musician and an indifferent student. "It sounds like I have a few minutes until I must serve my time," Rollo said with a sigh. Henry forced him to learn piano, as well, and only managed to get him to tolerate it by telling him that music was essentially mathematics.

"Go in and do your homework while you wait your

turn," I said, nudging him toward the family parlor where the piano was. With the children occupied with art and music lessons, I sought out Henry. He should have been back by now.

I nearly ran into him on the stairs. "How did it go?" I asked.

"He wasn't nearly as shocked as I would have liked. I suspect he sees it as a way to observe me up close."

"So we're going?"

"We leave next Monday. I'll tell the children at dinner."

I started to continue up the stairs to my room, but turned back. "Oh, I almost forgot. It sounds like someone at Rollo's school reads the *World*. He mentioned information he heard at school that was only printed there. You could try talking to him about his friends. There might be someone sympathetic within the school."

"His friend's parents need to have a talk with their son. It could be quite dangerous to let something like that slip at that school. The majority there are loyal royalists. If any other boy at the school brought home that story, there could be trouble. It might even be considered sedition."

"When you say things like that, it makes me want this revolution even more," I said with a shudder. "To think that merely saying something unpopular could cause real trouble."

"That's the way it's always been. We may seem to have privilege, and we certainly do, but we're watched more carefully than the fellows downtown. They can preach revolution in the taverns without catching much notice, but if I tried that sort of thing in the drawing rooms of the magister set, I'd find myself in prison. Do your Mechanic friends realize that I'm taking a bigger risk than they are?"

"That's why we're changing things. Our new country won't be that way, will it?"

"I think that most of the people who might side with us feel the same way."

From the preparations required for our journey, I'd have thought we were invading a distant country. We didn't have a specific itinerary, so we had to pack clothing for just about any occasion. That was easy for me, as I had one ballgown, one nice party frock, and several day dresses. Flora, on the other hand, wanted to bring the entire contents of her wardrobe. She only got to bring as many items as she did because the rest of us didn't come near meeting our weight limits for the airship. Henry tried to "forget" to bring evening attire, but his valet noticed the omission and corrected it just in time.

When the morning came to set out, most of our baggage had been sent ahead to the airfield on Long Island. The first leg of our journey, to Boston, would only take half a day, so we wouldn't need anything with us in the cabin other than whatever items we brought to pass the time. For once, I was the one most heavily laden, as I had books and school assignments for the children.

The governor met us at the airfield. "Good, you're

on time," he said brusquely. "The weather looks ideal for our voyage." He led us into the massive barnlike hangar, where I found myself gazing in awe at the leviathan inside. I knew this ship was far smaller than the military vessels I'd watched pass overhead, but it was still a lot larger than the rebels' *Liberty*. "Your first time to travel by air, Miss Newton?" the governor asked, and I was so startled to be addressed by him that I almost told him it wasn't, until I remembered that wasn't something to share with him.

"I've never traveled like this before," I told him, and it was true. The gondola on the *Liberty* was little more than a wicker basket. This ship had an enclosed gondola that looked like the cabin of a luxury yacht. Inside its hangar, the ship hung low to the ground, so we only needed a short flight of stairs to board through the nose of the gondola. We were seated in the passenger lounge, where windows were angled for a view of the earth below.

Rollo was too excited to sit. "Grandfather, please, may I watch the takeoff from the control room?" he begged. "And may I have a tour of the ship? I want to see it all!"

"Let's see what I can do," the governor said with a chuckle. The man was still intimidating, but I was beginning to see a different side of him. Although he represented the oppression of the colonies, he seemed to truly care about his grandchildren. He went forward for a few minutes and returned, beaming. "The captain would be delighted to have you as his guest, but you must stay out of the way and be very quiet."

"Outstanding!" Rollo cried out, sprinting forward.

Olive settled herself into one of the seats beside the windows. "I'm going to look out from here," she said. I noticed that she was very pale. There had been many a night when I'd had to soothe her nightmares about the airship accident that had killed her father. I wasn't sure how much resemblance her dreams bore to reality, so I sat beside her and took her hand.

"I've never flown like this before, so may I hold your hand?" I asked softly.

"Yes, Miss Newton. I would like that very much," she said, and the grip of her tiny hand on mine was likely to leave bruises, it was so fierce.

Even Flora seemed at least a little interested as the great ship began moving slowly forward. We burst out into the light upon leaving the hangar, and the ship drifted upward. The city gradually grew smaller beneath us, and we went out over the open water, turning to head northward. I realized I'd been holding my breath and made myself let it out slowly. I wasn't sure why I'd been so tense, unless I'd picked up on Olive's fear. I'd flown on a smaller, unproven nonmagical airship before, without even the security of a closed cabin. This one flew higher and moved faster, which might have accounted for my unease.

Once we'd stopped climbing and were drifting along far enough above the earth that I had less of a sense of speed, I managed to relax. It was quite peaceful, without the whipping wind I'd experienced on the *Liberty*. I might have enjoyed it, under different circumstances.

However, the presence of the governor was unsettling. Here I was, a rebel operative and a magical half-breed sitting just a few feet away from the person who embodied what we were rebelling against and who had the power of life or death over me. I'd been around him before when I chaperoned Flora at parties, and he'd paid brief visits to the Lyndon home, but now there were only a few of us in a relatively small space for the next five hours. I was afraid to speak, lest I accidentally reveal something incriminating.

On the other hand, I needed to do my job, which was the reason I'd been brought along, and now I had to do it in front of an audience, including my employer. "Olive, are you ready for some lessons?" I asked.

"Oh, yes!" she said enthusiastically. "I want to show Grandfather what I've learned."

I got out her schoolbooks and had just opened the science text when Rollo came bouncing back from the control room. "It was amazing!" he said. "I got to see how they released the tow cables and controlled the ascent. Then they showed me the charts."

"You're just in time for your schoolwork," I said.

His face fell. "Aw, really? In an airship?"

The governor chuckled. "I think perhaps we can postpone the schoolwork for the duration of the voyage. He can catch up later, once we've arrived."

"Thanks, Grandfather!" Rollo said. "Can I take that tour, instead? One of the crewmen said he'd show me the whole ship."

"I'll need a report about it," I said as sternly as I could

manage when his enthusiasm was so delightful. "And your schoolwork must be completed at some time today. I'm not the one who made those assignments."

"I believe your uncle has final say," the governor said.

"Please, Uncle Henry?" Rollo begged.

"I don't see why not, as long as you do your work in the evening, and you'll owe Miss Newton a favor for making her work a longer day."

"I don't mind," I said. "This isn't going to be a particularly arduous workday." Though, really, it was more difficult working under those circumstances. I could feel the governor watching us as I read along with Olive and quizzed her on her lessons. Fortunately, she was keen to show off, which made me look extremely competent.

Midmorning, the steward and maid brought around tea and pastries. At noon, the big table in the middle of the room was laid with fine china for a light luncheon. We were just finishing dessert when we began our descent into Boston.

There was only a slight jolt when we moored at the airfield. We exited down a flight of steps wheeled up to the nose of the gondola and boarded the carriages that waited for us. The younger children and I were in one carriage, while the governor, Henry, and Flora rode in the other.

"That's the only way to travel," Rollo said. "No bumps or jolts like in a carriage or a train. Maybe they should have smaller airships for traveling around town."

"They'd block out the sky if there were too many of

them," Olive said. "Why couldn't we ride with Grandfather and Uncle, like Flora did?"

"We're just kids," Rollo said, but he didn't sound like it bothered him. "They couldn't fit everyone in one carriage, and this way, we don't have to act too nice."

"Oh, really?" I asked, raising an eyebrow.

"Aw, Miss Newton, you're not like Grandfather. I may not act any different with you, but I *feel* like I'm acting better with you."

The carriage brought us to a stately townhome that wasn't quite as large as the governor's mansion, but it was a palace compared to the Lyndon home, which I had considered palatial when I first arrived. Looking at the outside, I thought this building must be a hotel, but once we entered, I realized it was a residence, and it was all ours for the week. Did the governor really keep a house like this just for his occasional visits to this city? I made a mental note to look further into the matter for a possible article.

The children and I were assigned to rooms on one of the upper floors—away from the governor's suite, much to my relief. I couldn't tell where Henry's room was, and there was no way to ask without looking improper. My room was much nicer than the one I had at home, which had clearly been designed for a governess. This room could have been for any guest. For a few days, so long as I was in my room, I might be able to forget my position.

Our bags and trunks were brought up, and while the housemaids were busy unpacking Flora's belongings, I hung up my own dresses in my room's wardrobe. When the maid entered, she startled me. "Oh, ye didn't have to do that, miss," she said, bustling in to take over. She was a sturdy girl about my age, with dark hair and dark blue eyes.

"I don't mind looking after myself," I said. "I'm only the governess."

"But ye're a guest in this house, miss."

"There's not much to do. I've done it already. Really, I don't mind."

Ignoring my objections, she picked up my bag and began unpacking. I tried to wrest it away from her, and something fell out of a pair of stockings, hitting the floor with a soft *ting*. I dove for the small gear with a red ribbon through it and hoped she didn't see it. I knew it had been risky to bring the symbol of the Rebel Mechanics with me while traveling with the governor and staying in his house, but Colin had mentioned arranging meetings with the local Mechanics, so I'd thought I might need it.

I'd hoped the maid hadn't seen it, but she bent to pick it up. She straightened and held the token by its ribbon, staring at it quizzically. "Ah, now that would explain why ye're so self-sufficient and don't like others waitin' on ye."

I couldn't tell if she meant that as a compliment or if she was implying that I'd wanted to unpack for myself because I had something to hide. A million responses flooded through my mind, ranging from threats to denial. Perhaps sensing my terror, she winked at me. "Oh, don't ye worry none, ye have nothin' to fear from me. I have one like it that I brought with me when I was hired for this job only just this week."

All my breath rushed out in a great *whoosh* of relief. "You're the local contact Lizzie set me up with? You could have said something before you gave me the vapors!"

She grinned. "And where's the fun in that?"

"You aren't related to Colin, by any chance, are you?" The sense of humor was certainly familiar.

"We're cousins of some sort. I've never tried to draw the family tree. I just know that my mother is somehow related to his father. And yes, I know that some things run in the family. I was lucky to get the wit and flair for the dramatic without the ginger hair and freckles."

"So if I uncover something I need to pass to the Mechanics, I give it to you?"

"Aye. 'Twill be a challenge right under the nose of his nibs, and that's what makes it fun."

"I'm sure I can count on your discretion."

"I've got as much to lose as you do. If it's your word against mine, you could throw me to the wolves."

"You don't have to worry about me."

I gave up fighting her about unpacking for me, since that gave her an excuse to stay and chat. She told me stories about Colin as a child that had me shaking with laughter. When she'd finished getting my room set just so, she surveyed her work with her hands on her hips and gave a nod of satisfaction. "There, just like home. Now, if you need me, pull the bell over there." I followed her gesture to a cord hanging on the wall over the bed. "My name's Mary, and I'll be taking care of you and the children. That Lady Flora's going to keep me hopping, isn't she?"

"Very likely, but if she gives you any trouble, let me know. Her uncle won't stand for it."

"He's the one who's helping? I take it he's the young one. Rather handsome, if ye like them scholarly. And if you can abide magisters."

"Yes, that's the one," I said, refraining from comment about how handsome Henry might or might not be. "He's not bad for a magister. You can trust him."

"Good to know. Well, I'd best be off. Plenty of work to do. Lovely chatting with you, miss. Shall I bring up some tea? We're letting the guests rest this afternoon, so a formal tea won't be served, but I can bring refreshments to your room. Dinner for the adults and Lady Flora will be at eight, but we'll serve supper in the nursery for you and the younger two at half-past six. And then if you're up to it, the Mechanics are having a gathering tonight. You and your Lord Henry are invited." She transitioned so smoothly into the invitation that it took me a moment to realize what she'd said.

"Tonight?"

"Yes, miss. Don't worry, it wasn't planned in your honor. The timing was merely convenient. But we'd love to have you there, you and his lordship."

"I'll have to speak to him. I'd also need to figure out how to get out of here and how to get there."

"I can help you with that, miss. Now, would you be wantin' some tea?"

"Yes, some tea would be lovely, thank you," I said. "Perhaps in an hour or so? I need to look in on the children and make sure they're doing their lessons, and if I get a chance to speak to Lord Henry, I can let you know then about the gathering."

"Very good, miss," she said, bobbing a quick curtsy. She gave me a wink over her shoulder as she left the room.

I took a moment to adjust my hair before going to check on Olive. She was lying on her back in the middle of a huge canopy bed. "It's a princess room!" she said.

"Just the thing for a princess," I replied. "Now, I want you to read that book I gave you on the history of Boston, before dinner. We'll talk about it then and plan what we want to see."

She dutifully got out her book and rolled onto her stomach to read, her chin resting on her fists. "I want to see everything," she declared.

"We have a week, so perhaps we shall," I said. "Now I'd better check on your brother."

I found Rollo examining every inch of his room, playing with the magical lights, and looking out the window. "I can't tell if this house has a central heating system," he said. "I don't find any ductwork. Could they really still be using fireplaces?"

"I have no idea. That might be something to ask your grandfather."

He flopped onto the bed. "What did you think of the airship, Miss Newton?"

"I found it to be a much easier journey than I've experienced on a train. Though I do like looking at the scenery from train windows. It's odd only seeing rooftops."

"That's why I think it would be great to have airships that travel just above the ground. No bumps, but you can still see out. I wonder why no one's done that yet."

"Perhaps you'll be the one to invent it. But first, before you forget any details, I'd like you to write an essay about what you learned on your tour of the ship today. I'll save your school assignments for tomorrow."

I expected him to protest, as he usually did any schoolwork, but he pulled out a notebook without complaint. "Good idea, Miss Newton. I don't want to forget any of it." I left him leaning over his notebook, his pen flying and his tongue sticking out from between his teeth as he concentrated intently.

I ran into Henry in the hallway outside. "Ah, Miss Newton, just the person I wanted to see," he said. "They've given you this room down the hall as a schoolroom." He escorted me to a sunny corner room that must have once been a playroom for little girls. I imagined the Lyndon children's late mother and their aunt, Lady Elinor, playing on the rocking horse and practicing the piano on the spinet in the corner.

Once we were in the room, he dropped his voice and said, "I'm afraid the governor is being conventional about dinner arrangements. You and the younger children will have an early meal in the nursery."

"I know. The maid told me. By the way, she's with the Mechanics."

He raised an eyebrow. "That's interesting. They got someone into the governor's house?"

"Apparently. She was just hired for our visit."

"I'll tell Olive and Rollo about dinner. Olive is bound to be disappointed, and I don't want you to have to be the bearer of bad news. I'm not sure Rollo will care." He smiled and added, "And I will have no one to talk to."

We were standing close together so we could speak without being overheard, and I knew that if we were seen like this, our relationship surely would be misunderstood. I wanted to take a step backward, but I couldn't bring myself to do so.

"I hope your dinner doesn't last too long," I said. "We've been invited to a gathering tonight."

"The local Mechanics?"

"Indeed. And you were specifically included in the invitation. Twice, now that I think about it."

"Do you know where or when?"

"The maid said she'll take care of that."

His lips twitched into a lopsided smile. "Well, now, sneaking out with the governess and a maid my first night in Boston. It's a pity I didn't choose 'incorrigible playboy' as my cover persona."

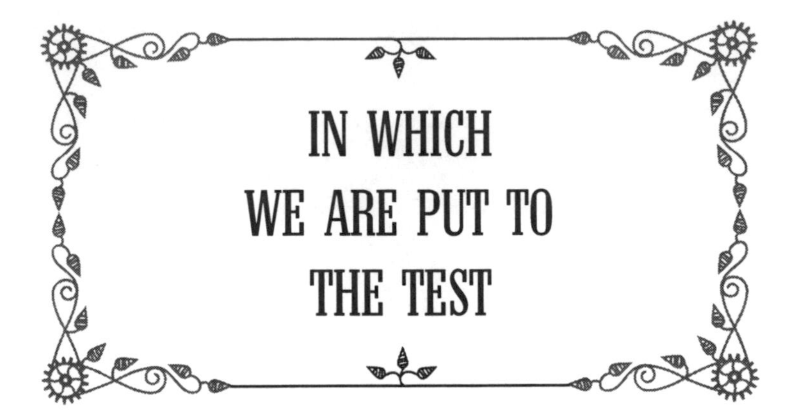

IN WHICH WE ARE PUT TO THE TEST

Mary brought tea to me at the appointed hour. She set the tray on the nightstand and poured into a pretty blue-and-white china teacup from a matching pot. "There ye are, miss," she said, handing the cup to me. "What did your Lord Henry have to say about tonight?"

"He accepts your invitation."

She beamed as she dropped a sugar cube into my cup. "It's good to hear that."

"You said you had a way to get us out of the house?"

"Aye, leave that to me. I'll come get you when they're through with dinner and it looks safe."

"What kind of gathering is it? How should I dress?"

"It's no big, fancy party, that's for certain. Dress plain."

A glance down at my simple gray day dress made me smile. I'd have to go out of my way *not* to dress plainly.

She left me alone with my tea, and I tried to force myself to relax. Mary obviously had things under control, so I had nothing to worry about in sneaking out of the house. I had no real agenda for the meeting other than getting acquainted, so there was no mission to succeed or fail. If the Boston Mechanics were anything like my New York friends, it would be more of a party than a real meeting, and that was something I realized I sorely needed. Aside from the recent show and party, my social life had disappeared with the rebel machines.

That evening at dinner, I was glad that I wasn't dining with the adults because it was a lot easier to hide my eagerness. Olive and Rollo were so excited about the day's voyage and being in a new place that they didn't seem to notice anything odd about my behavior. My bearing might have drawn more attention among the adults.

It was worse when dinner was finished and I'd seen Olive to bed, because then I had nothing to do but wait. I tried reading, but barely registered the words. I jotted a few notes about the airship voyage and the Boston house, but I didn't have enough information to make it into an article.

When Mary tapped lightly on my door, I jumped in shock, barely stifling a scream. This was no way for an experienced operative to behave, I told myself firmly as I forced my breathing to return to normal.

Mary grinned as she eased her way into my room, but whether she was amused by my reaction or by something else, I wasn't sure. "Shouldn't be long now, miss," she said.

"Your Lord Henry was forced to join the governor for port and cigars after dinner, but he declined the cigar. He was out of there within half an hour."

"They don't have much to talk about without arguing," I said, trying not to smile as I imagined the awkward scene. I wasn't sure which of them would have hated it the most.

"Both of them went off to their rooms, and I believe the governor's valet has already left him for the night."

I put my book down and stood. "So it's time?"

"It is."

"I'll get my coat and hat."

"You won't need that. Just come with me." She stuck her head out into the hallway before gesturing for me to follow.

I was curious about where I was going and how, without a coat. The weather was quite brisk. Did the Mechanics here have tunnels like in New York? Or did they have some fantastic conveyance that kept us out of the elements?

The truth proved to be rather disappointing. Mary opened the hidden door at the end of the hall that took us into the servants' staircase, where two black coats hung over the railing. Mary handed me one of them, along with a black felt hat, and said "You put that on, and I'll go get your handsome lord." She went back out into the hallway.

I slipped on the coat, which was plain and made of rough material. The hat, likewise, was simple and unremarkable. I realized that she must be disguising us as servants. With so many temporary staff brought in for the governor's visit, no one in the household was likely to notice an unfamiliar face.

Mary returned with Henry a moment later. He'd changed from dinner attire into the kind of tweed suit he usually wore to go searching for insects. He put on his plain coat and a black Derby hat, and we followed Mary down the stairs to the servants' hall.

There, we waited while she put on her own coat and hat. She paused for a moment, studying us, before giving us a curt nod. "You'll pass, I think." We joined the flow of temporary staff who weren't living at the house as they left for the day. If they suspected there were impostors among them, they showed no sign of noticing, though I doubted they cared all that much. As we passed through the servants' door, Mary signaled to a boy standing nearby. He ran over to us.

"These are the friends I told you about," she said to him. "When they come back, you're to let them in and get them to the servants' stairs, without lettin' anyone else know. Have ye got that?"

"Got it!" he said, snapping to attention like a soldier who'd been given an order.

Henry took a silver coin out of his pocket and handed it to the boy. "Here's to thank you for your trouble, and there'll be another just like it once we make it safely back to our rooms."

The boy's eyes went as wide as the coin as he studied it carefully. "Yes, sir!" he said. "You can count on me. My name's Harry. Ask for me if you need me, but I'm the hall boy tonight, so I'll be the one to open the door."

"Harry, eh?" Henry said. "My name's Henry, but my brother used to call me Harry."

Harry beamed. "We Harrys have to stick together, sir."

Mary gave Henry an approving nod before nudging us to get going. The servants' door opened into a space under the house's front steps, and we had to climb a short flight of stairs to reach the sidewalk. We walked past a row of grand mansions like the one we'd just left, and I hoped Henry was sure of the address because they all looked alike to me. I wouldn't know which one to return to.

After a few blocks, the houses were a little less grand. They were tall and narrow, shoved together in a row. A few more blocks, and we reached a neighborhood of shabby tenements. The streets were more lively here, with people out and about. Some shops were still open, and loud voices came from within pubs. Henry edged closer to me, and his glance darted warily around our surroundings.

Mary led us to a set of steps down to a basement apartment and rapped on the door in a distinctive sequence. A moment later, the door opened, and we entered into a darkened vestibule. A bright light suddenly hit me in the face, blinding me. I threw up a hand to shield my eyes from the glare.

"Are these the ones?" a voice behind the light asked.

"Yes, they're the ones from New York," Mary said. "Colin vouched for them."

"This way," the voice said. Abruptly, the light swung around and lit the way for us down a short hallway to another door. I blinked, trying to readjust my eyes to the darkness so I could follow.

Once that door opened, we found ourselves in a large room lit by electric lights. I saw then that the light that had met us was set into the band of a top hat worn by one of the most attractive men I'd ever encountered. He looked like something out of one of the paintings hanging in the halls of the Lyndon mansion. His cheekbones were chiseled, his jaw strong and square, with the slightest hint of cleft in his chin. When he swept the top hat off his head to bow to me, he revealed wavy golden hair. Although he wore the eclectic mix of styles favored by the Rebel Mechanics, he seemed to have visited a tailor after taking items from the rag bag, for his clothes were perfectly fitted to his form. And what a form! He had broad shoulders and a barrel-like chest, with his torso tapering to narrow hips.

I distrusted him immediately, not so much because he was attractive but because of the way he smiled as he bowed to me. He knew he was attractive and counted on that affecting me. I'd been burned by flirtatious Mechanics before, so I steeled myself against his charms.

"Ah, the infamous Miss Newton. Colin didn't tell us how lovely you were," he said, taking my hand to kiss it.

"That's because Colin respects me as an ally and as a valuable operative," I said, withdrawing my hand from his. "My appearance is not relevant."

He smoothly recovered. "Well, of course he mentioned how valuable you are." Barely missing a beat, he turned to Henry. "And your lordship, as well. I understand we owe the survival of our movement to you. We are honored to have you among us. I'm sure you'll understand if we don't share our names, but you can call me Adonis."

I had to restrain myself to keep from snickering. I hoped he was aware of how ridiculous he seemed. It was hard to believe he might be sincere.

Either I'd done a good job of hiding my amusement or he was oblivious, because he didn't react to my barely hidden snort. With a practiced smile, he said, "May I take your coats and hats and offer you refreshment?" If he was being at all sarcastic to Henry, I couldn't detect it. Either he was more open-minded about magisters than most Mechanics tended to be, or he was the rare man who was even more glib than Colin.

As I unbuttoned my coat, I took stock of my surroundings. The large basement room seemed to be one part shabby but gracious parlor and two parts laboratory. There were upholstered chairs that could have come from a fine house decades ago, and pieces of machinery covered all the tables. Only about half a dozen people were present, with no musicians, no dancing, and no elaborate machines dispensing drinks. Unlike the New York Mechanics' raucous parties, this seemed to be more of a polished salon, for conversation about social issues.

None of the other Mechanics made any move to speak to us, and no one other than the greeter introduced themselves. That much I was accustomed to. It could be dangerous for us to know their identities, and I couldn't much blame them for being uncertain they could trust us.

Adonis took our coats and handed them over to another Mechanic before escorting us to a seating arrangement. He gestured me to a wingback chair and Henry to a velvet settee across from me. "Would you like coffee, wine, sherry, hot chocolate?" Adonis offered.

"A cup of chocolate would be lovely," I said.

"The same for me, thank you," Henry said. His posture was tense, and he sat on the edge of his seat, most of his weight still on his feet, as though he was ready to spring up at a moment's notice. I didn't feel like we were in danger, but I also didn't feel entirely comfortable. There was something odd about this situation.

Adonis sent one of his people to get the chocolate and sat next to Henry on the settee. I noticed that he wore the most elaborate Rebel Mechanics insignia I'd ever seen. Most of the members merely put a red ribbon through a gear, but he'd put together multiple gears inside one larger one in a complex pattern, and instead of a simple red ribbon, he had an intricately braided lanyard holding his gear. I couldn't help but wonder what would happen if he and Colin ever ended up in the same room with each other, and I made a mental note to never let this man go anywhere near Flora.

"Did you have a pleasant journey to Boston?" he asked. "I assume you came by airship."

"Yes, we did, and it was pleasant enough," Henry said.

"If your people keep making progress on the electrical storage battery, you should soon be able to make trips this far with your ships." I felt a subtle shift in the mood of the room and had a feeling Henry had just scored some points by suggesting a hint of mechanical knowledge and interest.

"We work on smaller-scale projects here," Adonis said. "The New York crowd has their big engines, but we have more esoteric interests."

A huge, bearded man wearing a plaid waistcoat in colors that never should have been put together entered the room bearing a tray and offered us dainty cups of chocolate that seemed much more normal-sized once they were away from him and in our hands.

"Clearly you have a dynamo," Henry said, indicating the electric lights with a gesture.

"Not of our own invention. We share technology with our brothers throughout the colonies. What we're working on is rather more specialized." His tone remained friendly and casual, but I didn't like the way he kept his phrasing so vague.

"How so?" I asked.

He gave a careless wave. "Oh, small devices to make daily life easier. Anything that saves us physical labor gives us more time to devote to our cause and less dependence on the thieving magpies. No offense," he added with a slight nod toward Henry.

"I'll assume you're not including me in that group," Henry said politely, but I thought his eyes looked a little harder than they usually did.

"But perhaps you have some connections with others of your class who share your beliefs."

"I might."

"You see, we're having a little problem with them here. They're quite active, but either they're pretending to be us or the authorities assume it's us, so every time they do anything, we get the blame, and the authorities crack down on us."

"You're sure it's not another group of Mechanics?" I asked.

"Absolutely," Adonis said, nodding firmly.

"I'll mention it to my friends and see if they know anything—" Henry began, but he cut off abruptly.

At the same time, I found it hard to breathe. My entire body was frozen. Even my ribs refused to expand with my breath, leaving me feeling suffocated. Once the initial shock wore off, I had the presence of mind to notice that none of the Mechanics seemed to be affected. I suspected that these feelings must have something to do with magic. I didn't want the Mechanics to know I was part magister, so I forced myself not to let any sort of reaction show.

Not that they would have noticed me. All their attention was on Henry, who sat perfectly still. His breath came in short, shallow gasps, and he hadn't managed to complete his sentence. I thought he looked a little paler than normal, but it was hard to tell under the unusual lighting.

I noticed then a tall, slender woman in a severe gray dress standing by a machine set on a table behind the settee. The machine consisted of tubes through which some glowing material flowed, all coming from and going to a central wooden box with knobs on it. A web of copper wiring surrounded it all. The woman kept glancing between her machine and Henry. I deduced that the machine had something to do with whatever was happening to us.

I soon found that I wasn't as frozen as I felt. I was perfectly capable of moving normally. Only my magical abilities had been affected, and that had made me feel paralyzed. Forcing myself to move, I bent to pick up my cup and took a sip of chocolate, as though nothing was happening. "What were you saying?" I asked Henry, keeping my voice light and even.

Instead of responding to me, Henry said to Adonis, "You've developed some sort of magical dampener."

The woman turned a knob on her machine and I felt like I could breathe freely again. She stepped forward to address us. "Yes, the machine affects the flow of ether to block the use of magic," she said, her voice lightly accented. I guessed that she must be a native of one of the African colonies, judging by her accent and dark skin. If our host looked like a painting, she looked like an onyx sculpture given life, with a high forehead and sharp cheekbones. The planes of her face were somewhat softened by the small round glasses she wore.

"Interesting," Henry said, turning to face her. "And very useful for a conflict against magisters."

"How did it make you feel?" she asked.

"Like it was more difficult to breathe and move. You

did something to the ether, didn't you? Something that makes it impossible to process into magical energy?"

She smiled, her teeth showing white in vivid contrast to her dark skin. "Exactly! The device sends a current through the ether that makes it magically inactive. This one works at only a short range—perhaps a hundred-foot radius. I have found that it stops magical devices from working, but I was not sure how it worked on an actual magister. Would you mind very much if I activated it again? And then you could try using magic."

Although I could tell that Henry was intrigued, and I knew he'd happily go along with the test, I was outraged on his behalf. "That's why you invited us here? You needed a test subject?" I snapped. "Did you consider just asking? Is there something in the Rebel Mechanics' charter that requires you to recruit assistance under false pretenses?"

Henry turned back to face me. "Verity, it's all right," he said. "I don't mind helping them."

"That's my point. You don't mind. If they'd invited you by saying they needed a magister to test a device, you'd have been happy to help." Addressing the Mechanics, I asked, "What would you have done if he didn't want to help after you sprang this on him? What if you'd hurt him?"

"I apologize. I meant no offense," the inventor said, giving us a slight bow. "I felt it important to the experiment for you not to know what might happen."

"Athena didn't mean any harm to your magister friend," Adonis said, favoring me with a smile that might have made me melt a few months ago before I'd become wise to the Mechanics' ways. To be perfectly honest, it still gave me a little flutter, and I was sure he'd calculated to get exactly that response. That made me trust him even less.

Henry stood and approached the inventor. "In the future, please just ask me for help directly. You'll find that I'm generally game for almost anything. But for now, what do you need to me do?"

"First, a control. Is there some bit of magic you can do to demonstrate that your powers are working normally?"

I made sure my magical shielding was intact. One of the first things I'd learned about magic was that a magic user could feel it when someone else nearby was using magic, and it was essential to learn to shield oneself from the sensation, especially if your magical abilities were a dangerous secret.

Henry held out his hand, and his cup of chocolate flew into it. He raised an eyebrow as he took a nonchalant sip. Athena smiled. "So, your abilities are working normally?"

"They appear to be."

"Now let's see what happens with the device operating."

He placed the cup back on the table in front of the settee and returned to his position. I braced myself as Athena turned on the machine and the tubes began to glow. Fortunately, the Mechanics were all too focused on Henry's reaction to notice what I did because I couldn't quite stop a small gasp when the machine took effect.

Henry reached out his hand for the cup in the same

gesture he'd used before, and I felt the ether becoming excited. It just didn't seem to work at his command. The cup only twitched slightly. The sense of the excited ether was like pinpricks all over my body, too faint to be truly unpleasant, but strong enough that I was glad I'd known to brace myself or I might have given away my secret heritage.

"You are trying and it is not working?" Athena asked.

"I'm doing the exact same thing I did before, but with different results," Henry confirmed.

With a satisfied nod, she turned a knob on her device, and I fought not to let out a relieved sigh as the atmosphere returned to normal. The cup suddenly flew toward Henry, and he barely caught it. "I suppose I should have stopped trying before you turned your device off," he said with a sheepish grin.

Adonis jumped out of his seat. "It works!" he said. "This calls for a round of drinks. Let's open that bottle we've been saving."

While the Mechanics celebrated with hugs and slaps on the back, Henry came over to me. "Are you all right?" he whispered.

I nodded just enough for it to be barely visible. "Yes. It wasn't bad, just...strange."

Our host brought us glasses of fizzing wine and turned to face Athena. "Here's to our brilliant and beautiful inventor, who may have just won us the revolution."

We raised our glasses and drank, but I felt somewhat unsettled. This surely changed the landscape entirely. While it wouldn't matter against nonmagical weapons and soldiers, it might be enough to allow the ragtag band of Mechanics to stand up to the Empire's magical might. I could also imagine less savory uses.

Although Henry went along with toasting the inventor, I could see that his smile didn't quite touch his eyes, which were troubled. Our handsome host also appeared serious when he returned to his seat and addressed Henry. "I'm sure you can see how important this device is. If anything we have needs to be mass produced, it would be this. But I don't imagine that's something you could get your magister friends to fund."

"It might be more challenging than getting them excited about steam engines and airships, yes," Henry said. "There would have to be safeguards in place about how and when it can be used, and how it might be used in the aftermath." I could see that he'd had the same misgivings I'd had.

Athena came over to sit in a straight-backed chair adjacent to the settee. "We have to live without magical powers. Why can't you?" she asked.

"Because that device doesn't merely render me the same as you. It alters me. I was born with my abilities. Dampening them is like me blindfolding you and forcing you to go without your eyesight. While it wasn't truly painful, I can feel the difference that device makes, and I suspect you could make it work in such a way that it would be painful." He raised an eyebrow. "And if that sort of thing were to happen, well, you'd not only lose some valuable allies, but you'd make some enemies."

"I would not use it to cause harm," she said solemnly, her words sounding like a vow. "But I might need to test it further to determine the precise thresholds at which power is affected with minimal other impact."

"What about the rest of your organization? You can understand why I might have concerns."

"Yes. That is why I must test and calibrate it precisely before I allow this device to be replicated, so it can't be used to cause harm."

Henry frowned, weighing this for a moment before he said, "I may be able to find you some test subjects among my local friends. You should test it on more than one person. All of us are different. I use my powers more than most, so the effect on me may not be the same as on someone whose powers are merely latent."

"That is good to know." She stood and nodded her head like a queen acknowledging her subject. "Thank you for your assistance."

Henry put down his glass. "Now, was there anything else you wanted to discuss tonight, or did you merely need a laboratory rat?"

"If you could get us some willing test subjects, that would be grand," Adonis said, rising from his seat. Now that Henry had served his purpose, our host was much less genial. He gestured for one of the others to bring our coats and Henry's hat.

"I really am sorry if I offended you, miss," Mary said as she helped me with my coat. "Perhaps I should have told you it wasn't a social occasion."

"I understand how important secrecy is," I said. "But if we're all going to work together, trust is equally important."

"I'll keep that in mind," she said. We made our way out into the dark vestibule, where she paused with her hand on the outside door. "Now, I'd better make sure it's safe." She was only out for a second or two before she stuck her head back in and gestured to us. "Can you find your own way back?"

"I believe so," Henry said. "I'm familiar with Boston."

"Good. Then I'll get home, myself. I have an early start in the morning. Take care not to get caught out by any patrols. Your name might get you out of trouble, but I don't think you want His Grace knowing what you've been up to."

I barely had a chance to ask, "Patrols?" before she was gone.

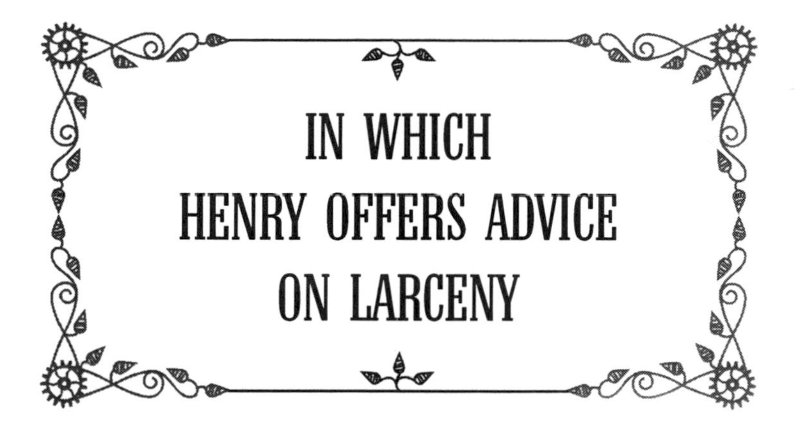

IN WHICH HENRY OFFERS ADVICE ON LARCENY

"Patrols?" I repeated to Henry.

"Things can get a bit...volatile here, so there's a sort of curfew."

"And we're out after curfew?" Panic made my voice shriller than I would have liked.

"It's not a very tight curfew. At least, it wasn't the last time I was here. It's mostly to give the authorities an excuse to question anyone who looks suspicious."

"No wonder there's a revolution brewing," I muttered.

"We look respectable enough, so as long as we appear to be ordinary people going about our business and don't give any indication that we're about to throw a rock through a window or start a riot, we should be fine."

"We were just helping plot a revolution," I reminded him.

"But we don't look like that's what we were doing. Now,

shall we return home?" He held his arm out to me, and I took it. As we walked, he said, "Do you want to tell me why you reacted the way you did when they tested that device? It seemed like a rather strong response to a minor faux pas."

I winced. I preferred not to let him know how easily I'd been duped, but if he was going to deal with the Mechanics, he needed to know how they worked. "This wasn't the first time I've seen them hide their true intent behind a veneer of friendliness. When they learned I was working for you, they decided I was in the perfect position to be an operative, so they created an elaborate scheme to recruit me. They set up situations to make magisters look bad and acted like they were rescuing me from those situations so that I'd side with them. It's quite appropriate that they were headquartered in a theater because they always seem to be playing roles." I couldn't keep the bitterness out of my voice, nor the faint tremble as I recalled how hurt I'd been by Alec's betrayal.

He didn't miss the emotion I'd let slip. "Is that all they did?" he asked softly.

I didn't want to tell him any more. The rest of the story made me look like a foolish girl whose head had been easily turned. But I didn't really want to hide it from him, either. I liked being able to be honest with Henry. "Part of their scheme involved Alec pretending to court me," I said, trying to keep my voice light so I would sound like it didn't matter to me. "He was most attentive." I blushed at the memory and was glad it wouldn't show in the darkness.

Henry stopped walking and turned to face me. "That

is ungentlemanly, and I don't care what class you're from, that's just not done."

"It didn't go very far. Mostly, he just paid extra attention to me and made me feel like he was interested. I was naive enough for that to turn my head. I should have known better." There had also been a few kisses, but I was definitely not telling Henry about that.

"Oh, come now, there's no reason for you to have assumed he wasn't being sincere," he said with a smile as he reached out and gently brushed my cheek with his fingers. "Why wouldn't he find you fascinating?"

His touch made me dizzy, even though I was sure he was just being kind. "Oh, I should have seen it. They created situations right out of a romantic novel. If you can believe it, Colin pretended to be a reckless magister who nearly ran me down with a magical roadster so that Alec could gallantly rescue me."

He laughed and hooked his arm around mine as we resumed walking. "Well, yes, that might have been a little obvious, although I must admit that some of the drivers are rather reckless."

"I think what made me angriest was that I had to figure it out for myself, even after I was part of their organization. They weren't planning to ever be honest with me. I have no idea how far Alec would have carried his courtship. He claims it became real, but how can I be sure?"

"And you're still willing to work with them?"

"I believe in the cause. It's bigger than all of us. The injustices are real."

"I can't condone the way they treated you, but I don't think tonight's incident was the same thing. There is some element of deception required in this situation. The risks are so high that it's difficult to be forthright."

A red-coated soldier rounded the corner ahead of us, heading our way. My grip on Henry's arm tightened. "Stay calm," Henry whispered. As the soldier approached, Henry nodded and said, "Good evening."

"Evening, sir," the soldier said brusquely. "You'd best be home. There's trouble brewing tonight."

"Oh, my!" Henry said. "Come along, dear, we'd better hurry."

I was dying to ask what kind of trouble there was, but Henry was already hustling me along the sidewalk. I supposed that your average person would be more concerned about getting home safely than about learning what was happening. We passed more soldiers along the way. "They're heading to the harbor," Henry noted. I was so turned around from all the twisting streets, unlike Manhattan's grid, that I wasn't sure where that was in relation to where we were going.

"Shouldn't we see what's happening?" I asked. "What if it's the rebel magisters?"

"It may be nothing to do with any group of rebels."

"What if it is?"

"What would we do? If we're to carry out our missions, we have to refrain from capture or discovery." He made a lot of sense, but it didn't stop me from wishing to know what had soldiers rushing to the harbor. "I suppose your journalistic self can't resist a possible story," Henry added with a fond smile that made me wonder if he could read minds.

We made it back to the house, and Henry knocked on the service entrance. Harry the hall boy opened the door, holding a finger to his lips. We nodded in understanding and waited while he went back inside. He returned a moment later. "It's clear. Let's go."

The servants' hall was deserted except for one last scullery maid finishing the washing up. She was too engrossed in her work to notice us moving down the hallway behind her. We made it to the back stairs without being noticed. Once in the stairwell, we removed our coats and hats and waited while Harry checked upstairs. He came back and gestured for me to go first. Though I encountered no one else along the way, I still breathed a deep sigh of relief when I shut the door behind myself. I quickly undressed and got in bed, both because I needed the rest and because the sooner I was exactly where I was supposed to be, the better I felt.

I attempted to keep to some sort of order the next day with the younger children. Flora was so eager to hold court as the lady of the house for her grandfather that it would have been impossible to make her do anything resembling schoolwork. I was content with letting her plan the week's meals and events with the housekeeper while I attempted to get Rollo and Olive to do their work.

When Henry came to the schoolroom that afternoon

and suggested a walk to the Public Gardens, I could have hugged him. "I'm beginning to think that it was unrealistic to expect their studies to continue uninterrupted on such a trip," I told him as we walked toward the gardens. "They're far too distracted."

"That was one of my objections to the trip in the first place," he said. "But don't worry, I won't hold it against you if you don't achieve miracles. Perhaps they'll absorb something along the way."

"Rollo did write a rather nice paper on the airship," I admitted.

"So all is not lost."

When we reached the gardens, we let the children run ahead while we walked more sedately behind them. "Would you be up for another excursion tonight?" he asked me, dropping his voice so it wouldn't carry.

"Your friends?"

"I received a rather cryptic invitation this morning from the friend we were talking about at the Mechanics' party. He said he and some colleagues need my expertise on a delicate matter."

"What kind of expertise? Insects?"

"Probably more like larceny."

"And you want me to come along?"

"I may need a chaperone to protect my virtue." More seriously, he added, "He was one of my more political friends in school. He was never a Masked Bandit because he lived in Boston, but he was part of the planning, and he was the one who first inserted the idea of revolution into the scheme. I imagine he and his local friends may be planning a similar venture. This might be an opportunity for you to present the Mechanics' perspective."

"In that case, I'll see if I can get Mary to arrange a similar escape for us tonight."

That night after dinner, we went through the same routine of sneaking into the back stairwell, putting on coats and hats, and slipping out with the servants. This time, though, we headed a different direction, remaining in the wealthier district. The streets were lined with mansions not much smaller than the one where we were staying. We went up the front steps of one of them, and Henry pushed the bell.

The door was opened not by a servant, but by a tall girl about my age wearing loose, heavily embroidered robes that I thought must have been the aesthetic dress I'd heard about. I'd never before met anyone daring enough to forego corsets and all the layers of clothing a proper lady required. "Henry Lyndon, you haven't changed a bit," she said.

"Camilla?" he asked, his eyes widening slightly. "You certainly have. You're all grown up."

"Be sure to tell my brother that. He refuses to see it." With a glance at me, she added, "And you brought a friend." She didn't sound angry about that, but she wasn't particularly welcoming, either.

"This is Verity Newton, who's part of my organization," Henry said. "Verity, this is Camilla Seton, the baby sister of one of my university friends."

"Baby, hmph," Camilla said. "I suppose you'd better

come in rather than us talking on the stoop." She turned and headed into the house, leaving us to follow her and close the door behind us. I couldn't help but wonder if she was so accustomed to having servants to do everything that she'd never learned how to greet guests and show them in.

From the entry foyer, I could hear the sounds of a wild party somewhere in the house. Music played, and there were shouts of laughter. Henry and I exchanged a glance, and he raised an eyebrow.

"They're in the ballroom," Camilla said, moving past us to lead the way up the stairs. She conjured a globe of light in the palm of her hand as she climbed into the darkness. Henry did the same. It seemed odd for there to be no light in the house, which also seemed sparse on furnishings. There were no paintings on the walls, and the niches were devoid of sculptures.

"Aren't your parents at home, Camilla?" Henry asked. "And what about the servants?"

"My parents are abroad. The house is supposed to be closed up, but Brad and I can get in." She turned to glance over her shoulder at Henry. The magical glow coming from below her face gave her a devilish appearance. "They think I'm at finishing school, learning to be utterly useless."

When we reached the top of the stairs, the party sounds were even louder, and light streamed into the hallway from the ballroom at the rear of the house. Henry and I followed Camilla, who didn't seem to care whether or not we were behind her.

I paused on the threshold to stare at the room. If I hadn't seen Camilla using magic, I'd have thought I'd stumbled upon a Rebel Mechanics party. Most of the guests were dressed like Mechanics, in an odd mix of mismatched working wear and formal attire. The women wore either the Mechanics' scandalous dress of shorter skirts and visible corsets or loosely flowing aesthetic gowns like Camilla's.

But the "Mechanics" didn't ring true to me. For one thing, they were too clean. Mechanics tended to be mechanically minded, so there were always traces of oil or soot on their hands and clothes. Some of their clothing might once have been of high quality, but it came by way of a thrift store, so it was worn and shabby. This clothing was all too new and clean. I also noticed that none of them wore the insignia of the Rebel Mechanics. I didn't think it was a secret, but it also didn't seem to be widely known among outsiders.

Henry and I exchanged another look. I could tell by his widened eyes and the slight wrinkles between his brows that he was as surprised by this gathering as I was. It did appear that the Mechanics had been correct about the rebel magisters impersonating them. Were they doing so to deflect suspicion, or were they emulating out of admiration?

Camilla led us to a group of young people sprawled on cushions—the only furnishings visible—in one corner of the room. "He's here," she announced.

A young man who was even taller than Henry rose quite

gracefully from his cushion and approached us. "Lyndon! It was good luck that you happened to be in town, right when I needed you."

"I was glad to hear from you. There was something I wanted to discuss with you, as well," Henry said, but his friend wasn't listening.

He veered slightly off course in his approach to Henry and went to me, instead, taking my hand and kissing my knuckles while bowing deeply. "The Honorable Bradford Seton, at your service, my dearest lady. If I'd known Lyndon was bringing someone so lovely into my presence, I'd have dressed for the occasion." It was the sort of thing Colin would have said, but he'd have said it with a cheeky wink to show that he knew it was outrageous and that he didn't expect anyone to take him seriously. I thought that this man might actually believe he was charming me.

I wasn't sure how to respond. I didn't want to insult Henry's friend, but I was suspicious of anyone who flirted so obviously. In fact, I was getting rather tired of men insincerely attempting to charm me. Henry spared me by stepping in between us, forcing Bradford to release my hand. "Really, Seton?" he said. "Do you never stop? We're here for business, and Miss Newton is no one to be trifled with."

Camilla sank onto one of the cushions. "Honestly, Brad, are you trying to embarrass me?" she drawled, sounding as though the topic bored her. "We have better things to do. Now, please take a seat." She gestured toward a couple of vacant cushions. Camilla might have been wearing loose, uncorseted aesthetic dress, but I was in proper attire for a governess, which made it difficult to sit on the floor with any grace. I had no idea how I would rise again. Camilla hadn't taken our coats, and I realized after I was seated how warm the room was. I shrugged out of the sleeves of my coat and let it fall off my shoulders. Across the circle from me, Henry took off his own coat, folded it over his arm, and lowered himself to perch uncomfortably on a large cushion. Bradford resumed his seat on the cushion beside Henry.

Camilla pointed to the girl seated beside me. "That's Maude." Maude also wore flowing robes, but hers looked suspiciously like she was dressed in a nightgown. Her fair hair hung in loose curls down her back. She sat as though someone was painting her portrait, her limbs perfectly arranged and her body positioned to best show off her figure.

"And there's Theo," Camilla added. The young man to my right raised a hand in greeting. He had dark hair falling across his forehead and a bushy mustache. His collar was open, with no necktie, and he wore no coat.

"For those who don't already know him, this is Lord Henry Lyndon," Brad said. "We were mates in school."

Introductions concluded, Camilla said, "We need to pick your brain, Henry. You might just hold the key to a little dilemma we have, and that will help us decide what we should do tonight." I was surprised to find that she was apparently the leader of their group.

"What do you need from me?" Henry asked.

"Since you're the expert bandit, we need your advice on how to break into a highly secured area to cause some wanton destruction of property."

"I'm far better versed in armed robbery, I'm afraid," Henry said. "There's not much finesse required in holding a gun to someone's head."

"But surely you indulge in some subterfuge to get into places you want to rob and get out of them without being identified or caught," Brad said. "I remember all the planning sessions. How do you sneak in before they have their guards up? And do you ever encounter magical security measures?"

"Normally we slip in as people who might be expected in such a place, put on our masks, re-emerge for the holdup, slip away, remove the masks, and then blend in with the rest of the people there. We don't usually have to worry about security measures."

"So you've never had to break into a bank vault? Or, say, board a ship that's under heavy guard?" Camilla asked.

"Never," Henry said. "What's this all about, anyway?"

"A small symbolic demonstration," Maude said. "It's time we sent a clear message to our Imperial overlords that we will no longer tolerate their tyranny, and with the governor in town, the timing is apt." It seemed strange to hear such fiery rhetoric coming from such a delicate-looking creature, but I supposed that must be her camouflage, the way Henry's absentminded amateur scientist persona was his.

"You know about the tea tax?" Theo asked.

"Yes, that's why the rebels won't drink tea," I replied.

"There's a ship in the harbor with a load of tea, and we aren't going to let it be unloaded to be taxed," Maude said. "We're going to reject British tea and all the taxes it represents."

"Only there's one tiny problem," Camilla said. "We can't get to the ship."

"That's what was going on at the harbor last night," I guessed.

"The mission was a failure," Maude said. "We couldn't get past the security, and we drew enough attention that I'm sure the security will be tighter now."

"Then perhaps you need to rethink this mission," Henry said.

"Says the man who robs trains," Brad said.

"Yes, and when we nearly got caught, we stopped for a while. We didn't go back to the same place to try again. What are you even trying to accomplish?"

A larger crowd had formed around us as people stopped their drinking and dancing to come listen to the discussion. The music stopped playing, and even the musicians joined the circle.

"Last night's failure doesn't have to mean the end of our venture," Camilla said, raising her voice to address the whole group. "We can still make our point about taxation. Yes, I know it's purely symbolic. Tea has been unloaded and the import duty paid before. But the royal governor is here in Boston, so he would surely hear of this action. We must make our voices heard!"

"And what happens then?" one of the few men not dressed as a Mechanic asked. "Do you really think we'll suddenly be granted seats in Parliament, or the social order will be altered? Or will they tighten their grip even more?"

One of the men dressed like a Mechanic stepped forward, and if I hadn't already been sure that he was no true Mechanic, his speech would have given him away. He sounded too polished, almost affected. "Oh, we might make the Empire angry? What will they do to us? Take away our representation in Parliament? We don't have any to begin with. Raise our taxes? How much higher can they go? Every good we could possibly need is already taxed. Control our press? Try publishing something without the official stamp. Limit our choices in the way we live our lives? That's been happening for centuries. What can they do to make our lives *more* miserable?"

There was a spattering of applause, and a few shouts rang out in the room. Once that response had died down, one of the more conventional-looking people stepped forward. "Ask the people in New York. They were under martial law, with movement around the city restricted."

"That was because of the Rebel Mechanics, not us," said a woman dressed as a Mechanic.

Her opponent didn't miss this fact. "And who do you think they're going to blame?" he asked, gesturing at her attire. "You're doing this dressed as Mechanics. That's going to make them clamp down on the city. We'll have warships in our skies and soldiers billeted among us."

"But that won't affect our people."

I could hold my tongue no longer. "That's not fair at all!" I blurted. "Do what you want, but be brave enough to take the consequences for yourselves. You can't go pretending to be Rebel Mechanics and then not care what ills might befall them while you remain unscathed."

The silence that followed my outburst was unsettling. Into it, Henry said mildly, "Verity is here as a liaison of the Rebel Mechanics. We've been trying to convince them that we have common interests and that they can trust us. Now, I'm not so sure. Really, wouldn't it make more of a statement to take action as magisters? The governor expects the Mechanics to make noise. I can assure you it would shock him to the core if he knew his own people were turning against him."

"It doesn't matter at all since we can't get to the ships," Brad said. "We were hoping Henry might have a solution, but it appears he doesn't, since he's rather more confrontational in his illegal actions."

"What, exactly, are you running into?" Henry asked.

"There's a magical barrier blocking access to the ship," Camilla said. "Nothing we tried could break it. We don't even know for certain what lies beyond that. My hope is that since the barrier is so secure, the ship won't be as tightly guarded."

I had an idea, but I wasn't sure I wanted to bring it

up. Would the Mechanics want to cooperate with the magisters, and what good would come of it for them? On the other hand, this might be a way to bring the two groups together in Boston and perhaps gain some funding for the Mechanics. I caught Henry's eye, and I could see from his face that the same thoughts had crossed his mind.

"If you'd thought to include the Mechanics instead of merely impersonating them, they could have taken care of this for you," I said.

There was a loud rumbling in response, as everyone in the room began discussing this among themselves. Maude put a stop to their discussion with one graceful wave of a delicate white hand. "How so?" she asked in the ensuing silence.

"They have a machine that dampens ether so it can't be used magically," Henry said. "I've seen it demonstrated."

The response to that was vehement. Shouts of "How dare they?" and "That is an outrage!" rang out.

"What are they supposed to do when magic is used to oppress them?" I demanded, shouting at the top of my lungs. "They must have a way to fight back, and they have more cause for revolution than you do. You sit here playing at it, making showy gestures while you lead lives of privilege. They're shut out of the entire system because of an accident of birth, and then are penalized for trying to make up for that with their ingenuity." I realized I was essentially paraphrasing one of Alec's speeches, but his points had been valid even if he'd been less than genuine in the context of that speech.

"You both have the same goal," Henry said. "We all want freedom from the British Empire and all the oppression that entails. Do you plan to exclude the nonmagical from our new nation? Or do you want to build an even stronger nation by combining strengths?"

"We are up against an Empire," Maude said. "And we've seen that we can't even make a small protest on our own. Do you think the Mechanics would be willing to help us?"

I felt every eye on me. "I don't know. They won't be happy that you were planning to implicate them. They're already unhappy about the trouble you've caused them. But this would be an opportunity for them to test their device. I imagine they might have some terms for their participation."

"Go ask them," Camilla said firmly. Her glare was enough to silence the grumblers.

IN WHICH I ATTEND A TEA PARTY

"Do you think they'll help?" Henry asked as we left the mansion.

"I hope so. But I'm concerned that rather than help the magisters, they'll take the idea and go off on their own."

"We'll have to remind them of the possibility of test subjects and money," Henry said.

The streets were much quieter this night, and I wondered if that had anything to do with the previous night's activities. If there was a tighter curfew, we might not be able to move so freely around the city. There were policemen and soldiers about, but they left us alone. They were on the lookout for a mob, and they weren't expecting anyone dangerous to come out of the magister district. There were a lot more uniforms once we were in the less exalted part of the city, near the Mechanics' place.

We waited until a pair of policemen had walked to the

end of the block before we approached the basement door and I knocked, remembering the pattern Mary had used. As we waited for an answer, I hoped that we'd even find them here, that this hadn't just been a place they'd used to meet with us.

Adonis soon opened the door. He favored me with an appreciative smile before saying, "Back so soon? Do you have news for us?"

"Probably more than you ever expected," I said. "We need to talk."

The parlor was slightly more crowded than it had been the night before, and the atmosphere was more social. We had to weave our way around small clusters of chatting Mechanics to reach the settee where Athena sat, surrounded by admirers hanging on her every word.

"They're back!" Adonis said. "And it sounds like they've got something interesting for us."

"How would you like a real-world test of your device?" I asked.

"I would like that very much," she said.

Henry and I explained the situation. "And so," I concluded, "they can't make their protest without your help. I thought it might be a good idea to make them aware that they need you. If they saw your device in action, it would be proof of what you could do. That might get you money from them."

"Or they might just exploit us the way they always do," Adonis said, sounding significantly less genial.

"They're doing that with or without your help," Henry

said. "They're dressing as Mechanics to carry out this scheme. You might as well be there."

One of the men said, "Yeah, we might as well be there, doing it ourselves!" That got widespread agreement from the Mechanics.

"But if you work with them, you'd have access to test subjects and money to allow you to produce more of your devices," I argued desperately.

"I don't know, that much tea on the black market would bring in a lot of money," Adonis mused, which got another cheer.

I turned to Henry, but I wasn't sure what I expected him to do. They were less likely to listen to a magister than they'd been to listen to me. "But working together…" I said, my voice trailing off as I realized how futile that argument was.

"What do they have that we don't?" Athena asked, rising to her feet. "They have magical power, yes, but that is what they wish us to remove for them. We have the device, we have manpower. We should claim our own victory."

That got a rousing cheer from the whole group, and a number of them hurried out, presumably to make preparations and rally more troops.

"Thank you kindly for the intelligence," Adonis said with a sardonic bow. "This time, perhaps the authorities will be correct in blaming the Mechanics. Or should we dress as magisters? Now, allow me to show you out. We have work to do."

"Well, that didn't go the way I hoped," Henry said once we were outside.

"What should we do now?" I asked. "The magisters will be waiting to hear from us."

"And they're not going to be happy that we failed."

"The tea will still be gone, and the authorities were going to blame the Mechanics, anyway," I said, trying to rouse an ember of hope in my heart. "Will it make that much difference to the magisters who actually does the work? This way, they can stay at their party."

"Who knows? Maybe they will see it that way," Henry said with a shrug. "But I suppose we'd better break the news."

When we arrived at the Seton mansion, the front door was slightly ajar, so we entered without ringing the bell. The party in the ballroom had grown even wilder in our absence, with more people present. The collection of weapons near the ballroom entrance suggested that this was more than a social gathering. They were here for a mission, and they weren't likely to welcome our news.

Camilla, Maude, and Theo still sat on their cushions in the corner, and Camilla rose to meet us as we approached. "Well?" she demanded. "Where are your Mechanic friends with this device?"

"On the way to the harbor," Henry replied.

"To meet us there?"

"To destroy the tea on their own," I said. "Or steal it. Since they were going to be blamed, anyway, they decided they may as well use the device to get past the barrier."

"They'll never succeed without us!" Camilla declared. "How can they, without magic?"

"They are rather resourceful," Henry said.

"You couldn't do it *with* magic," I added.

"And they're going to steal the tea? That's all wrong. We're making a statement about taxes, not being common thieves." She whirled, shouting out, "Maude! Theo! Where's Brad? We must go, now!"

Theo pulled himself rather unsteadily to his feet. "Go where?"

"The Mechanics are going to the harbor!"

"Without us?" Maude asked from her pose on her cushion.

"We have to stop them!" Camilla said. "They're going to steal the tea, which will ruin everything."

"What do you propose to do against them?" Henry asked, his voice remarkably calm. "Their machine neutralizes your magic."

"We have weapons," Theo said, reaching for one of the shotguns resting against the ballroom wall.

"You can't fight them!" I cried.

"Why not?" Theo asked, one eyebrow raised.

"Because you're on the same side. You're fighting for the same thing, against the same people. You should be allies. You certainly shouldn't be shooting each other."

He didn't acknowledge my objections. I watched helplessly as the magisters streamed out of the ballroom, picking up weapons as they went. "A few at a time!" Camilla called out. "Don't look like a mob."

I turned to Henry. "We have to stop them, or warn the Mechanics, or do *something*!"

He checked his pocket watch. "If we go, we'll be out very late. You should probably head back. You've done your part, and this is risky."

"I've been in far more dangerous situations before," I protested.

"I'm aware of that. I'm not worried about your physical danger, but I'm worried about what could happen to you if it's discovered that you've been out all night."

I tried to smile. "Somehow, I don't think my employer will mind."

"If we were in our own house back home, that would be fine. But at the moment, we're under the governor's roof, and even if I didn't dismiss you, he could send you home."

"The same is likely to happen to you if you're caught."

"I'm a young bachelor. I'm expected to be out on the town. I won't be suspected of rebellion."

"But your fitness as guardian of the children might be questioned if you're discovered to be out at all hours. You know he's only looking for an excuse to take the children from you."

"Are you suggesting that both of us go home and stay out of this operation?"

"I'm suggesting that neither of us wants to miss it and we both have something at stake."

"You just want to write the article," he teased.

"And you've missed danger since giving up banditry."

"There, we understand each other," he said with a

broad grin. "Now, shall we head to the harbor?" He held his arm out to me.

With a grin of my own, I took it. "Yes, let's."

The front door had been left open because constant opening and shutting was more likely to attract notice in the dead of night than a door remaining ajar. The streets were even quieter now than they'd been earlier. The only people about were policemen. We avoided most of them by keeping to the shadows, but every so often I felt a slight brush of magic from Henry that suggested he was doing something to keep us from being noticed.

Once we'd made it to the harbor district, there was more action. Soldiers were more evident, as were workers. The docks never shut down entirely. The first task would be to get past the initial perimeter, but it didn't appear as though they were checking credentials. They were ready for a mob, not for individuals.

"I don't see them," I said as I scanned the docks anxiously for signs of the Mechanics.

"You can't expect them to ride in on a steam engine, singing 'Yankee Doodle' at the top of their lungs." He paused, quirked an eyebrow, and added, "Well, perhaps your friends in New York might, but I suspect this lot will be different for this operation. It's the magisters who are more likely to make a spectacle of themselves."

Ahead of us, I spotted what appeared to be a well-bred couple dressed for an evening at the opera. They were so out of place that they drew my eye, and then I recognized

Mary as the woman. "Over there!" I whispered to Henry, and he followed my gaze.

"Well-spotted!" he said, and we picked up our pace to follow them to a warehouse on the docks. I quickly took the Mechanics insignia out of my pocket and pinned it on my lapel as we approached the warehouse. I wasn't sure if it was my gear and ribbon or if I was recognized, but no one questioned our entry.

The Mechanics were already gathered, most of them dressed like ordinary workers rather than in typical Mechanics garb. Adonis and a few others had put on evening attire, like a magister might wear. Athena stood next to a small roadster that had a canvas-draped object sitting in the passenger seat.

"Should we warn them about the magisters?" I whispered to Henry.

Before he could answer, there was a sharp whistle from outside. "It's time!" Adonis called out.

Athena got into the driver's seat of the roadster. It moved forward silently with its magical engine. I hoped its owner wasn't among the magisters heading toward the tea ship. With a glance at each other, Henry and I fell in with the crowd. He caught my hand and held it tightly, keeping us together in the mass of people. Most of the crowd hid in the shadows, only the roadster with its lady driver visible to anyone who wasn't looking for us.

The crowd of Mechanics stopped and took cover behind crates and the various structures on the dock. I noticed a faint shimmer in the air, blocking the pier that led to a ship whose masts looked naked with their sails furled, like winter-bare trees. Guards stood behind that shimmer, looking alert.

A few of the Mechanics crept forward, lurking behind the roadster as Athena called out, "Excuse me! I seem to be quite lost."

"You aren't supposed to be here, miss," the nearest guard told her.

"I'm not even sure where 'here' is," she said with a girlish laugh. "I must have become very turned around." She leaned over to the passenger seat. "I have a map around here somewhere."

I knew she'd activated her device when I got that now-familiar feeling of being frozen and Henry's hand tightened on mine. I forced myself to breathe normally so I could pay attention to what was happening.

The moment the shimmering barrier came down, the Mechanics rushed from behind the roadster and swarmed the guards, knocking them down and silencing them before they could sound an alarm. It took Henry and me a moment to recover from the jolt of the device and join the Mechanics.

Once we were all past the barrier, Athena turned a dial on her device, and I felt like I'd been freed from chains. Next to me, I heard Henry let out his breath in a long sigh. "That barrier should hold anyone from coming after us until we're done!" Adonis called out. "Now, let's have ourselves a tea party!"

"Not so fast!" another voice challenged, and all of us turned to see that Maude, Camilla, Theo, Brad, and about a dozen other magisters stood behind the reactivated barrier. Most of them were dressed like Mechanics, making the whole gathering seem like a world turned upside down. Camilla strode forward almost to the barrier, her eyes flashing. "What do you think you're doing?"

"We're stealing some tea," Adonis said. Giving her a sweeping bow, he added a sardonic, "Milady."

"You can't steal it!" she protested.

"Why not? It still keeps the Empire from collecting taxes on it."

"But you're playing right into their hands. If you steal the tea, you're just a bunch of thieves, and they can pretend it's merely the action of common criminals. If we destroy the tea, it's a statement about our refusal to pay unfair taxes."

"Says the person who's never had to worry about paying for anything," Adonis shot back.

She shook her head and moved closer, keeping her eyes locked on his. "You don't know anything about me. Why do you think I'm putting myself on the line for this cause? My family is so burdened with taxes that we've had to sell almost everything we own. We have a grand mansion that's empty, and it will soon be sold, as well. I can't remember the last time I had a cup of tea."

The Mechanics laughed at her. "I'm so sad that you're uncomfortable in your mansion," Adonis said, his voice heavy with mock pity. "That must be terrible for you."

Maude moved forward to join her, linking her arm with

Camilla's. She'd put a heavily embroidered opera cloak on over her flowing white gown, and she reminded me of a Greek goddess from a Renaissance painting. "We can help you," she said, her voice soft and earnest, but still carrying. "Wouldn't it be interesting if the governor learned that it was a crowd of magisters who protested his government's policies by destroying the tea?"

He gestured at his attire. "He's going to think that anyway, especially since we were able to get past the barrier. If you lot join us, we'll just be blamed."

Camilla stomped her foot. "But it was our plan! You got the idea from us."

"What will you do if we don't cooperate?" Adonis asked. "Put a hex on us? As you've seen, we have a way to stop that."

"We have other weapons," Camilla said, her voice dropping to a growl.

The Mechanics laughed again, and Adonis held his arms out. "Do your worst, milady."

"We'll—we'll call the authorities."

Henry and I had been lurking in the crowd of Mechanics, but Henry moved forward at that. "Don't tell me you'd really be that petty, Camilla," he said.

"Henry, what are you doing with them?" Brad asked.

"I was hoping to get all of you to listen to reason." He turned to Adonis. "They can help, really."

"Why should we trust them?" Adonis asked. "Can't you do the same things they could?"

"I can, I suppose." Henry worried his lower lip in his teeth for a moment, then moved toward the barrier. "Look, you haven't given them much reason to trust you," he told his friends. "Let them deal with the tea. You can manage a perimeter and help them escape afterward. Maybe that will help them trust you in the future. Are you after glory or results?"

The magisters all looked at each other, then Camilla said, "Very well," to Henry before turning and walking away. The rest of the magisters joined her.

Behind us, the Mechanics had already boarded the ship and subdued the crew, who weren't putting up much resistance. "They may be right about one thing," Athena said. "If we steal the tea, they can say it was merely a criminal act. They won't have to admit it was a political act of defiance. Throw the tea into the harbor."

Adonis nodded, then shouted, "Let's brew ourselves a giant cup of freedom tea! But damage nothing else!"

The rest of the Mechanics boarded the ship, and Henry and I joined them. A few men went below and began passing up crates. When the crates reached the deck, the rest of us went to work smashing them open and dumping them overboard. Henry and I didn't have any tools, so we helped kick any spilled tea off the deck and into the harbor.

Although I appreciated the cause and understood what we were doing, I still couldn't help but sigh at the thought of all that tea going to waste. I liked tea, and I was grateful that my position in Henry's house and the need to maintain my cover as a loyal subject of the Empire required me to continue drinking it.

As we worked, some of the Mechanics began singing their version of the "Yankee Doodle" song, changing the lyrics to suit the occasion. "Yankee Doodle went to town, to have a big tea party. Beat the magpies and made some tea, enough to serve an army." It perhaps wasn't the most poetic turn of phrase, but it made everyone laugh, and soon the rest of the group picked up the chorus. The atmosphere became rather festive, and it was almost a disappointment when the hold was emptied.

One of the men pulled a flask out of his coat pocket and passed it around the assembled conspirators. I took a sip when it reached me and gasped as the harsh liquid burned my throat and made my eyes water so badly I could hardly see to pass it on to Henry. He gently took it out of my hand to take his own sip.

Adonis called for attention, and the crowd grew silent. "We've struck a major blow tonight. Now, let us disperse or hide as quietly as possible." He turned to the crew. "We apologize for any inconvenience this may have caused you."

All of us filed off, down the gangplank, and approached the barrier. Now that the deed was done and my elation was fading, I began to worry about how we'd get away and get back to the house. Surely someone would have noticed the activity at the docks, and that would mean the authorities were on their way.

The device did its work in lowering the magical barrier

once more. Some of the magisters were still waiting outside the barrier, though not all who had come from the party. Once we were all through and magic was working again, Camilla approached Adonis. "Do you want us to do something about the guards?"

"Like what?"

"I can subdue them so you can untie them, and we can adjust their memories so they won't know for certain what happened here."

"I think we'll leave them tied up. The shift will change soon, and that way they'll know what happened."

"You want the authorities to know about your device?"

"They didn't see anything other than a bunch of people who looked like magisters rushing at them. They don't know how we did it. See, we managed to do all this just fine without magic."

"We can help you escape."

"Don't need the help. Thanks for the offer, though." He gave her a mocking bow. "Have a good evening, milady."

The Mechanics appeared to melt into the darkness. I didn't even see where Athena's roadster went. I wasn't sure they'd gone anywhere. Were they hiding at the docks?

"I can't believe you sided with them," Camilla snarled at Henry.

"I didn't side with anyone. Someday, everyone will realize that we just need one revolution, and we'll get nowhere if we fight each other." He turned to me. "Now, come on, Verity, we'd best be going."

Now that our mission was accomplished, it seemed like our real danger began. There were very few legitimate reasons for people to be on the streets at this time of morning. It was too late for most honest people to be coming home, and too early for even those who worked very early in the morning to be going out. It would be another hour or so before the bakers were at their ovens, and the scullery maids were still sound asleep.

Near the docks, there were taverns open, men spilling out of them, and a few women waited under lampposts. All of that made me uncomfortable and grateful for Henry's presence, but it became worse as we drew closer to the magister neighborhood.

There, the streets were completely deserted, other than the occasional policeman on foot patrol. I was sure that anyone out at this time would be taken as a thief. We didn't even have the option of using Henry's name and title because that would reveal that he was out with his governess late at night, and that would create a scandal that would jeopardize my position. I was starting to understand why he'd suggested that I go home earlier. He could have played the role of dissolute young nobleman staggering home after a night out with friends, but my presence added a complication.

Instead, we tried to avoid the patrols. We moved as quietly as we could, keeping to shadows and not moving into the light until we were sure no one was nearby. We both used our magic to blend into the shadows whenever we were near others. I had seldom used magic outside Henry's study, and I hadn't realized how draining it was to use this much power in a real crisis.

When we reached the governor's house, we encountered another problem: There was a sentry at the house. Henry barely pulled me behind the front steps of the adjacent house before the guard turned toward us.

IN WHICH I APPEAR *EN DISHABILLE*

"Word must have come about what happened," Henry whispered into my ear. His breath was warm on my neck, but it made me shiver.

"How will we get in?" I whispered in reply.

"I don't know."

I couldn't help but think of another time I'd hid with a young man while patrols went past. Alec had sheltered me like this when he'd pretended we were being pursued so I would sympathize with the Mechanics. This time, though, it wasn't a game. We really had done something illegal, and there really was a danger of being caught.

"What we need is a diversion," I said. "If we can draw his attention elsewhere long enough for us to reach the service entrance, we might be able to sneak in."

"Excellent idea, Verity. I'll go around the corner and make some noise, and you rush for the door."

He started to head out of our hiding place, but I caught him by the arm. "What about you? How will you get in?"

"Through the front door. No one will think anything of me having been out late with my friends from school. They're all respectable people. You're the one at risk."

"You could get in trouble with the governor."

"I believe I'm allowed at least one night out while the children are safely under the supervision of their grandfather. Now, wait until the guard turns away, and then rush for the door."

The sentry approached us, then turned and walked the other direction, and Henry took that moment to dash around the corner. He must have gone around the entire block because it was several more minutes before a loud noise came from the opposite direction. The sentry ran to investigate, and I flung myself out of the hiding place and down the steps to the service entrance, where little Harry was already opening the door to see what was going on.

"Get me in, quick," I told him.

Without hesitating, he pulled me inside and shut the door softly. He hustled me down the empty hall to the back stairs. I removed the coat and hat while I waited for him to check my hallway, then tiptoed down the hall to my room when he told me the way was clear.

Once inside my room, I tore my outer clothes off as quickly as possible and pulled my nightgown over my head. I sat down for a moment to remove my boots and stockings, grabbed a shawl to throw around my shoulders, and pulled the pins from my hair and shook it loose as I ran down the stairs.

I flung open the heavy front door and stood silhouetted in the doorway. A figure moved toward the house from the shadows nearby. Wishing that my magical powers included some sort of silent communication, I hoped Henry would hold back rather than revealing himself to the guard. I stepped farther out onto the front steps. When I was sure the sentry had seen me, I blinked as though I'd been awakened from a deep sleep and said, "Whatever is that noise? It sounds like the city is exploding."

He came up the steps to speak to me. "Nothing to be alarmed about, miss. There's been some ruckus in the harbor, and it sounds like the culprits are celebrating."

Out of the corner of my eye, I saw the figure dart from the shadows to the servants' entrance below the front steps. "Oh, that's good to know," I said. "The sound woke me, and I wasn't sure if I needed to do something to protect the children."

"No, you're perfectly safe, miss. We're keeping an eye on the house. Nothing to worry about."

"Thank you so much. I'll rest better knowing you're out here."

I hoped that had given Henry enough time to get inside unnoticed. I made my way back up the stairs. When I reached my floor, I heard a soft hiss from the landing above. I looked up to see Henry leaning over the railing. He gave me a salute, which I returned with a smile before heading to my room.

Once I was inside, I became aware of the scent of tea and noticed that the hem of my skirt was coated in tea dust. Mary was in on the cause, so I doubted she'd give me away, but would she be able to explain getting tea out of my clothes?

I took my petticoats off from under my nightgown and took them and my skirt into the bathroom. I couldn't rinse them out without brewing a sink full of tea, so instead I shook them out as well as I could over the bathtub. After a little brushing, my clothes might have passed for regular wear that included a walk in the park. Only if you sniffed carefully would you know it was tea rather than dirt that soiled the hem.

I searched the floor for signs of tea dust, and I didn't see anything obvious. I hoped I hadn't left a trail down the hall that would lead to my room. It appeared that I'd made it without my clandestine activities being detected.

The sound of my door opening woke me the next morning, and for a moment I was disoriented, uncertain where I was. I sat bolt upright, ready to deal with the intruder, until I saw that it was Mary. "Sorry, miss, didn't mean to startle you," she said. "I just came in to make up the fire."

I rubbed my eyes, trying to clear my vision. "I'm not too late for breakfast, am I?"

"You can still make it without anyone noticing anything amiss."

"Thank goodness!" I jumped out of bed and hurried to the wardrobe to find a dress I could wear.

"Late night, miss?" she asked, though I knew she knew exactly what I'd been doing, as she'd been there, herself.

"I stayed up far too late utterly engrossed in a novel."

"I'm sure it was very exciting," she said, her twinkling eyes ruining her attempt at a deadpan expression. "Would you like me to take your dress for cleaning?"

"I would appreciate it."

She picked it up from the chair where I'd left it and raised an eyebrow. "I might be able to get a nice pot out of it while I'm at it."

She helped me finish dressing, and I thought I looked somewhat presentable, if perhaps a bit hollow-eyed, when I went downstairs to breakfast.

Henry, Olive, and Rollo were in the breakfast room when I arrived. "Good morning, Lord Henry, Rollo, Olive," I said as I headed to the sideboard to serve myself breakfast. "I trust you slept well."

"Quite well," Henry said, barely looking up from the newspaper. "And you, Miss Newton?"

"I'm afraid I was up far too late reading."

"That's funny, because stories always put me to sleep," Olive piped up.

"That's because the stories you like are boring," Rollo countered.

"I like my stories," Olive said, her jaw jutting stubbornly and her eyes narrowing at her brother.

While the children argued, Henry looked up and caught my eye over the tops of his glasses. I smiled, then tried to school my expression. I took a seat across from him, next to Olive, and forced myself to focus more on the children than on him.

Conversation became even more impossible when the governor joined us. He seemed to be in good spirits, humming to himself under his breath as he loaded his plate with food. Henry and I exchanged a look behind his back. Would he be that cheerful if he'd received word of the destruction of the tea?

"Good morning Miss Newton, Lyndon, children," he said as he seated himself at the head of the table. "Miss Newton, did you have plans for this afternoon?"

"Nothing more than lessons, Your Grace," I said.

"Would you mind receiving calls with Flora? Today's the day for her to be at home. I'm sure a number of the local ladies and young people will call on her, and she needs to be suitably chaperoned."

"I will assign work for Olive and Rollo during those hours and conduct the rest of the lessons this morning," I said.

"Work?" Rollo moaned.

Henry opened his mouth to chastise his nephew, but the governor spoke first, saying, "Keeping up with your schoolwork was one of the terms of you coming along on this trip. You'll have plenty of time to see things later."

With a deep sigh, Rollo poked around on his plate with his fork.

"I like to do my schoolwork," Olive said. "May I have an extra assignment, Miss Newton?"

Just as Rollo opened his mouth to respond, the butler

entered and presented a card on a silver tray to the governor. The governor read it, a flush rising from his collar. He gave a loud snorting cough and said to the butler, "Is he still here?"

"He is waiting in the hallway, Your Grace."

The governor rose, shoving his chair back violently, and stalked toward the doorway, pausing to mutter a gruff, "If you will excuse me," to us before leaving.

Even the children were silent as we all strained to hear. The governor's deep voice carried throughout the house, but I could still only make out phrases like, "Are you sure?" or "Magisters? Really?" and "What kind of counterspell?"

Henry and I looked across the table at each other. He raised one eyebrow, and I gave a slight shrug. The children were so busy staring at the doorway that I didn't think they noticed our reactions. I thought it was a safe bet that the governor had learned about the tea party.

He didn't return by the time we had finished our breakfast. The children left first, then Henry excused himself. I waited an appropriate amount of time before taking my leave, even though the only person left in the room was a footman.

I found Henry waiting for me in the hallway outside the schoolroom. "The governor must know what happened," I whispered.

"Yes, and I'm trying to decide if I should brave the bear in his den to ask about that or if I should ignore it. What would I do if I were entirely innocent?"

"I believe that the Lord Henry who studies insects

would be curious enough to ask questions. It would seem uncharacteristic of you to ignore it."

He grimaced and sighed. "I suppose you're right. If I encounter him, I'll have to ask him whatever's the matter without sounding too interested."

I barely stifled a yawn. "I hope we're staying in tonight."

"Had your fill of intrigue, have you, Miss Newton?" he asked with a wry smile.

"I merely need to rest between clandestine operations."

With that, I swept into the schoolroom to begin the day's lessons. Keeping Rollo's attention engaged was a challenge, but I hated to see the classroom time end because social calls were my least favorite activity. At the appointed time, I put on my one tea dress—the one for the occasion, not the one that was currently covered in tea—and tidied my hair before joining Flora in the parlor.

Much to my surprise, the governor met me outside the parlor. "Might I ask you a favor, Miss Newton?" he said.

"Of course, Your Grace."

"There have been recent events involving some young people among the magister class. We can't permit destructive behavior to continue. I would appreciate it if you would keep a watchful eye on any visitors today and see if you notice anything unusual. I'll ask the same of Lady Flora, but you're a level-headed young woman, and I trust you to observe details."

I was so stunned by his request that I had to blink a few times to be sure I was actually awake. "Of–of course

I can do that for you, Your Grace," I stammered. "But I don't know any of these people well enough to know what behavior is unusual."

"I trust you to tell if anything strikes you as odd. Thank you, Miss Newton."

It was rather flattering that the royal governor of the American colonies had asked for my assistance, even though it put me in a difficult position. Obviously, I couldn't actually report on anyone who was involved. If he weren't making the same request of Flora, I might have been able to get away with claiming not to have noticed anything, but any report I made would have to match Flora's report. It was easy to assume that Flora would only notice her visitors' attire, but I'd learned not to underestimate Flora's intelligence.

"Flora, my dear," the governor said as we entered the parlor. "Might I ask you to keep your eyes and ears open as you visit with callers today?"

"I don't expect them to say anything interesting," she said.

"There have been some unusual events here that might be related to magisters. Young people would be more likely to talk to you about their activities."

"Only if they're foolish. Who would tell the governor's granddaughter about unseemly behavior?"

She had a point, and that made me feel better. Even firebrands like Maude and Camilla were unlikely to parade their exploits in this house, and besides, no matter what they'd planned, they hadn't actually done anything.

The governor smiled fondly at his granddaughter. "That's likely the case, but I would like to hear about your visits, nonetheless. Miss Newton will provide a report, as well."

He left us, and I took a seat in the back corner and began to knit. I would have preferred to read, but that was apparently considered rude, even if I was being treated like I was invisible. I still wasn't sure what I was supposed to do as a chaperone if anything untoward did happen. I imagined hurling myself bodily between Flora and a caller and had to smile. It was more likely that my presence was expected to serve as a deterrent. My existence suggested that chaperones weren't just a useless social custom, though I suspected that my mother's magister paramour had been beyond an age to be chaperoned. That proved how foolish the rules were. How many others like me were there?

Much to my surprise, I recognized our first callers. When Camilla and Maude were escorted into the parlor, I barely remembered not to greet them, and they didn't openly acknowledge me, though I thought Maude darted a glance at me. They wore aesthetic dress, which I thought rather daring when visiting the governor of the colonies, and Flora barely managed to get through the initial social niceties, she was so dumbfounded by their loose clothing.

"I don't suppose dear Henry is in," Camilla said. "He and my brother were such good friends in school, and I would dearly *love* to talk to him today." I thought I detected a hint of menace in her voice and tried not to wince. The magisters probably weren't too happy with Henry at the moment.

"I have no idea where Henry is," Flora said. "If you know him at all, you know how little use he has for social conventions."

"But I would hope he has use for old friends," Maude said. "We hope we'll see him at the ball. Such exciting things have been planned for that night. I'd hate for him to miss it."

I was glad I was sitting behind Flora because I wasn't able to stop myself from flinching. Maude's tone and the glint in her eyes suggested that the exciting plans had nothing to do with gowns, music, or dancing and everything to do with making up for not being able to carry out their own tea party. But would Flora pick up on that, or was I only getting that impression because I already knew about Maude's affiliations?

"I'm sure Grandfather will force him to attend," Flora said. Her tone made her sound like she didn't much care.

"We're quite looking forward to it," Camilla said, and her smile was fierce enough that I thought surely it would be obvious that she had dangerous intentions, even to one who didn't know her. I hoped that Flora was so distracted by talk of a ball that she wouldn't notice if her guests did handsprings around the room.

"I'm afraid my heart isn't in a ball," Flora said with a deep, dramatic sigh. "Alas, the one I love will not be there. I'll likely never see him at a ball."

I barely managed not to groan out loud. I'd thought she'd have forgotten Colin by now. I bit my tongue and bent my head over my knitting, glancing upward to peer at our guests.

"Oh, do you have a beau?" Maude asked with a trilling laugh. She did such a good job of portraying a vapid society girl that it was hard to believe she was the same person who'd been rallying the troops and arguing with the Mechanics the night before.

Again, I wished I could see Flora's face. "Not exactly," she said. "But there is a man I admire who's likely far more worthy than any pampered nobleman." She hurried to add, "But you can't tell anyone!"

"You can trust us," Maude assured her. "Pampered noblemen are nice to dance with, though."

Both visitors stood. "We look forward to seeing you again, Lady Flora," Camilla said. "We're sure you'll find our Boston ball quite diverting."

"Well, they were certainly suspicious," Flora said when they were gone.

My heart thudding painfully, I tried to keep my voice from shaking when I replied, "What makes you think so?"

"Did you see the way they were dressed? They might as well go out in their nightgowns. It's positively scandalous."

"I hardly think that indicates that they're troublemakers," I said as mildly as I could manage.

"But they aren't proper ladies."

"I don't think that's what your grandfather is concerned about."

"True. He cares little for ladies' fashions. I honestly have no idea what he expects me to tell him."

The rest of the visitors were far more conventional, and far more boring. I couldn't find even the slightest thing that I thought Flora might report to the governor. At the end of the afternoon, the governor rejoined us. He moved stiffly, like he was too tense for his limbs to function normally. "Well?" he demanded, skipping all pleasantries.

"Nothing more than terrible fashion sense, Grandfather," Flora said. "I never thought I'd see someone paying calls wearing aesthetic dress."

"And you, Miss Newton?" he asked.

"I noticed nothing untoward. No one mentioned any activities that sounded suspicious."

"Hmmph. I suppose it was unlikely, but it was worth trying. Thank you both."

Once he'd gone, Flora mused out loud, "If that's the way Boston women dress, I won't have to do anything to my ballgown, after all, and I'll still outshine them all." She rose and drifted out of the room, leaving me to sigh in relief.

Henry spoke to me later that afternoon in the guise of checking up on the children's schoolwork. "No one's saying anything specific," he reported, "but there's been a steady stream of official visitors and some raised voices."

"I think your friends have something planned for the ball," I told him. "You should have seen the way Camilla looked when she spoke of it."

"That may just be Camilla. She's always been rather combative, about everything. She may merely have a romantic conquest in mind."

I put my hands on my hips and glared at him. "Are you implying that a young lady is unlikely to have thoughts other than romance? That seems very unlike you."

He winced. "Touché, Verity. I should know better. After all, she planned the event last night."

"They didn't get to make their big move with the tea ship, so I think they're planning to use the ball to make a political statement."

"I'm not sure what they could do without revealing their identities, since everyone there will know everyone else. Even dressing like the Mechanics won't make for much of a disguise."

"You should find out. You can visit your school friends. Though I imagine you'll get quite an earful when you do. I think they're angry at you."

"They probably see me as a traitor," he said with a wince. "But you're right, I should go, and maybe I can learn something or talk some sense into them. I wish you could come with me. You'd probably be better at dealing with them than I am."

"Alas, I am a mere governess, and I can think of no reason to go, unless Flora also comes with you. But if Flora comes with you, then you can't talk openly. So you'll have to go alone and bring me a full report."

Although I tried to sound like I was teasing him, it

reminded me yet again that I didn't fit into his world. He was my closest friend, and yet I couldn't go out in public with him without the children also being there or without sneaking around. Even if his friends had revolutionary leanings, I couldn't openly socialize with them.

That afternoon, I wrote an account of the rebel "tea party." I wasn't sure how much credit the Mechanics wanted to take or how public they wanted to be about their magic-dampening device. I settled for saying that "unknown parties" had carried out the raid, using "mysterious means" to defeat the magical security measures. When Mary came to alert me to dinner being served in the schoolroom, I handed it to her to pass on to her contacts within the Rebel Mechanics. I definitely didn't want my "Liberty Jones" pseudonym to go on that one, and I tried to change my writing style so the authorship wouldn't be obvious.

The next day, I forced myself to focus on lessons with the children and a brief outing to a museum with them, even though I longed to hear what Henry had learned from Maude and Camilla. He was home when we came back from the museum, but we didn't have a chance to speak without an audience until teatime, when I brought the children to the parlor.

Flora played the piano and the other two eagerly told their grandfather about everything they'd seen in the museum, which gave Henry the chance to ask me how the children had behaved on our outing. When it was clear that no one was paying any attention to us, he said softly, "I'm afraid I have no news. They played innocent with me, claiming they had no plans, even though I could tell they were lying. They probably suspect I'll run straight to the Mechanics to tell them everything."

"That's better than them suspecting you'll run straight to the governor."

He gave a wry grin. "True. I suppose we'll have to wait and see what they do. That should make the ball more interesting." He raised his voice slightly to normal conversational level and added, "Perhaps you should assign an essay about the museum. Or would that make museum visits seem too much like a chore?"

"I would prefer that the children learn to think of museums as fun, though Olive has already announced plans to write a story about the visit, and Rollo sketched weapons while we were there."

"That should suffice for educational merit," he said with a nod. "Thank you, Miss Newton." He returned to the family, and I felt a pang at his departure. Even though he was only on the other side of the room, he may as well have traveled to another country. All I could do was look at him, and I didn't even dare do much of that with the others present.

When the night of the ball came around, Mary helped me dress while a proper lady's maid was hired to prepare Flora. Mary was able to lace my corset and do up all the buttons

I couldn't reach, but she wasn't much better than I was at arranging my hair. The two of us laughed as each of her attempted fancy styles failed horribly. Flora would have been in tears and probably hurling hairbrushes, but I knew my appearance mattered little, as long as I didn't embarrass the family.

"A ball must be a lot of fun," Mary mused as she tried to anchor a twist with hairpins.

"I'm going there to work," I reminded her. "As a chaperone, I'll mostly sit along a wall and keep my eye on Lady Flora. At my last ball, I danced one dance." It had been with Henry, and I could still recall every moment, every sensation.

"That's not right at all," she said with a sniff. She studied my head and added another hairpin. "You should get that Lord Henry of yours to dance with you."

"He might be kind enough to do so, but I'm sure he'll be much in demand as a partner for the other ladies." I thought he'd also be dancing with them as a way to converse about recent events under the governor's nose.

"But you can still look at all the pretty dresses. I bet it's like something out of a fairy story."

"The one ball I've gone to was," I admitted.

"Well, I think you look lovely, miss," she said, admiring her work in the mirror. I had to agree with her. The simple style she'd managed to create suited me better than any of her more elaborate attempted concoctions would have. "You have a grand time."

Henry was already waiting downstairs, dressed in white tie and tails, his unruly sandy hair somewhat tamed for the occasion. He greeted me with a big smile. "You're wasted as a chaperone, Miss Newton. You may be too busy dancing to keep an eye on Flora."

"I hardly think that's likely," I said, hoping my cheeks didn't look as red as they felt.

"You have to promise me one dance."

"If you insist." I added a hasty, "Sir," when I realized that the governor had joined us.

"Still waiting for Flora, are we?" he asked Henry. "My daughters would have missed the first half of every ball if I'd let them take all the time they wanted getting ready."

"I believe Flora's too eager for this ball to risk missing any of it," Henry said.

Only then did the governor seem to notice that I was present. He turned as though he'd only just caught a glimpse of me out of the corner of his eye, and he smiled in the way he'd greet an old friend he was glad to see. But once he turned to face me, he appeared to realize who I was, and his smile faded. "Miss Newton," he said with a brusque nod. "You are aware of your duties?"

"Yes, Your Grace." I bobbed a slight curtsy.

"And you'll do what I asked you the other day? Keep your eyes and ears open."

At that moment, Flora appeared at the top of the stairs and paused for us to admire her before she made her way slowly down the staircase. I wasn't sure why she bothered making a dramatic entrance with only her uncle, her grandfather, a couple of servants, and me to witness it, unless perhaps she was practicing for the entrance she planned to make later that evening.

"Good, there you are," the governor said with a grunt. "Now, stop dillydallying and come on. The carriage is waiting."

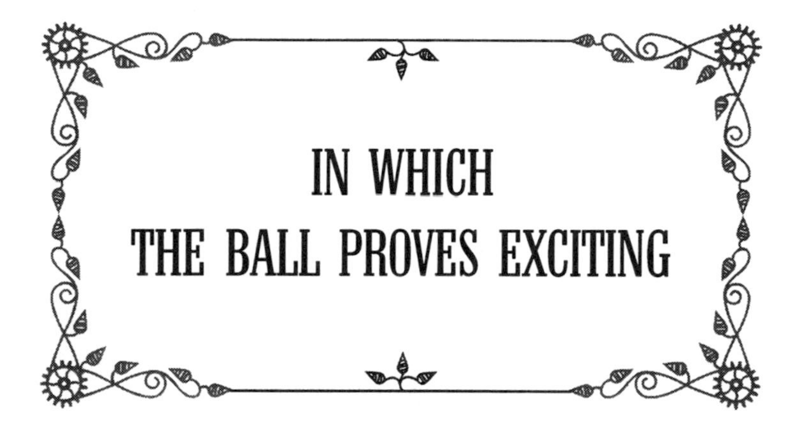

IN WHICH THE BALL PROVES EXCITING

The ball was held at a nearby mansion even larger than the place where we were staying. The ballroom might have held the house where I grew up, and its gilded and painted ceiling was so high I could barely make out what the fresco depicted. When we entered, the governor, Flora, and Henry were announced with much pomp. I hung back behind them as the assembled crowd cheered the governor's entrance. He escorted Flora down the steps into the ballroom, Henry a few feet behind them and me trailing after the whole group. Henry shot a few glances over his shoulder at me, so I knew I wasn't entirely forgotten.

We had seats on a dais at one end of the room, as guests of honor. The governor's was practically a throne, and those for Henry and Flora were also grand, with velvet cushions. I had a modest chair at the rear of the dais, in

Flora's shadow. I quietly lowered myself onto it and willed myself to be invisible.

I'd thought that the last ball I'd attended had been an elaborate affair, and had scoffed at the idea that it was considered a very modest event. Now I understood why Flora had described it that way, for this ball outstripped it. Everything about it was larger: the flower arrangements, the refreshment tables, the orchestra, and the guest list.

In fact, I wasn't sure how anyone could dance, there were so many people there. They were packed in, shoulder to shoulder. Yet somehow space cleared on the floor when the governor and Flora stepped out to begin the dancing. After the first minute or so, the floor filled again, all the dancers moving around the floor and miraculously not bumping into each other.

Flora had barely returned to her seat after the first dance when a line of young men formed to beg a slot on her dance card. She didn't respond with much enthusiasm to any of them, but I didn't notice her rejecting anyone. Her heart might still be with Colin, but that wasn't going to stop her from enjoying the ball. I presumed that anyone who was invited would be considered suitable, so my presence was purely ceremonial and to show that her family was following the custom for her class.

Both Brad and Theo were in the group asking Flora to dance, which meant at least some of the rebel magisters were present. The room was too crowded to spot anyone else while they were dancing.

Flora was off on the floor again as soon as the next

dance began, and it appeared that the governor was making the rounds, dancing with the various noblewomen. Henry stood and said, "I suppose I'd better ask enough women to dance that I don't look rude. And maybe I can find out what Camilla has planned."

"Have fun," I instructed, trying not to feel and sound jealous. I finally spotted Camilla when she danced with Henry because both of them were tall enough to stand above much of the crowd. She wore more conventional attire, corset and all, tonight, though her gown was out of fashion. She must have been honest with the Mechanics about her family's financial position.

I soon spotted Maude because she was definitely not dressed like anyone else at the ball. She wore a flowing Grecian-style gown that veiled her figure when she was still but that draped around her, outlining her body, as she moved. She wore her hair loose and no jewelry. I was rather impressed at the confidence it must have taken to appear like that, but she didn't seem to notice the stares or the mutters of disapproval. I had to wonder what her rank was. Only someone immune to societal censure could get away with flying in the face of convention to that extent. She didn't lack for dancing partners, though. Young men seemed utterly entranced, possibly because of their mothers' disapproving scowls.

Flora returned to her seat, fanning herself, and waited for some swain to bring her a cup of punch. "That gown is practically obscene!" she said.

"Which one?" I asked.

"Lady Maude Winters—the one who called earlier in the week."

"She seems to be properly covered. She's showing far less décolletage than most of the ladies present." Including Flora and even me.

"She's clearly not wearing a corset. Aesthetic dress is fine for at home, but this is not the occasion for being such a Bohemian." She watched for a moment longer, then said somewhat vaguely, as though she was unaware of speaking out loud, "It does look very comfortable, though."

Flora's partner came to claim her for the next dance, and I was left alone again. I watched the crowd, trying to determine what, if anything, the rebels might have planned. Maude was easy to track, mostly because I could follow the stares, but I couldn't find Camilla anymore. Theo and Brad were impossible to detect in that throng because all the men were dressed alike.

Henry returned from his rounds of the dance floor and sat in Flora's chair, closer to me. "Camilla still denies they have anything planned, but she's a terrible liar, and she looks far too smug."

"I think Maude might be the diversion," I suggested.

He grinned. "You may be right. She's certainly being noticed. We should split up and work our way around the room to see if we can overhear or see anything. Don't worry, you're not expected to just sit there all night. In fact, moving around to better keep an eye on your charge is customary. Go get yourself some punch."

I rose, smoothed my skirts, and made my way down from the dais and into the throng lining the perimeter of the dance floor. It was like trying to swim upstream. As I moved, I didn't see anyone I recognized from the night of the tea raid, and no one showed signs of recognizing me.

No one did anything so obvious as saying, "Now let's carry out our plan." I didn't expect them to, though it would have made my life much easier. I made my way to the refreshment table, and an older gentleman gallantly filled a cup for me. "How are you enjoying the ball?" he asked.

"It's rather crowded," I said without thinking as I continued studying the faces of the people around me.

"Yes, it is. It seems everyone who's anyone wants a glimpse of our illustrious governor. But I suppose that's no novelty to you."

I turned then to face him, and he smiled. "Yes, I did notice you. You're chaperone to the granddaughter, aren't you?"

"I am."

"And here I am, forgetting my manners, though it wasn't proper for me to speak to you in the first place without a formal introduction. I hope you'll forgive me. I'm Baron Pierce."

I gave him a slight curtsy. "I'm Verity Newton."

"A pleasure to make your acquaintance, Miss Newton. Let's just pretend that some mutual friend introduced us."

"I don't really have friends here. Only my employer."

"And most of my friends have died. I wouldn't have come at all, but this is something of a command appearance for someone in my station. Have to support the Empire, and all that. I do hope you don't mind if I don't ask you to dance. My dancing days are long behind me."

"I'm not much for dancing, myself. Not in this crowd, at least. I'd be sure to cause a collision."

"Ah, but the right partner would take care of that. In my youth, I could have steered you without incident around the floor." He grinned wryly. "Though in my youth, dancing like this would have been quite scandalous. We did patterned country dances. None of this holding each other so closely."

Although I'd enjoyed being treated like I was visible, I needed to move on and see what I could learn. I was just about to make a polite farewell when a sound like a series of small explosions shook the room. In spite of his age, the baron managed to leap in front of me, shielding me with his body. All around us, people screamed. A couple of ladies fainted. Someone nearby dove under the punch table.

I looked around for the source of the noise and saw the word "Freedom" hanging in the air over the dance floor. I noticed then the sense of magic in use. Had this been the rebels' plan, a demonstration at the ball?

"Those young fools," the baron muttered, seemingly forgetting my presence. "Just making a spectacle, no thought for consequences. That'll make it harder on the rest of us."

That took me aback. It wasn't the response I'd have expected from a member of the nobility. I considered asking him about it, but he didn't seem to realize he'd spoken aloud, and I didn't want to put him on his guard. Instead, I said, "It was lovely meeting you, but I must find Lady Flora."

I fought my way through the crowd, searching for Flora's golden curls and hoping she was safe with her grandfather. Was the single word exploding magically over our heads the extent of the demonstration, or did they have something else planned?

"Ver—Miss Newton!" I whirled and saw Henry squeezing between people to get to me. "Do you see Flora?"

"No. You're taller than I am. Can't you see her?"

He got closer to me and put his hand on my shoulder, gripping tightly enough that we couldn't easily be separated. "This must be what they had planned," he murmured into my ear.

"Do you think there's more?" I asked, turning to face him.

"I hope not."

I suddenly felt that paralyzed sensation that came with the magical dampener. Before I could react, the room suddenly went dark. Not only did the "Freedom" vanish, but all the lights in the room, which presumably were powered by magic, went out.

As had happened to Henry and me the first time we'd experienced the device, everyone froze at first, but soon they realized that they could move and were only hampered magically, and then they panicked. Henry pulled me closer against himself so that I was partially shielded from the mob. We had the advantage in knowing what was happening, but I imagined it would be terrifying to face the effects of the device in that setting with no warning. A dull roar rose from the crowd as people gradually found their voices again.

Then a single female voice rose above the din, singing clearly, "The colonies are free, to live in liberty. This is our cause." The tune was the anthem of the British Empire, but the words were quite different. Other voices, male and female, joined the song. "Free from the tyrant's tax, free from all Parliament's acts. Free from the governor on our backs, let freedom ring!"

There were more voices than I would have expected, but then I remembered how many people had been at Camilla and Brad's house, preparing for the tea raid. If all those people were at the ball, the rebels might outnumber the loyalists, especially among the young people. If I wasn't entirely mistaken, I also thought I heard the baron's voice joining in, very softly.

"Should we go find them and get them to turn it off?" I whispered, directing my voice at where I thought Henry's ear might be. The range of the device meant it had to be very close.

"They've made their point, and now it could get dangerous," he murmured in reply. He began moving, guiding me and shielding me from the crush of humanity as we made our way very slowly through the crowd. My eyes had grown more accustomed to the darkness, and now I could make out the windows along the rear of the ballroom, as well as a faint light that I assumed was the entrance. That at least gave us a target to aim for.

Before we were halfway across the room, the sensation of being stifled lifted and the lights came back on. "I guess they won't need persuading," Henry muttered, and he changed direction, fighting our way to the governor's dais, where the governor was having words with a few other nobles and some uniformed soldiers. As we approached, I caught the governor saying, "...the tea, and now this. You need to get things under control."

"Of course, Your Grace," the man he was speaking to said, bowing. "It's probably just a prank. You know, those Rebel Mechanics are quite active here."

"This is magic, so I doubt they had anything to do with this," the governor snapped. "This was done by our people. I want to know who."

Flora's dance partner got her to the dais. Both of them looked somewhat the worse for wear, their clothes crumpled from the crush. "I'll go bring you some punch, Lady Flora," her partner promised as I took her arm to help settle her in her chair.

"Are you all right?" I asked her.

"What is this?" she asked.

"It seems to be a little political demonstration, but

there doesn't appear to be much more than this display. We should be perfectly safe."

"I'm sending you home, right away," the governor said. "Lyndon, you escort the ladies. I'll sort this out here."

Henry and I exchanged a glance. If the Mechanics had used the dampener, that meant they were likely outside, so leaving might not be the best way to keep Flora out of danger. Or had they brought the device nearby secretly and then hurried away with it? Surely the soldiers would have noticed if there were an angry mob outside. I couldn't help but wonder if the timing of the device had been lucky coincidence or if they'd coordinated with the magisters.

Henry straightened and moved decisively toward Flora and me, acting the way I had seen him directing the Bandits or interacting with the rebels, but then he remembered that he was supposed to be the vague, absentminded amateur scientist, especially in front of the governor. He stopped and wavered, even swaying slightly. "Oh, dear!" he said, blinking rapidly behind his glasses. "I suppose I should have the carriage brought around."

Before he could leave I called out, "Lord Henry! We need to get our wraps."

"Of course! I'm sorry. It completely slipped my mind. I should escort the two of you to the cloakroom." He took Flora's arm and I prepared to follow behind them, but he gestured with his other hand, and I hoped I didn't blush as I stepped forward to clutch his elbow. "Now, both of you hold on," he said. He nearly tripped on the bottom step of the dais as he left, and I had to bite my tongue to keep from laughing.

He might have been playing his role to the hilt, but he was quite adept at maneuvering us through a panicking mob. I barely brushed against anyone as we crossed the ballroom. All three of us paused to catch our breath when we reached the stairs where we'd entered. "We'll go to the cloakroom and meet you back here," I told him, and then I took Flora's arm to guide her. It wasn't nearly as chaotic here as it was in the ballroom, but there were still people frantically trying to leave.

"What is all this, Miss Newton?" Flora asked me as I draped her cloak around her shoulders. "Is there really a rebel group among the magisters?"

I was about to reassure her that it was nothing when I noticed that her eyes were bright and her face flushed. She was excited, not scared, which was both surprising and troubling. "There appears to be, though how serious they are remains to be seen. All they did was make a statement about freedom, when they could have done far more in this crowd."

"But why would magisters want to rebel?" she asked, knitting her brow.

"I wouldn't know. But perhaps you could write an essay on the subject for me, speculating on possible reasons."

I expected her to protest the way she usually did about anything even resembling schoolwork, but she nodded as her eyes went unfocused in thought, as though she was already mentally composing.

When we made it back to the foyer, Henry was just returning. "It's something of a madhouse out there, with so many people trying to flee all at once, and there seems to be a bit of a crowd outside, as well. There's no chance of the carriage getting anywhere near us."

"We're not that far from home," Flora said. "Couldn't we walk? We'd be there sooner."

Coming from Flora, that was like her announcing that she didn't much care for fashion, and both Henry and I turned to gape at her. Oblivious, she began walking forward, forcing us to hurry to catch up with her.

Henry took both our arms once more. If it was a madhouse in the ballroom, it was even worse outside. The street was clogged with carriages jockeying for position. Ball attendees and their servants milled about on the sidewalk in front of the mansion, searching for their carriages. Across the street, barely visible in gaps between the carriages, a crowd of people stood, watching the spectacle.

I couldn't tell in all the chaos who that crowd might be, until a voice rose in song. "Yankee Doodle went to town, riding a steam pony." More joined in on the Rebel Mechanics' theme song. They didn't seem to be doing any more than standing there and singing, but their presence was obvious.

Henry tugged at us, pulling us down the street and away from the scene, but Flora hung back. "What is that?" she asked.

"I believe it's the Rebel Mechanics, and you can be sure they're up to no good," Henry said. "Now, come on, we should go before they start causing trouble."

She began walking again, but she looked back over her shoulder. "They're just singing. So, there are magisters rebelling and there are these Mechanics who also want to start a revolution. I don't think people like the government much."

We were silent for the rest of the walk home. Flora still seemed to be lost in thought, and Henry and I didn't dare talk in front of her. The trip really was quite short, and I was sure we were home in less time than it would have taken to find our carriage. When we made it inside, I asked Flora, "Do you need any help?"

"I can ring for a maid myself," she snapped before stalking up the stairs.

Henry normally would have scolded her, but he was preoccupied. He sighed as he took off his glasses and rubbed his eyes. "I don't know what they were thinking," he murmured. "Now the governor knows for certain that there are rebels within the magister world. That will make my job more difficult."

"Surely this isn't the first time magisters have expressed dissent."

"Never quite this blatantly. Between this and the tea, which the authorities seem to be blaming on magisters, we will no longer be above suspicion, which eliminates our advantage among the rebels."

I glanced around, making sure we were still quite alone,

but even the butler had gone away. "Speaking of which, do you know a Baron Pierce?"

"I know of him. Why?"

"When the message appeared, he said something a lot like what you just said, that this would make things more difficult, and I think he was singing along with the rebel song. Is it possible that there are dissenters higher up in the ranks, not just among young people?"

"I've hoped it was the case, but I've never seen any evidence. I expected it to be more among the middle-class magisters, the ones who are doing most of the work and providing the magical power without having the titles and privilege, but I suppose people with titles might also get involved at that level."

"You did," I reminded him. "Someone doesn't have to be young to see a need for change."

"The question is, how do I approach him? It's not as though I can just start talking about revolution. What if he meant something different when you heard him?"

"I was the one talking to him, so I could bring it up without you putting yourself at risk."

"But then you'd be putting yourself out there."

"He was already sympathetic to me as a chaperone, so he might not think anything of me being curious about his political views, even if I was mistaken. But you can't reveal your role. The real problem is, how do we even speak to him again? Is he someone you could call upon?"

"Not really. The rules are rather touchy about who can

do what. If he called upon the governor and didn't leave a card for me, then I can't call on him directly." Noticing my skeptical look, he smiled and said, "See, this is why some of us are rebelling. All these silly rules will be swept away in our new nation if I have anything to do with it."

"It's a pity we can't manage to just bump into him," I said. "Is there someplace in Boston that everyone goes?"

He grinned. "There's church on Sunday, and all the nobility will likely attend the same one in this neighborhood. We're sure to pass him before or afterward, and you could greet him. We'll just have to find a way to be away from the governor and the children when you do so."

"That sounds like a rather vague plan."

IN WHICH I ENGAGE IN EAVESDROPPING

Not that I was able to come up with anything better. We loaded up two carriages for the short trip to the church, where the governor made a grand entrance before taking his place in a reserved pew. I wasn't sure whether I was more relieved or insulted when I learned that I wasn't expected to sit on the family pew. It was nice to be away from the governor and my duties, but I felt very alone sitting at the back of the church.

However, my position allowed me to watch most of the congregation. I spotted the baron a few rows back from the family and wished I had a way to point him out to Henry. It was difficult to concentrate on the sermon when I was trying to come up with excuses to talk to the baron without the governor noticing anything. Normally, my position in that household made me ideally situated as an operative, but too much proximity to the governor hampered me when it came to taking action.

I saw my chance at the end of the service when the governor's party was allowed to leave first while everyone else had to wait. I was on the end of a pew, so I waited until the baron came along as the church emptied from the front and made eye contact with him as he passed.

Much to my relief, he recognized and remembered me. "Why, it's my friend from the ball," he said, holding his hand out to me. I took it and walked out with him. "Did you ever learn anything about that event?" he asked as we walked.

"I'm afraid not." Dropping my voice, I added, "But between you and me, I have a feeling I know who was responsible, and I think they were still in high spirits after their activities earlier in the week." I made sure to keep my tone light enough that he could tell I didn't disapprove.

"Do I take that to mean that you'd decline an invitation to tea?" he asked, a twinkle in his eye.

"I suppose that would depend on how and where it is served, though I must say, I had my fill of it this week."

He grinned. "What an astonishing young woman you seem to be, and just as I was giving up hope in the next generation."

Neither of us could speak openly when surrounded by people who very likely wouldn't sympathize, but I was now fairly certain we'd sounded each other out on our political views and found agreement. "I have some friends

I'd love for you to meet," I said. "I believe you'd find them invigorating. Do you ever get to New York?"

"Not too often, but if I do, I'll have to pay you a visit. Though I don't suppose that calling upon the governess would be welcome at the governor's home."

"But I don't work for the governor. I work for Lord Henry Lyndon, who is guardian of the governor's grandchildren, and I can assure you that you would be welcome in that home."

He raised an eyebrow. "Oh?"

As if on cue, Henry nearly ran into us when we came out the front doors of the church. "Oh dear, terribly sorry, Miss Newton," he said. "It seems Olive left her favorite handkerchief in the church. I told the governor to go on ahead with the children in the first carriage while I go back to look for it, and then I can come home with you."

I waited until he finished his explanation before introducing him to the baron, who immediately said, "Allow me to help you search."

The church was now nearly empty, so we could talk somewhat more freely as we searched the pews, but we kept our voices low. "I get the impression from Miss Newton that we might be kindred spirits, Lord Henry," the baron said.

"You're hoping to make a change in the way the colonies are governed?" Henry asked.

"I'm looking to shed the mantle of colony and become a nation," the baron replied.

"Then I wish we had time to talk. I suppose you could say I'm active in a movement, and Miss Newton is associated with the Rebel Mechanics. We have multiple groups who could work together to accomplish something, but what we're missing is leadership, someone who could actually help create a nation."

"There are more of us than you'd expect. I can give you names throughout the American colonies. May I have a note sent by courier?"

"It will have to be soon. We leave tomorrow."

"I will send it this afternoon, and I will notify my friends that they may hear from you."

Henry enthusiastically shook his hand. "I am very glad to make your acquaintance, sir."

"You can thank your governess for looking so pretty at the ball. I couldn't allow such a lovely young lady to be left so utterly alone."

"Miss Newton has a knack for meeting people and adding them to her legions," Henry said. "She'll end up in charge of this nation, you can bet. She's already got all the forces in place."

"I merely move in a variety of circles," I demurred, even as I felt a flush rise up my neck to my cheeks.

The baron's manner abruptly changed. "I should warn you not to expect an enthusiastic response, even from those sympathetic to the cause," he said, his eyes grim and his mouth tight. "They are reluctant to commit themselves to action or to take risks. They may be unhappy with the present situation, but don't expect it to change. They're willing to wait and see what happens while grumbling to themselves."

"Perhaps they'll be inspired by the younger generation and what we've accomplished," Henry suggested.

"We may have to wait until your generation is in power before anything happens."

"I don't think that's likely. Things are brewing even now," Henry said. "The displays here recently are merely a sign of more serious events that are afoot."

"I pray that may be the case," the baron replied, but his expression showed no sign of optimism.

There was a long, uncomfortable silence, and then Henry sighed. "We've lingered about as long as would be believed for a search for a handkerchief." With a wry grin, he pulled an embroidered handkerchief out of his pocket. "Oh, there it is! Imagine that!"

The baron and I laughed, and the gloomy mood was broken. We said farewell to the baron, who walked away rather than taking a carriage. Henry and I boarded the waiting carriage, and he sat beside me. "You've done it again, Verity," he said, taking my hand. "I don't know where we'd be without you. This may be just what we need."

I could barely focus on his words, I was so distracted by his hand gripping mine. He seemed to have forgotten that he was still holding onto me and appeared unaffected by the contact. I wondered if I should ease my hand out of his to avoid any potential awkwardness, but he was holding too tightly for me to do that without being obvious and looking like I was trying to escape him, which I certainly wasn't. I rationalized that it was easier and less uncomfortable for me to keep my hand in his, and he was the one likely to bear the brunt of any embarrassment once he realized what he was doing.

While I fretted about our proximity, he went on excitedly about his plans to get his friends throughout the colonies to contact the baron's list of potential allies. "Are you sure you can trust them all?" I asked.

"The baron's list or my friends?"

"Both. One false ally on that list or among the people you contact, and the movement could be jeopardized."

"I don't intend to tell everyone about everyone. I'll assign one person to contact one person."

"And all of them will know about you."

He squeezed my hand, which told me he hadn't forgotten he was holding it, after all. "Dear Verity, haven't you noticed that I lead a charmed life? Besides, all my friends already know about my revolutionary proclivities. If I haven't been arrested by now, I should be safe. All I'm doing now is writing letters and talking to people. It's far less hazardous than armed robbery."

The sick knot in the pit of my stomach disagreed with his assessment of risk.

As we prepared to depart Boston, I was too busy with the children to know whether the baron had fulfilled his promise to deliver the list of names to Henry, and I wasn't able to spend enough time with Henry to ask. It was only as we loaded the carriages to depart for the airfield that he caught my eye and patted his breast pocket.

This journey, to Charleston in the Carolinas, was an overnight voyage. That meant I had to spend all day in the passenger lounge with the others, a night in a cabin shared with Olive, and then another half day with everyone else. I wondered if I could suggest an afternoon nap. We were making an early start, after all.

While we made our ascent, we were all too occupied with looking out the windows to worry about making conversation. Once we'd reached the cruising altitude, though, we had to interact with each other. I assigned work to Rollo and Olive, who took their books and papers to the dining table. Flora paged through a fashion magazine, and Henry sketched. That left me with the governor, who brought out no amusements. I would have loved to read, but I felt it would be rude to leave him alone.

Much to my surprise, the governor cleared his throat and addressed me. "I did mention that I'd met your parents, didn't I, Miss Newton?"

"Yes, Your Grace, you did. And Lady Elinor told me a little more about that event."

"Your mother was very kind to Elinor, who was quite a bother. I remember your mother fondly. I was sad to hear of her passing. It was recent, you said?"

"Yes, just before I came to work for Lord Henry."

"Your father let you leave home so soon after your bereavement?"

That was a difficult question to answer politely. My father hadn't *let* me leave. He'd ejected me from his house upon my mother's death, saying I was no daughter of his. But I didn't want to tarnish the governor's fond memory and good opinion of my mother with a hint of scandal, so I said, "My father insisted upon it. I had nursed my mother through her illness, and he believed a change of scenery would be good for me."

"You were well-educated, it seems. Your father instructed you?"

"Yes, Your Grace. He taught me the way he taught his university students, even though I was much younger."

"You seem to be doing an excellent job with my grandchildren." Much to my relief, he picked up a newspaper and buried his face in it.

I looked up and caught Henry's eye. He raised an eyebrow, as if to ask, "What was all that about?" To which I replied with a faint shrug, indicating, "I have no idea." Perhaps the governor was merely being polite, since we were set to spend many hours in very close quarters. I checked on Rollo and Olive's progress, corrected one of Rollo's Latin conjugations, then resumed my seat and picked up a book.

We passed the next couple of hours in companionable silence until the steward brought midmorning refreshments. "We must have the last tea in Boston," Henry quipped as the steward poured from the pot. The governor's glower suggested he wasn't at all amused. I was surprised Henry had brought it up, but then I supposed that it would be odd for him not to discuss such a notorious event. It was in keeping with his public persona to treat it as an amusing joke that he'd likely forget about the next time he encountered an interesting specimen of insect.

All of us went back to our respective solitary pursuits. Flora finished her magazine and became restless. She got up and paced the lounge, pausing to look over Henry's shoulder at his sketchpad. "Henry, why are you drawing Miss Newton?" she exclaimed.

Everyone looked up from what he or she was doing and stared first at Henry, then at me. "Look at the way she's sitting," Henry said, gesturing toward me. "She's set just so against the window, and the angle of the light is perfect. I had to sketch her. Apologies, Miss Newton, if that makes you uncomfortable."

Flora leaned over the sketch, frowning. "It is a very nice rendition, though you might have been a bit too—" She broke off abruptly, glancing guiltily at me, and quickly retreated to her seat, picking up her magazine again. I wondered what she'd been about to say.

Henry flipped the page, turned, and began drawing again—something other than me, I hoped. Though I would have liked to see how he'd depicted me.

That was the only uncomfortable incident for the rest of the day. We passed over New York as we ate lunch, then had a long afternoon before dinner was served. I was included with the family in these meals, and we didn't have to change into evening attire. I found at dinner that the governor had quite an interest in the classics, and we discussed Homer, much to the dismay and boredom of the children.

Even so, bedtime came as a great relief because I'd be able to relax. "I want to sleep on the top bunk," Olive declared as we headed to our cabin, where the steward had made up our beds. One look at the upper berth, however, and she changed her mind. "You can have the top bunk, Miss Newton," she said. "Or you can join me in the lower bunk if you're too scared to climb up there."

I helped her out of her clothes and into her nightgown, and she crawled into the bunk and curled up in the corner while I undressed. When I was in my nightgown and had brushed and braided my hair, Olive said, "Before you climb up, can I have a story?"

I'd packed a few of her favorite books, and she snuggled against me as I read to her. She was asleep before I finished the story, and I hated to disturb her to move to the other bunk. Chancing one bit of magic, I used my power to turn out the light.

I found it hard to sleep, however. I had too much to think about: the rebel magister and Mechanic groups, the possibility of finding an elder statesman to lead the movement, the governor's interest in me, and whatever was happening between Henry and me, if it wasn't purely in my dreams.

I didn't remember falling asleep, but Olive woke me early in the morning when she crawled over me to get to a window and look out. "Do you think we're almost there?" she asked when she saw that I was awake.

"I think we still have several more hours to go."

"Charleston must be very far away. Will it be different from New York?"

"I imagine it will be, but I've never been there."

It did turn out to be different from New York. The buildings were lower and more colorful, and the streets were lined with palmetto trees I only recognized because I'd seen illustrations in botany books. The carriages that met us at the airfield took us to a mansion on the Battery, facing the ocean. Although it was early November, it was still quite warm and very humid. I could only imagine what it must be like in the summer.

The room I was given was at the rear of the house, overlooking a kitchen garden and outbuildings, though I was pleased to learn that the room to be used for lessons had a view of the sea. When Henry came to inspect the schoolroom and discuss my lesson plans for the week, it was the first chance we'd had to talk privately since that carriage ride in Boston.

"I'm going to go out and send some ether messages to my friends," he said softly while we leaned over the array of books I'd laid out on a table.

"I thought that wasn't secure," I said. I didn't know how the magical long-distance messaging system worked, but I knew that anyone could tap into the Mechanics' telegraph, if they knew the code and how it worked.

"I wouldn't dare send anything from this house, but if I word the messages carefully and send them from a public venue, it should be safe," he said. "Anyway, I'm merely suggesting that my friends call upon some people on my behalf. Tomorrow I'll call on a few local people."

"I wish I could go with you."

"So do I," he replied with a grin. "You have a talent for getting people to listen, but I can't think of any excuse to bring you with me, other than bringing the children."

"I'm not sure I'd inflict Olive and Rollo on any statesmen we're trying to impress."

"That's too true. But don't worry, I'll give you a full report."

It was two days later before I saw Henry again, in the breakfast room. We were alone for the moment, so as we stood at the sideboard together, serving ourselves, I whispered, "How did it go yesterday?"

He sighed. "The baron was right. They don't see a need to act now. They're unhappy, but not willing to take the risk of doing anything about it."

"Perhaps your friends will have better luck."

"I hope so. This city isn't exactly a rebel hotbed. I have no university friends from that set here, and the people I do know have given every appearance of being staunch loyalists. Have you heard anything from the local Mechanics?"

I shook my head. "I haven't been so fortunate as to have a maid introduce herself as my liaison."

The governor entered the room then, cutting off the conversation. Henry immediately began to talk about the impressive array of tropical bugs that might be found in this region. I had a hard time stifling giggles. "So, if you don't have anything you need me to do, Your Grace," he said to the governor, "I'd like to go do some exploring and see if I can find some specimens. It's warm enough that they might even still be active."

"No, no plans today. I have meetings. Miss Newton, I would appreciate it if you kept the children quiet and out of the way. We'll have luncheon served for all three in the schoolroom, as I have guests coming."

"Yes, Your Grace," I said with a nod.

He looked rather grave, and that made me curious as to what his meeting was about. Rebel activity didn't seem to be very high here, so there must have been other governmental concerns.

I didn't relish being trapped in the schoolroom with all three children all day. Fortunately, Flora remained in her room, and although I checked in on her to suggest that she read a book, I didn't try to make her do anything too much like work. It was challenging enough keeping the other two occupied. Rollo had his assignments from school, and I had my planned lessons with Olive, but our days were usually broken up by art and music lessons or walks.

By lunchtime, they had already completed everything I

had planned for the day, and only an afternoon rainstorm kept them from demanding to go outside. I couldn't even supervise piano practice, since the governor had asked us to be quiet. I set them to drawing the view from the window while I headed down to the house's well-stocked library to find a book to read aloud that would entertain both of them.

Unfortunately, the library was very short on novels, focusing primarily on local history. I finally settled upon a book of biographies, thinking that there might at least be some interesting personages to discuss with the children. As I was well aware, real life could be as exciting as any novel.

I was making my way toward the stairs when I heard raised voices. After making sure no servants were nearby, I tiptoed closer to the room the governor was using as a study and strained to make out what the voices were saying.

"How did it get this bad?" the governor boomed.

The other person spoke more softly, so I had to move even closer to hear what he said, and I still only caught the occasional word. "...oversight. We caught the discrepancies, but...more widespread than we realized."

I held my breath. This sounded like something that might be useful to our cause. "In every colony?" the governor shouted, accompanied by a pounding sound, as though of fists on a desk.

"It appears so, Your Grace."

"How did this happen?"

"We've conducted a thorough investigation."

"And?"

"We still aren't sure."

"The money?"

"Unsure. But the treasury is dangerously close to empty. You'll have to raise taxes, I'm afraid."

"We already have magisters joining the revolt. We don't dare do that. Who else knows about this?"

"No one, Your Grace."

"Keep it that way. I may be able to secure a loan. I'll write to a few people I can trust, and perhaps we can get the funds back with more investigation."

It sounded like the meeting was wrapping up, so I didn't dare linger outside the door, even though I was dying to learn more. I hurried up the stairs to make sure I was out of sight before either man left the study.

Now I really needed to talk to Henry. I had a feeling I had just what we needed to spur even the least ardent revolutionaries into action.

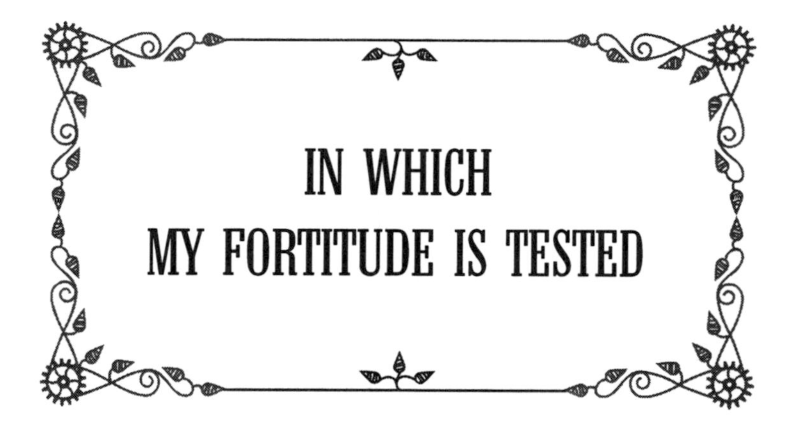

IN WHICH MY FORTITUDE IS TESTED

I was so anxious that if I hadn't managed to find Henry before I went to bed, I might have resorted to sliding a note under his door, even if that would have been quite scandalous if someone else saw it. Once the children were in bed and all the governor's guests were gone, I played the spinet in the schoolroom, hoping that would catch Henry's attention. I knew he played when he needed to think, so surely he would pick up on the clue.

He did come into the room, still dressed for dinner. "Did you find any good specimens today, Lord Henry?" I asked as I played a Bach étude.

"Yes, I did. Some of them are absolutely horrifying. You wouldn't believe the size of the bugs here. I'll have to plan another visit in warmer weather. And how was your day? I know we asked quite a lot of you."

"The children got restless, but I believe I managed to keep them occupied."

He came over to the piano and leaned against it. Still playing so that the music might mask our discussion, I lowered my voice and said, "I overheard something interesting today." As quickly and as softly as I could, I told him about the conversation in the governor's study.

His eyes widening, he sank onto the piano bench next to me. "Are you sure?" he asked, his voice barely above a breath.

"No," I admitted. "I was missing the context entirely, and I didn't hear everything that was said. I missed the beginning of the conversation, and I don't know who was meeting with the governor. But the part I did hear sounded suspicious."

"If there's been some kind of corruption or mismanagement, that might be enough to spur the reluctant revolutionaries to take action. An empty treasury and higher taxes because of this is good reason for revolution."

"Or is the treasury empty because someone has been robbing the government?" I asked with a smile.

"Well, if they want to keep their money, they should do a better job of guarding it, so it's still mismanagement. The difficulty will be proving this. I can't just tell people what my governess overheard. I need evidence."

"He's writing to his friends to try to get loans to cover it up until he can find the missing money. If we could just get one of those letters…"

"That sounds like a job for the Masked Bandits."

I was so shocked that I stopped playing. "Henry, no!" I exclaimed.

Fortunately, he had the presence of mind to get his hands on the keyboard and continue the music so that my outburst didn't ring through the house. "Robbing couriers is child's play. You've seen me do that."

"I'm not worried about you getting the documents away from the courier. I'm worried about *you* getting away. And you can't go robbing people while you're in the governor's house."

"The couriers may get letters in the house, but they have to go elsewhere with them, and then I can carry out a quick robbery and be back home. The governor will hardly search my room when looking for missing documents."

"But you're on your own. Your gang isn't here."

"It doesn't take more than one person to take documents off a courier. And don't even ask to come with me. Both of us being out would only look suspicious. I need you to be entirely aboveboard."

"We both went out in Boston," I reminded him.

"Yes, and that was probably a mistake, as we were nearly caught. You don't have a friend among the staff here, either."

"Yet. Give me time."

"We don't have time. The letters will probably go out soon."

The front bell ringing was loud enough to be heard

over the piano. "Or possibly tonight," I said, gulping down the lump that had formed in my throat.

He stood up. "That would be my cue."

I managed to catch his sleeve before he got away from me. "Be careful."

"Of course!"

But I knew he wouldn't be. He might play the mild-mannered amateur scientist, but Henry loved danger.

I went to the window and watched as a man carrying an attaché case left the house about ten minutes later. Almost immediately afterward, a tall, lanky man followed him. I didn't notice the courier turning around, so he must not have realized he was being shadowed. Within moments, they were both out of my sight. I doubted Henry would do anything so close to the house. He'd have to wait until the courier was in some area where it would look like an ordinary robbery.

If I could have thought of a way to follow him or go along with him, I would have, but he was right about that being difficult in this house. There was no maid who was an agent of the Rebel Mechanics—that I knew of—to sneak me out, no friendly hall boy to let me back in, and no proper governess would venture out alone at this time of night. Henry had it so much easier because young bachelors were expected to go out on the town.

With a sigh of frustration, I returned to the piano. I had to give up playing when it became late enough that it would have been rude to keep the household awake. I retreated to my room and paced for at least an hour. Surely he'd find a way to let me know when he was home, I thought. He'd said that stealing documents from a courier was easy, so even if he'd taken precautions, shouldn't he have been back by now?

I finally decided I might as well go to bed. I knew it was sheer superstition, but I was afraid my waiting up was keeping the watched pot from boiling. Much to my surprise, I'd no sooner settled into bed than I heard a tapping at my window. I knew there wasn't a tree anywhere nearby, so I jumped out of bed and ran to throw back the curtains. The window glass was spattered with rain, and I thought I saw a face pressed against it. I opened the window, and a body tumbled through and onto the floor.

I swallowed my instinctive scream of shock, but I couldn't stop myself from scrambling back, away from the intruder. I heard a gasp that sounded like pain, and then there was a rough whisper, saying, "Verity, it's me."

"Henry? What on earth?" I asked as I moved to kneel beside him.

"I'm so sorry, Verity, but I didn't dare go through the front door, there's a watchman on the street and he'd have seen me, and your room is the one at the rear, there's a trellis nearby, and I need your help." All the words came tumbling out at once, as if he was verging on hysteria.

"What happened? Did something go wrong? Did you get the documents?"

"I got them, but there was a little problem getting

away." His voice shook as his teeth chattered. He was soaking wet and chilled, probably from having been out in the rain, but there seemed to be more than that wrong. I realized what that must be when I noticed that the hem of my white nightgown where I'd knelt next to him had a dark stain on it.

I conjured a small light in my hand, the way he'd taught me, so I could get a better look. "You're bleeding!"

"I think this one might be a little worse than the last time you helped me," he admitted.

It was too dark, even with my light, to examine the wound. "Should we send for a doctor?" I asked.

"How would we explain a gunshot wound?" He sounded more like his normal self. "The first thing we need to do is get me out of your room. I don't want there to be any evidence that I was ever here."

I pulled myself together. I prided myself on being good in a crisis, and this would be a test of my fortitude. "First, some towels, so you don't go dripping down the hall." I grabbed some from my bathroom and blotted him as well as I could. It was alarming how much blood ended up on the formerly white towels. I'd have to figure out later what to do about that. "Can you walk?" I asked.

"I'll need some help." He held his right arm out to me, and I pulled with all my might to get him to his feet. As soon as he was upright, he fell against me. I got my arm around him, and he draped his arm around my shoulders. He seemed to be trying his best to carry his own weight and walk, but I felt like he was doing well to move his feet as we made our way to the door.

I propped him against the wall and checked up and down the hallway before hauling him across to his room. There, I threw one of the towels that was still draped around him onto the floor in front of the fireplace and lowered him to the ground. With a wave of my hand, I made the fire flare up because I was afraid he was going into shock, he was trembling so badly.

I was less worried about a light causing suspicion in his room—being an eccentric young bachelor covered so many behaviors—so I turned on the lamp and moved it closer to him. "It's the shoulder," he said.

I eased his overcoat away from his shoulder. The white shirt underneath was dark red with blood. I lifted him somewhat to check his back, but the shirt was all white. "The bullet must still be in there," I said.

"You'll need to get it out," he said through clenched teeth. "Look in my trunk. I have a medical kit."

"You brought a medical kit on this trip?"

"I'm notoriously accident-prone. And isn't it good that I did? Improvising this sort of thing with tools you might find lying around would be difficult."

I didn't think it would be easy *with* the right tools, but I forced myself not to think so I wouldn't panic. I found the kit, which looked like a doctor's bag, and brought it over to him. He motioned for me to help him sit up, and he rummaged through the bag, bringing out a bottle. "Open this," he ordered. After I did, he took a long swig from it and handed it to me. "For the pain," he explained. "I suspect I'm going to need it." He took out another bottle, some instruments, and a great deal of gauze, then lay back down, breathing heavily, like the effort had cost him a great deal.

"You'll need to take those forceps and probe the wound for the bullet," he said. "Do you think you can do that?"

"Of course I can," I said, trying to convince myself as much as him.

"Of course you can," he echoed, a faint smile on his lips. "I should never doubt you, Verity."

I used the scissors from the kit to cut his shirt away from the wound, forcing myself not to think about seeing that much of his bare skin, and moved the lamp closer to light my work. He clenched his jaw and squeezed his eyes shut as I put the tips of the forceps into the wound. I immediately came upon something solid. "I think I have it," I said and tugged as gently as I could. He gasped and went limp. Working quickly before he could regain consciousness, I pulled the bullet free. Remembering a novel I'd read about stagecoach robbers, I put the forceps back into the wound and probed for a scrap of cloth that might have come with the bullet. I was surprised to find it, and it seemed to match the hole in his shirt. "See, Father, pulp novels are good for something," I muttered to myself. I poured a generous amount of disinfectant over and into the wound, then pressed a wad of gauze onto it, putting on pressure to slow the bleeding.

He moaned and stirred then. "Are you done?" he asked groggily.

"I need to get you bandaged, but I removed the bullet and the cloth it took with it, and I've cleaned the wound."

"You have a future in medicine if you get tired of being a governess," he mumbled.

"Especially if I keep working for you. I'm getting plenty of practice." I wrapped a bandage around the wad of gauze, holding it tight against the wound. "Now, we need to get you warm and dry."

His overcoat had actually kept his body fairly dry. It was just his hair that was soaked. He seemed to have lost his hat somewhere along the way. I wished his valet had come with us because Matthews was far more experienced in this sort of thing. I might not have quailed at removing the bullet, but I was very uncomfortable with the prospect of undressing him. I found a dry towel in his bathroom and gave his head a vigorous rubbing, pulled a nightshirt over his head to hide the bandage, then wrapped a blanket from the bed around his shoulders and made him lie down again.

"There should be a teapot and some tea and sugar in the trunk," he said.

"Do you pack expecting to encounter a tea emergency?"

"Strong, sweet tea is very good for shock. Get water from the bathroom, and you know how to boil it."

"Do you think it's safe for me to use so much magic?"

"They'll think it's me if they notice anything."

I filled the pot, then concentrated on the ether surrounding it. Soon, the water was bubbling, and I added tea leaves. After the tea had steeped thoroughly, I strained it into a cup I found in the trunk and added a generous dose of sugar. Kneeling beside him, I helped him sit halfway up and held the cup to his lips for him to drink. When he'd finished, I lowered him back to the ground. "You should probably have a cup, yourself," he said, his words starting to slur, perhaps from the painkiller he'd taken. "You've had a bit of a shock in dealing with this."

"I need to clean up first. We don't want that blood to set." I gathered the towels and his overcoat and took them into the bathroom. I set the towels to soak in the bathtub in cold water and attempted to dab the blood out of his coat. It looked like the worst of it was on the lining, so the real problem was the obvious hole. He only had the one overcoat with him on the trip.

After draining the water from the tub and giving the towels another rinse, I realized that my white nightgown looked as though it had been through a war. I managed to rinse the blood out of the hem, but by the time I'd done that and wrung out the towels to leave them to dry, my thin cotton gown was so damp as to be transparent. I couldn't go out to face Henry like that, so I took his dressing gown off the hook on the back of the door and wrapped it around myself.

I returned to the bedroom to find him dozing. I checked his pulse and found that although it was weaker and more rapid than would be considered healthy, it was stronger and steadier than it had been earlier. "Yes, I'm still alive," he said sleepily without opening his eyes. "Now, have some tea and let's see if it was worth all my spilled blood."

I didn't need urging to pour myself a cup of tea and add plenty of sugar. Now that the immediate crisis was over, I could feel the shock setting in. My legs felt watery and my hands shook. I downed the whole cup before picking up the packet I'd found in Henry's overcoat pocket. "Don't tell me you don't know what's in it," I said, trying to keep a light, teasing tone in my voice to hide the tremor.

"I was too occupied with fleeing for my life to stop to look. It would be just my luck if it's nothing more than birthday greetings to a friend."

With trembling fingers, I opened the package and pulled out several sheets of paper covered in bold handwriting. When I saw Henry trying to sit up so he could read, I moved closer to him and held the pages so that he could see by the light of the fire.

The contents were more astonishing than I anticipated. The governor admitted that there had been some kind of fraud or mismanagement that was about to bankrupt the colonial government and begged his friend for a loan to tide the colonies over until the matter could be investigated and resolved.

When he'd finished reading, Henry let out a low whistle. "And to think, it's in his own handwriting. This is exactly what we needed, worth every drop of blood. Even all those fence-sitters should be up in arms about this. I need to take this letter around to all those who denied me before."

"You won't be doing that for a couple of days, not if you don't want anyone to find it suspicious that you've got a bad shoulder right after the governor's courier shot someone who stole these documents."

With a sigh, he said, "I'm not sure I can safely do it ever. Being specifically linked to this letter would put me in great danger."

"So, it takes large doses of pain medicine to make you think rationally," I teased. More seriously, I added, "I can get it to the Mechanics, to go in their newspapers. We know there are magisters who read them."

"You can't be linked to it, either."

"Liberty Jones is willing to cede this scoop to some other reporter."

"We need to put this directly into the hands of people we know we can trust. As dangerous as it may be to hold on to this news, let's wait until we get back to New York."

"You can't keep this sort of thing all that time, in the governor's house!"

"I know. But you can."

"Me?"

"No one is going to search your room. Why would a governess who's never out of sight of her charges have incriminating evidence in her possession? And you're less likely to have servants pawing through your belongings in the name of being helpful."

He closed his eyes and took a long, deep breath through clenched teeth. "Though if you are to remain above suspicion, you should probably get back to your room and make sure it shows no signs of intrusion. I'll need you to help me up and into bed first, though."

As I got my hands under his good shoulder to help him sit up and then get to his feet, I said, "You know you're not going to be anything like back to normal by tomorrow. How will you explain your condition?"

He leaned heavily on me as we walked around to the head of the bed, where I pulled back the covers and allowed him to fall onto the mattress. "I have come down with a terrible case of the flu."

"You really do need a doctor," I said as I pulled the covers up over him.

"Believe it or not, I've had worse. Armed robbery is a dangerous business." He grabbed my hand and squeezed it. "Thank you for being my rock. We would all be doomed without you."

"That medicine has gone to your head," I chided. I reluctantly slipped my hand out of his, but I couldn't resist brushing the hair off his forehead.

I thought he smiled ever so slightly, and was that a sigh, or a moan of pain? "Now go to bed, Verity," he murmured, closing his eyes.

I checked the room one last time for signs of blood and made sure the medical supplies were all packed away in the trunk before I slipped out of Henry's dressing gown and left it draped across the footboard. I picked up the stolen letter and tucked it up under one sleeve of my gown, then listened for a long moment at the door before opening it. When I detected no signs of life in the hallway, I darted across to my room.

I'd hidden things before, but never anything quite this important or damning. Being caught with this letter in my possession would likely be considered treason, even if they could find no evidence of my participation in the robbery, and I was in an unfamiliar house being run by the governor. I couldn't think of any reason for anyone to deliberately search my room for contraband, so in devising a hiding place I tried to think of places no servant would have any reason to look while packing, unpacking, or arranging my wardrobe. I thought for a moment about one of my books, but there was the risk that one of the children might look there. I encouraged them to borrow books from me.

My first step was to disguise it, so it wouldn't be obvious at first glance. I found an envelope in the drawer of my desk and slid the letter into it. On the outside of the envelope, I wrote my name in my best impression of masculine handwriting. As an afterthought, I added, "To my dearest" above my name. I sealed the envelope, waited about a minute, then eased it open.

Now that it looked like a love note that had been read, I hoped that no one who wasn't prying into my life would take a closer look. I stuck it between the pages of my Bible, as that was one book no one was likely to need to borrow from me, and with any luck, that would add a dash of guilt to anyone tempted to read my letter.

It wasn't until I'd settled that matter that I realized the window was still open. It was warm enough outside that the room hadn't become badly chilled, but it still felt very damp, which made me shiver now that I wasn't active. I made a quick check to ensure that no blood was evident in the room or on the windowsill and that no one was likely to suspect I'd had a midnight visitor, then crawled into bed and tried unsuccessfully to quiet my mind enough to get some rest.

IN WHICH I MUST MAINTAIN APPEARANCES

After a night of tossing and turning and startling at every sound within the house, I got out of bed at the crack of dawn. In the daylight, I couldn't find any traces of Henry's visit, which relieved me a great deal. I made my own bed and tidied after dressing so that the housemaid would have no reason to linger in my room.

I was alarmed to find the governor already at breakfast when I went down. I felt as though every word I said to him amounted to a lie when I was hiding such a huge secret from him. Of course, I'd been hiding things as long as I'd known him. I'd been spying on him the first time I visited his home. But this felt greater, somehow.

The governor greeted me with a gruff, "G'morning," as I entered the room, but he didn't look up from his newspaper. He was always gruff, and even more so at breakfast, so I couldn't tell from his manner if he yet knew that his dispatch had been stolen. I was immensely relieved when Olive joined us soon after I sat at the table. Her chatter kept an uncomfortable silence from forming. Rollo joined us not long afterward, and he had his own way of steering a conversation.

"Have you heard that there's a ship that travels under water, and they think it's in this harbor?" he said, his eyes shining with excitement.

"Where did you hear that?" I asked. He'd had no opportunity I was aware of to talk to anyone local.

"One of the footmen is as interested in engineering as I am, and we were talking about it. I told him all about the airship, and he told me about this underwater boat."

"I doubt such a thing exists," the governor said from behind his newspaper.

Rollo's eyes went wide. "If you don't know about it, Grandfather, then that means it must be something invented by the Rebel Mechanics."

The governor lowered the newspaper and looked at Rollo over the top of it. "The Rebel Mechanics are nothing more than red ribbons and bold talk. Have they ever actually made anything? Has anyone seen one of their miraculous devices?"

I focused on my toast and hoped that my invisibility as governess would count in my favor because it was hard not to react when I was well aware of exactly what the Mechanics had created.

"They made a steam engine," Rollo protested. "It was in the newspaper."

"It was in an unauthorized scandal sheet," the governor corrected. "That is not a reliable source." I knew he was not only incorrect but was actually lying to his grandson because I knew he'd sent soldiers to seize the machines, and British soldiers, including the governor's friend General Montgomery, had seen the slum children fleeing an altercation in omnibuses pulled by a steam engine.

Rollo set his jaw defiantly in a way that for a moment made him look remarkably like his uncle, but he wisely said nothing more, even as his eyes said, "I know it's true!"

Clearly changing the subject, the governor asked, "Where's Lyndon? He should be down by now. Rollo, go check on your uncle. He's usually more punctual than this."

Rollo got up and ran off. He returned a few minutes later, frowning. "He's not feeling well. He's all pale and sweaty."

I was rather surprised that the governor actually looked concerned. Henry was convinced that the governor didn't approve of him, especially not as guardian of the children, but it looked to me like the governor didn't wish him ill. "I should send for a doctor."

"He says he just has the flu and said he wants some tea and to be left alone," Rollo said.

"I will go read him a story," Olive declared.

"You'll leave him alone, as he asked." The governor turned to the footman who was in charge of the breakfast room. "Have some tea sent up to Lord Henry. And get someone to check in on him every so often to see if he needs anything."

I tried to convey the right degree of concern, something appropriate for an employer who had the flu rather than for a good friend who'd been grievously wounded. I had to settle for a mild, "Oh dear, I hope he feels better soon," even though I wanted nothing more than to stay by his side and soothe his fevered brow.

With Henry out of commission, I had sole charge of the children, which made it difficult to check on Henry or learn what the governor was doing. Up in the schoolroom, I couldn't hear any explosive outbursts that would indicate that the governor had learned the letter had been stolen. The morning seemed very normal, and I had to play chaperone that afternoon, as Flora received callers welcoming the governor's family to Charleston.

Just before dinner was served in the schoolroom, Olive insisted on checking on her uncle and presenting him with a drawing she'd made for him, and I didn't protest at all. Although we wouldn't be able to speak freely, I could at least check on his condition.

We found him drowsing, propped up on pillows. He was pale and had dark hollows under his eyes, but I thought he looked somewhat better than he had the night before. I let Olive be the one to approach the bed while I hung back by the door. "I made you this picture to make you feel better," she announced, handing him the drawing.

He took it from her with his good hand. "Why, thank you, Olive, this does make me feel much better. I'll put it on my nightstand so I can see it." His voice sounded rough and shaky, but I couldn't tell if that was genuine or if he was feigning illness to disguise his true condition.

"You look terrible," Olive declared. "Miss Newton, do you think he needs to see a doctor?"

It was a good excuse for me to check on him. I stepped forward and placed a hand on his forehead. I barely stifled a sigh of relief when I found it neither too warm nor too cold. "He doesn't appear to be feverish, so likely all he needs is some rest," I declared. "And we should leave him to it."

"Thank you for your visit, Olive," he said. "And Miss Newton? I know you have quite the collection of light reading material. Would you mind lending me a novel?"

"I would be happy to. I'll bring you a selection after dinner."

I ushered Olive out with a glance over my shoulder at him. He flashed me a slight smile before closing his eyes.

Reassured by the visit to her uncle, Olive was in better spirits during dinner, back to arguing with her brother. It took me a little longer than I would have liked to get both of them into their rooms for the night, but finally I was free to get a selection of pulp novels to take to Henry.

I left the door open as I visited him, for propriety's sake, so we had to keep our voices low as we spoke, interspersing more normal conversation in case anyone passed by. I started by presenting the books to him. "I've finished all of these, and you should like them. They're entertaining, but not very demanding of the intellect."

While he made a show of examining the books, I whispered, "I can't tell that the governor knows about the letter yet. If he does, he's taken the news rather well."

"I doubt he does know."

"How do you mean?"

"Didn't I tell you last night? Oh, I probably didn't. It's all rather a haze, I'm afraid. I didn't rob the courier who came to the house. I robbed the man he handed it over to, who added it to a satchel with a larger number of items. I took the satchel and managed to get the piece I wanted before he took the satchel back from me." He gave a rueful wince. "That's how I got shot—I was letting him get the satchel back. I'd have been free and clear if I'd just taken the whole thing. But with any luck, it could be days or even weeks before anyone realizes that one letter went missing. The governor will first assume that his friend is ignoring his request. It's such an awkward thing that he may hesitate to follow up, for fear that his friend is letting him down gently by merely not responding."

I thought I heard footsteps coming down the hall, so I said out loud, "That one was my favorite, but I'm not sure it would be quite to your taste. You might enjoy this one more. It's more diverting."

"Right now, anything other than this wallpaper would be more diverting," Henry replied hoarsely with a weak laugh. It might have been my imagination, but I thought the footsteps paused briefly outside the door before moving on.

When I could no longer hear any sound outside, I whispered, "That was insane!"

"And rather brilliant, you must admit."

"You could have been killed, and then where would we be?"

"His aim was a bit better than I expected. I was hoping he'd merely wing me. And you don't have to worry about anyone thinking to search for the letter that no one knows is even missing. I just wish we could get back to New York right away and get this news out."

"You'd better hope you have at least another day to recover before you're forced to spend an entire day with the governor."

"If I'm still ill, I can stay in my cabin for the voyage."

I stood. "I hope you enjoy those books. I don't have any others with me, so you'll have to make them last the rest of the trip. Get well soon."

"Thank you for your kindness, Miss Newton."

I forced myself not to look back over my shoulder at him as I left his room and closed the door behind me. Once I was alone in my room, I sank onto my bed and buried my face in my hands, allowing myself to shed a few tears. He'd taken such a horrible risk, and I was amazed that he'd actually planned it, putting himself on the line to help keep our efforts as secret as possible. He seemed to be doing well now, but I had the strongest suspicion that if a revolution did, in fact, occur, Henry Lyndon was unlikely to survive it.

Any ease I'd gained from knowing that Henry had acted so as to keep the governor unaware of our plot was lost the next morning at breakfast when the governor announced that we were cutting our trip short and would be returning to New York that afternoon. "I have had some unexpected business come up that I must attend to," he said. Had he learned about the letter, or was he merely dealing with the situation behind the letter?

I was too busy helping the children pack and getting their trunks loaded on the baggage carriage to spend too much time fretting. My next worry was about Henry—could he successfully hide an injury while feigning illness, all while so close to the governor?

That turned out not to be a concern at all. The governor offered to let Henry stay until he recovered from his "illness" and then travel home on his own when he felt well enough. Much to my surprise, the governor had already sent for Henry's valet to look after him, which made me feel much better. Matthews was used to having to deal with Henry's scrapes, and he would arrive not long after we departed.

I made one last visit to Henry under the guise of making arrangements for the children's activities for the next few days. "You know what to do," he whispered.

"Yes, as soon as I get the chance. It will be much easier once I'm home."

"You can write the story based on the letter and show the letter as proof to your contacts, but don't hand it over to anyone. I imagine I'll get inquiries in the aftermath, and I want to be able to show it. This is a story you'll want to hand over as directly as possible. No leaving it in a drop."

"I know. I also won't write it under my regular pseudonym."

He leaned his head back against his pillow and closed his eyes. "I know. You're well-versed in this activity, perhaps even more than I am. But this is so critical. This could be the spark that begins a revolution. We can't do anything to jeopardize the opportunity. I just wish I could be there."

"It's probably better that you aren't. That's less suspicion on you."

"And perhaps more on you."

"Nonsense. I'm practically invisible. No one suspects me of anything."

In spite of what I told Henry about being above suspicion, I felt acutely conscious of my deception while in the governor's presence on the airship. I kept telling myself that he barely noticed me, so there was little chance of him being able to tell merely from looking at me that I had his letter detailing the scandal tucked between the pages of my Bible.

The problem was, he did notice me. I felt him watching

me throughout the day as I reviewed lessons with Rollo and read with Olive. "You are quite a good teacher, Miss Newton," he said when we took a break for afternoon tea. "I must say that I initially doubted Lyndon's choice when he hired you. You seemed far too young and inexperienced when he could have employed so many fully qualified, experienced tutors, but you do seem to have a knack for it."

There was a genuine compliment buried in there somewhere, so I meekly said, "Thank you, Your Grace. They are capable and eager students."

"I imagine you were a good student, yourself."

"I suppose I was. I liked to read. I still do."

"Any thought of following your father into academia?"

"I'm not sure that's the life for me." I had been considering applying to a women's college before my mother became ill, but since that avenue was no longer an option for me and since I had other interests now, it was probably best not to get into those details.

"I'm surprised your father let you get away without at least a try at it."

I was sure he was trying to be complimentary, but now he was pushing right where I was trying to evade. "He believes that this experience is good for me," I said, keeping my tone neutral.

"You have siblings, don't you? I seem to recall your parents saying something about children."

"Yes, Your Grace. But they are all much older than I am. They left home while I was still a small child."

God bless Olive, she kept the governor from pressing further by saying, "You're the baby, too, Miss Newton? Were your brothers as mean to you as Rollo is?"

"Hey! I'm not mean!" Rollo protested.

"Sometimes you are," Olive said, quite somberly. "You make fun of me and you hide my dolls."

"I hid your dolls once! And I gave them right back."

Their grandfather, who probably hadn't experienced sibling bickering in decades—if ever—abruptly hid himself behind a magazine once more, ending the uncomfortable conversation. As relieved as I was, I also felt rather guilty that I would be airing his dirty linen when he was trying so hard to be kind to me. It was hard to imagine a man in such a lofty position taking such interest in a mere governess. I had to remind myself that he represented a regime I despised, and he had the power to make life better for so many people, but did not do so.

We began making our gentle descent into New York the next morning while we were finishing breakfast. The children ran to the windows, and I forced myself to follow in a more dignified manner, although I was almost as eager as they were to see the view.

My previous flight over Manhattan had been in the Mechanics' much smaller vessel and at a much lower altitude. Even though we were coming in for a landing, when we crossed the island we were still higher than the *Liberty* had traveled. I couldn't see details on the ground, but I could see the pattern of the streets and the occasional larger landmark. "Can we see our house?" Olive asked.

"We're in the wrong part of the city," Rollo replied.

Very soon, we'd reached the airstrip and settled down to the mooring mast. The governor bid us farewell and sent the children and me directly home, saying he had business to attend to right away. The baggage would be delivered later.

I was surprised by just how much like home the Lyndon mansion looked when we pulled up in front of it. Not too long ago, it had seemed as remote and imposing as a European castle to me. I never would have imagined then that I would look at it with the warm affection of home. Mrs. Talbot, the housekeeper, met us in the foyer. "Welcome home! Luncheon will be served in an hour."

"Thank you," I said. "I hope our early return wasn't too great an inconvenience."

"Nonsense. We're glad to see you back. The governor sent us a message, so we had time to prepare. I do hope Lord Henry isn't too terribly ill. Matthews went off in such a rush."

"He's already on the mend. The concern was that the rigor of travel might hamper his recovery. It's best for him to get his strength back before making that journey."

"That is so good to hear."

I sent the children up to their rooms and went to my own room, eager to move my incriminating evidence to a safer hiding place. With Henry's help, I'd created a false bottom in my desk drawer for hiding articles and documents, and I wasted no time sliding the governor's letter, still in its disguise as a romantic missive, into that spot. It was in a place that would incriminate me if it were found, but it was far less likely to be found there, even accidentally.

I'd need more time to study the letter before I could write an article, but I didn't dare do that while the children were awake. It would be disastrous if Olive came looking for me while I was working. As impatient as I was to get this news out, I had to do this properly and take no chances.

IN WHICH I MAKE HEADLINES

Only after the children were in bed and sound asleep that night did I sneak the letter out of its hiding place to study it. Henry and I had skimmed it the night he stole it, but I hadn't picked up or retained many details. I took notes on the most important and incriminating facts as I read. When I was sure I had it all straight, I hid the letter again. Working from my notes, I drafted an article, then edited it to make it sound like it came from some other pen than that of Liberty Jones.

When I was done, I wished that the Lyndon home had fireplaces in the bedrooms because that would have made it easier to destroy my notes and drafts. Then again, why should I worry about the notes and drafts when I had the letter itself, which was far worse? I hoped that once Henry came home, he would think of a better place to hide it.

He'd told me to hold on to it, but I wondered if it might be wiser to send it to the Mechanics who were outside the city. I wasn't sure what place would be safe once this news hit print. I just knew I preferred it not to be in my bedroom.

My next task was to find a way to hand the article over to my contacts. This time, I needed to observe all precautions and give no one any reason to believe that I was meeting with anyone connected with any radical group. That would be difficult while I had sole charge of the children until Henry returned home.

Much to Rollo's dismay, I insisted on him going to school the next day, even though we were home sooner than we'd planned. "You can tell all your friends about riding in an airship," I reminded him at breakfast.

"And I got a tour," he said, perking up somewhat. Olive joined us for the walk to school, and she was the one to suggest walking home on the street with all the shops. I'd hoped to find Nat there selling newspapers, and I'd even practiced what to say to indicate I needed to arrange a meeting, but he was nowhere in sight.

The art and music teachers hadn't been scheduled since we'd returned early, so I didn't have that excuse to get away in the afternoon. It was so maddening that I was sharper than normal with the children. Even Flora noticed. "You must still be tired from the journey, Miss Newton," she said from the piano as I supervised Rollo's homework that afternoon. "You're not usually this short-tempered. Or are you worried about Henry?"

"I'm worried he'll leave me alone with you three for

much longer," I retorted. "I hadn't realized how much easier his presence makes my job."

"I'm being good," Olive said.

"And I thank you for it," I replied, patting her on the shoulder. "I'm sorry, Rollo, if I sounded snappish. I will try to be more patient."

It was raining, so I couldn't even take an afternoon stroll in the park and hope to run into someone. What I really needed was an excuse to head downtown to meet with any of my usual contacts.

Henry himself provided it. The next day at lunch, Mrs. Talbot came into the dining room to announce that she'd received a message from Henry, who had departed that morning on a passenger airship. "He should be home by tomorrow morning," she said.

"We should get some flowers for his room!" Olive declared.

I couldn't hold back a grin. "Yes, Olive, that's an excellent idea. We should go this afternoon to buy some. I know just the place."

I considered bringing the article with me, for I trusted the girl at the flower shop, but I wanted to be able to talk about it, and I couldn't do that with Olive present. Instead, I wrote a short note requesting an in-person meeting.

My friend greeted us at the shop. "Hello, miss, what can we do for you today?" she asked, darting her eyes from Olive to me, then raising a quizzical eyebrow. I'd never brought one of the children here with me before.

"We need flowers for my uncle," Olive informed her.

"He's been sick, but he's coming home, and I want to make him happy."

"That is very kind of you," the shopgirl said. "Do you know what his favorite color is?"

Olive gasped. "I don't know! Do you, Miss Newton?"

"I'm afraid it hasn't come up in conversation," I said.

"Do you know some things he likes?" the girl asked.

"He likes bugs," Olive said.

"Bugs?"

"He studies insects," I explained.

"Then what about something in the colors of a monarch butterfly?" the girl suggested. She moved around the shop, pulling stems in shades of yellow, orange, and gold from buckets of flowers. She arranged them all in a bouquet. "Like this?" she asked Olive.

Olive clapped her hands. "Yes! It's perfect. May I carry it home, Miss Newton?"

"Yes, but you must be very careful."

Olive was so busy staring at the bouquet she held that I was certain she didn't notice me passing a note to the shopgirl along with payment. "Mrs. Talbot will help us find a vase for the flowers, won't she?" Olive said as the shopgirl read the note and nodded to me.

That errand accomplished, I wasn't sure which I anticipated more, Henry's return or the response from my rebel contacts. I was a little worried about the timing, since the publication of the article coinciding with Henry's return from the place where the letter had been stolen might look suspicious.

That anxiety was eclipsed when Mr. Chastain brought me a note while Olive, Mrs. Talbot, and I were putting the flowers in a vase. "This was just delivered for you, Miss Newton," he said.

Frowning, I opened it. Ostensibly, it was from my sister, but my sister had made no effort to contact me since I'd left home, and I didn't think any member of my family even knew where I was. The handwriting was wrong, and it was signed, "Your loving sister," with no name.

"What is it, Miss Newton?" Mrs. Talbot asked, sounding concerned. I supposed that my confusion might have resembled distress.

"My sister is in town, and she's invited me to join her for tea at the Astoria this afternoon."

"That's very short notice."

"It must have been an unexpected trip."

"You must go, then. I'll get Rollo from school."

"But you have so much to do, preparing for Lord Henry's return."

"Now really, do you think Lord Henry expects much of anything? You know he'd tell you to visit your sister. Go!"

Since I didn't believe for a moment that it really was my sister, and I was fairly certain this sudden invitation was a response to my request for a clandestine meeting, I was sure of what Henry would say. I changed into a nicer dress, put on my best hat, and hid my article in the lining of my reticule.

When I came downstairs, Mr. Chastain had secured a cab for me, and I felt like a grand lady as I journeyed to the hotel. Once there, I glanced around, feeling somewhat lost. I would recognize my own sister, of course, but I knew I wasn't likely meeting her, and I didn't know who would be playing that role.

A tall, elegant woman in a rather spectacular feather-festooned hat rose from a table tucked away in a corner behind some potted palms. "Verity, darling, there you are!" she said, crossing the room to take my hands. "You're such a dear to meet me. I must apologize for the short notice, but I didn't know until we arrived that I would have time to see you."

It took all my self-control not to gape, for my "sister" was Lizzie, but as I'd never seen her before. I might not even have recognized her. Not only was she dressed in the height of fashion, but the hair that showed beneath her hat was a brown that matched mine rather than her usual fiery red, and her freckles had been so skillfully covered with cosmetics that I only knew artifice was involved because I knew what she normally looked like. I supposed the theatrical society the rebels hid behind had its uses. She'd managed to disguise her usual slight Irish lilt so that she spoke very much like I did.

"Of course I'd make time for you," I said as soon as I recovered my wits.

She led me to our table, and as I sat, I whispered, "This is all rather elaborate, isn't it?"

"Your message sounded urgent. Our florist telegraphed as soon as you were gone."

"It is urgent. It's the most urgent thing I've done yet."

"Now I am intrigued." As a waiter approached with a teapot, she raised her voice slightly and said, "I hope you don't mind if I already ordered. You like Assam, as I recall."

"Yes, that's lovely, thank you."

When the waiter had gone, she grinned and added, "You certainly dumped enough of it in the harbor."

"I'm surprised that you're drinking tea now. I thought that was off-limits."

"How better to disguise our clandestine activity? You needed a meeting that wouldn't be at all suspicious."

"This is perfect," I admitted.

Our conversation was interrupted once more as we were brought tiered stands of sandwiches, scones, and cakes. "Oh my, I'll never be hungry for dinner," I said.

"I suppose you dine early in the nursery with the children, as a governess," she said, adopting the tone of a slightly condescending older sister.

"Yes, I'm afraid I do, especially while their uncle is out of town."

When the waiter was out of earshot, she whispered, "I wonder if they'd notice if I stashed whatever we don't eat in my purse. I could feed the girls in the boardinghouse on this for days."

The room was fairly noisy, and our table was isolated, so I thought it might be safe to speak when the waiters were well away. I leaned forward, on the pretense of taking a sandwich, and said, "We have evidence of corruption at the highest levels in the government. The governor had to ask friends for loans to keep the colonies functioning until he can find the lost funds."

I thought she would choke on the bite of cucumber sandwich she'd just taken. "Really?"

"We have the letter from the governor himself. Henry stole it from a courier."

"Are you sure it's genuine, that it isn't a trap? If we publish it, will he know he has a mole and who it's likely to be?"

I froze, considering the terrible consequences if that were to be the case, then shook my head. "No. He had no way of knowing what I overheard or that I would even have been in a place to overhear, and I don't think he yet knows that the letter was taken. The courier got his bag back without knowing anything was missing."

She nodded, thinking. "Well, then, perhaps it is real."

"Henry believes this is what we need to make those who are reluctant ready for action. There are some in very high ranks who sympathize but who are unwilling to become involved. If they know this, then…"

"Then they will feel compelled to act."

"I've written the article. I have the letter as proof if anyone needs to see it, but it remains with me."

"I understand." In a more conversational tone, she added, "Your new position sounds quite fascinating, though I never imagined you as a career girl. And working for the governor's family! You must tell me what he's like."

"He's been very kind to me, and he loves the children very much, but I don't see him that often."

We spent the rest of the time in sisterly chat. It felt surreal to me, as I'd never had such a conversation with my own sister. We'd never been close even before she'd sided with her father and denied my place in the family.

I barely suppressed laughter when Lizzie managed to tip the least messy sandwiches and a scone or two into her bag. "Oh, I have something for your children," I said once the waiter had taken away the empty plates and cups. I handed her the envelope from my bag.

"How very sweet of you. I'm sure they'll love hearing from their auntie." She hooked her arm through mine as we left the tea room and went to the hotel lobby. There she kissed me on the cheek. "It was so good to see you again, sister dearest. We really should stay in touch more often."

"You must let me know the next time you plan to be in the city," I said, playing along.

I allowed myself a deep sigh of relief once I was in a cab on the way home. I hadn't realized just how tense I'd been ever since Henry's escapade to steal the letter. Now I knew the truth would come out.

It was probably just my imagination, but as Olive and I escorted Rollo to school the next morning, I fancied that I sensed an extra energy in the air, a buzz like an electrical current between people when they met. Were they talking about the scandalous news about the government? I hadn't yet seen the newspaper, so I wasn't entirely certain the news was out. It had been somewhat past the deadline to make it into the next morning's edition, but I thought for something this important, they'd have delayed printing.

When the boys left their chaperones at Rollo's school, they rushed to each other as though sharing exciting news, and I had to remind myself that this wasn't the sort of news that would excite young boys. They'd thrill about a new machine, not financial mismanagement.

I finally saw a copy of the newspaper when we ran across a newsboy with an armload of papers. Instead of standing on a single corner, he kept on the move, letting the top of the front page peek out from under his coat. People dropped coins in his pocket and grabbed copies as they passed. The stream of customers was so steady that I couldn't get close enough to buy a copy. I settled for attempting to read other people's papers as they passed.

It was fairly obvious from the giant headline that the news was, indeed, out. "Scandal in Colonial Government" the headline blared in letters a couple of inches high. In only slightly smaller letters, the paper asked, "Where Is the Money?" I knew what the article said because I'd written it, so I didn't try too hard to read it once I knew it was there.

"Miss Newton, slow down! You're walking too fast," Olive complained, making me realize that this development had put a real spring in my step. Now surely people would be willing to rise up. It wouldn't just be a few wanting change.

When we came within sight of the Lyndon home, Olive forgot about wanting to walk more slowly. There was a carriage in front, unloading a passenger. Olive cried out, "Uncle Henry!" and ran forward, dragging me behind her. Though I had to admit, I was probably as excited to see him as she was.

Mr. Chastain was just helping him out of the cab when we reached it. Henry looked much better. His color was almost back to normal, and his eyes had lost that sunken, hollow appearance they'd had right after his injury.

"Uncle! Are you better?" Olive asked, throwing her arms around him.

"Much better, Olive, thank you," he said, returning her hug with his good arm.

"Wait'll you see what we got you!"

"I can hardly wait." He caught my eye and smiled. "I presume the children have been good for you, Miss Newton?"

"They've behaved admirably," I said.

"I'm glad to hear that."

He made it up the front steps and into the house without help, much to my relief. He didn't use his left arm much, but if one didn't know to look for an injury, one wouldn't notice anything in the way he carried himself. Only when we reached his room after climbing the staircase did he show signs of weariness. He sank onto the edge of his bed and let out a long, slow breath, but I couldn't tell if he really was tired or if he was maintaining the illusion of recent illness.

"See, we got you flowers!" Olive pointed out, gesturing to the bouquet on the nightstand.

"And so you did," Henry said. "Those are lovely. Did you pick them out yourself?"

"Miss Newton and I did. You like them?"

"I like them very much. Thank you, Olive." He looked up at me and smiled. "And you, Miss Newton."

Matthews came in, directing the footmen with Henry's trunk. "You need to rest, sir," he said. "Perhaps you can have visitors again later."

"We need to get to our schoolwork," I said to Olive.

She kissed her uncle on the cheek before we left. I noticed in passing that Matthews had a newspaper tucked under his arm, so I thought it likely that Henry already knew I'd carried out my mission. I paused at the doorway and looked back. Henry met my eye, nodded, and grinned. I smiled in response before following Olive to the schoolroom.

Henry must have truly felt much better, for he joined us for dinner that evening. I'd missed these family meals during our journey. To be honest, I'd missed dining with Henry and being treated like part of the family. We couldn't talk about our work in front of the children, but it was nice just to have him there.

"What was the airship you took like?" Rollo asked. "Was it bigger than Grandfather's ship?"

"I didn't pay much attention because I remained in my cabin the entire time," Henry replied. "I must say, it was a restful way to travel. I fell asleep soon after I boarded and woke feeling quite renewed just as we landed."

"Perhaps they should advertise airship travel as medicinal," I said.

"Perhaps," he said with a smile. "Though I think a lot of it had to do with knowing I was on my way home."

As we left the dining room, I thought Henry and I would finally have the chance to talk, but Mr. Chastain approached with a stack of messages on a tray. "These have come for you, my lord," he said. "Several via ether, and the rest delivered personally."

"Word of my return must have spread. Miss Newton, do you think you could assist me by playing secretary? I would most appreciate the help."

"Certainly, sir. Let me get Olive into bed and I'll join you in your study."

Olive was so excited by her uncle's return that it took me longer than usual to get her settled down, and I could hardly blame her. I was rather excited, myself, and eager to find out what all those messages were about.

When I joined him in the study, he was beaming. "It worked, Verity!" he said, waving a message. "Of course, no one has outright said they're supporting revolution, but would they really have messaged me if their stances had remained the same? They must have spread the news throughout the colonies because I've also heard from the crew in Boston that they made some new friends today. I shouldn't be surprised because that was quite an article."

"The subject matter was the important part."

"But you put it in a way that made it clear what was happening and why it was important. I don't think I'd have had this kind of response from a dry recitation of facts. If this is what I'm hearing already, we may be on the verge of something big. I just wish I knew what the governor thought. Unfortunately, our relationship isn't such that I have any excuse to pay him a visit."

"But I do!" I realized. "Not him, exactly, but Flora and I are supposed to visit Elinor tomorrow."

He grinned. "That should do just fine. You can count on her to let you know if he's been particularly unhappy. Meanwhile, are you free tomorrow evening?"

"Of course. Why?"

He gestured toward the small stack of envelopes on his desk. "Some of my friends have mentioned coming by, and we might need an extra hand for whatever game we want to play. At least, that will be my excuse for sending for you. I have a feeling the Mechanics may have just gained some funding and support, and we'll want your report on the governor's reaction."

"Are you sure you feel up to company?" I asked.

"I'm really doing much better. All I needed was some rest and a little healing energy from the ether. I'm fine as long as I avoid one or two uncomfortable positions and don't make sudden moves."

I let out a relieved sigh. "That is good to hear. I was worried that you'd suffered from amateur medical assistance."

"You did an excellent job. And how could I not feel better when we're doing so well?" He reached over and took my hand, staring directly into my eyes. "We've done it, Verity. How does it feel to know you've sparked a revolution?"

"I'll let you know when it really starts," I replied.

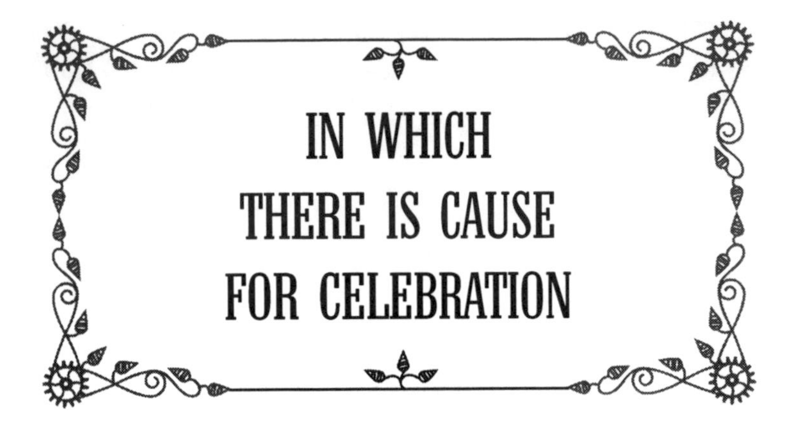

IN WHICH THERE IS CAUSE FOR CELEBRATION

I'd halfway expected Elinor to cancel our tea because of the controversy surrounding her father, but I'd had no word of a change in plans by the time to depart. I thought I sensed an air of extra tension in the governor's mansion when we arrived, but it was likely just my imagination at work. The governor himself made no appearance as Flora and I were escorted up to Elinor's room.

Elinor was in her usual spot, ensconced in her massive canopied bed, a lace bed jacket around her shoulders. "I am so glad you were able to come," she said when we entered. "I was about to die of boredom. Father's been such a bear the last few days that even if he had time to spend with me, he'd be far too unpleasant for my delicate constitution." I had to bite my lip to keep myself from smiling at that, for Elinor was the healthiest-looking invalid I'd ever seen.

Henry had mentioned to me that her primary ailment was being sick of society. By taking to her bed, she avoided having to play hostess for her widowed father and all the paying and receiving calls, going to dinner parties, and attending balls that would have entailed. Only the people she really wanted to see were admitted to her sickroom.

"I'd heard that there was some kind of scandal," I said tentatively. The news was so widely discussed that I thought it would sound more suspicious if I hadn't heard it.

"Oh, yes. It seems that one of Father's trusted appointees has betrayed him. He'd hoped to deal with it before word got out, but somehow that story is now everywhere."

"I don't know why everyone's making such a fuss," Flora said as she took a seat and arranged her skirts around her. "Don't we expect people in the government to use the money for their own purposes?"

Both Elinor and I turned to stare at her. "My, but that's a rather cynical view," Elinor said, echoing my own thoughts.

"Everyone in any position of power is quite wealthy," Flora said, and I found myself reevaluating whether she might be suited to Colin, after all.

"But that's because it's the wealthy and powerful who get appointed to high positions," Elinor said.

"They all somehow become even more wealthy while doing a job that supposedly doesn't pay well and that tends to make them neglect their own estates." Perhaps sensing our surprise at her views, Flora tossed her hair over her shoulder and said defensively, "You make me read. Is it so odd that I would form opinions?"

"Not at all," Elinor said. "This is exactly why your uncle wants you to be educated. I'm sure he'd be proud of you, and happy to discuss these things."

"Just don't tell anyone else. They'll think I'm a boring bluestocking."

Thinking of the magisters I'd met in Boston, I had a feeling she would actually fit in quite well in that set. I just wasn't sure Henry would want his niece mixed up in those activities. "I do hope this hasn't made things more difficult for the governor," I said to Elinor.

"There have been calls for his resignation, and he's worried about the rebel movements gaining traction."

"And we just came out from under martial law in the city," I said with a sigh.

"It doesn't seem as though anyone's marching on the government buildings yet. If there's no insurrection, there's nothing to suppress. But enough talk of politics. What did you think of the book?"

I wasn't sure this was the intelligence Henry needed, but I couldn't think of a way to ask for more without sounding like I was seeking information for a specific purpose. Elinor had a knack for giving me just the nuggets of gossip I needed, to the point I sometimes wondered if she knew exactly what I was up to, so I hoped if there was more, she'd find a way to share it.

After we'd had tea and discussed that month's book to

Elinor's satisfaction, I tried to steer the conversation back to the governor. "Please give your father my regards," I said. "He was very kind to me on our trip. I hate to think of him in distress."

"I'm sure he'd be pleased to hear that," she said. "And I think, more than anything, what's distressing him is the sense that he's been betrayed, first by his official, and then by whoever spread the news. In fact, I think he's more worried about finding who's responsible for giving that information to the newspapers than he is about dealing with the corruption. Someone seems to have intercepted some correspondence, and he wants that person found."

I forced myself not to gulp in fear at the knowledge that the missing correspondence was currently in my desk. "I can imagine that," I said as mildly as I could manage. "It must be terrible to suddenly feel you can't trust your friends."

For a moment, I even felt bad for the governor and what we'd done to him, but I reminded myself that it was his own policies that had led to these events.

I didn't get a spare moment alone with Henry to report what I'd learned, but that evening after dinner, Mrs. Talbot knocked on my door. "Miss Newton, Lord Henry has asked me to invite you to join him and some friends in the parlor. He says they need one more hand to make up a game. I'm not entirely sure it's proper, as they are all young gentlemen."

"I trust Lord Henry completely, and do you think he'd allow his friends to take liberties with me?" I said.

"I suppose, when you put it that way..." Her expression was pained, but she eventually sighed and said, "It's good for you to spend time with people closer to your own age, and I doubt those young men would even look at a nonmagister girl."

She was probably right, I thought as I headed downstairs. Henry's friends accepted me as a party to their cause, and they respected my abilities, but I doubted they even saw me as a girl. As for Henry, it was hard to tell. How much of what I thought I saw in the way he related to me was merely the product of my own fancies and wishful thinking?

I found Henry and his friends seated around a card table, looking just enough like they were playing to satisfy any servant who might look in, but anyone who watched long enough would know that no game was actually in progress.

Henry started to get up to greet me when I entered, but Geoffrey put a hand on his shoulder before coming over to hand me a glass of champagne. "It's the woman of the hour!" he said, raising his own glass.

"All I did was write the article and pass it on," I protested. "Lord Henry did the hard part."

"I think I'd rather pull off the robbery than have to write," Philip said with a grin. "Even with people shooting at me."

Henry motioned for me to take the seat next to him. "The response has been more than any of us could have hoped."

"Even my father is talking about there needing to be change," Philip said. "Old Scratch must be strapping on his ice skates about now."

"I'm worried that it may be premature," Geoffrey said. "It might have been better for this news to come out when we were more prepared."

"On the other hand," Henry argued, "this may be what we need to get enough funding and support for the cause. I'm hearing from people all over who want to join up. Someone else has even invited me to a meeting, not knowing I'm already involved." He turned to me. "Now, what's the word from the governor's home?"

"Apparently, there have been calls for his resignation, and there's a lot of concern within the government," I said. "The governor wants to track down the people who leaked this information. Lady Elinor suggested that the betrayal seemed to have angered him more than the corruption."

Henry winced guiltily. "It is a kind of betrayal, isn't it? I was his guest, and I've exposed him to public criticism."

"He's the one who was keeping secrets," Geoffrey said. "If he'd been running things the way he's supposed to, he wouldn't have been in any danger."

"Do you think he'll trace it back to you?" Philip asked Henry.

"I don't see how he could. For all he knows, I was

coming down with influenza that night and was too ill to get out of bed the next morning. I was traveling when the information was published in the newspaper. He'd have to already suspect Verity and me to put the pieces together and find any kind of pattern."

Philip stood and raised his glass. "Then we should all stop worrying and celebrate. A toast to our glorious and righteous cause, which may now come to fruition, thanks to the daring and skill of the greatest bandit in the colonies and the intrepid reporter who spread the news." He drained his glass and said, "And now, to formally launch our organization. I've been to see the locksmith, and here are our first keys." He pulled small, ornate keys hanging on blue ribbons from his pocket and handed one to each of us. "I have more for when we gain new members, but I would suggest a magically binding loyalty oath before we issue a key, and I have the lock to use for testing when you meet someone new with a key, to ensure it's genuine."

I held my key in the palm of my hand. As small as it was, its importance weighed heavily. The Rebel Mechanics were an illegal group, but they weren't taken entirely seriously by the authorities. This key represented rebellion at the highest levels of magister society. And to think, I now was part of both groups. "We probably shouldn't get in the habit of openly wearing these," I suggested.

"No. We'll just bring them out discreetly," Geoffrey agreed. "We'll need to begin vetting our recent contacts."

"That's work for later," Philip said. "Tonight, we're

celebrating. Henry, do you have a music player in this place? I'm in the mood for a dance."

Henry waved his hand at a finely carved box sitting on a shelf, and piano music, slightly tinny, began playing. Philip listened for a moment. "Not quite what I had in mind, but it'll do," he said with a shrug. "Miss Newton, would you do me the honor?"

He hardly waited for me to agree before he whisked me away in an exaggeratedly stately waltz. He made each move with a gallant flourish, and his expression was a perfect mockery of the nobles I'd seen at balls. Soon, I was laughing so hard I might not have been able to stay on my feet without someone else holding me up, and it took me a moment to notice when my partner had changed.

I stopped laughing long enough to catch my breath and looked up to find that Henry was now the one who held me. "I really can't allow my staff to be treated in such a way," he said with a crooked smile and raised eyebrow. "I shall have to give Verity extra pay for subjecting her to the torture of that dance."

Henry's waltz was still stately, since that was the only way to dance to that music, but I didn't get the impression that he was mocking anyone. He was merely dancing, steering me carefully around the furniture. I'd danced with him once before, at the ball at the governor's house. Then I'd been intensely conscious of our surroundings and the fact that we were planning to warn the Mechanics of an impending raid as soon as we were able to get away from the ball.

Now, though, it was just us and Henry's two friends, and soon I even forgot about the friends. It felt like we were alone together in a world where we both belonged. When the music ended, it broke the spell. Both of us stood there, blinking. I knew I was coming back to the parlor and the reality of the separate worlds in which we lived. Henry looked equally lost, but I couldn't read his face to tell what he was thinking.

"I don't suppose you have a different reel for this thing," Philip said. "Something more lively."

Henry blinked again and released me, stepping away as though just then realizing that we'd been standing there in each other's arms for what had seemed like hours. "Oh, yes, um, in the cabinet there. They were supposed to be sorted, but I have no idea what the children might have done. Flora likes recordings of the works she's learning to play, so there's a lot of piano music."

The reel Philip found was still more piano music, but it was a jaunty polka. He spun around the room with an imaginary partner as the rest of us laughed. Henry glanced at me, raising an eyebrow in invitation, and I smiled as I took his hand and let him lead me. I had little experience with this dance, so I stumbled and trod on his feet far too often, and soon we were both laughing so hard we couldn't dance any longer. I leaned against his shoulder, making sure it was the uninjured one, to catch my breath, and then I didn't want to move, but I knew I had to.

Hoping the flush on my cheeks would be attributed to

my dancing, I forced myself to back away from him. "Oh my, I haven't danced like that, ever," I said, fanning myself with my hand. Geoffrey filled a glass for me, but I shook my head. My wits were already addled enough. Champagne would not help matters. "And it is getting very late for me, so if you gentlemen will excuse me?"

I felt like I barely had to walk up the stairs to my room. I seemed to float upward on a cloud of bliss at the memory of being in Henry's arms like that. I knew it couldn't go much beyond that unless we managed to change things, but we'd made some important steps. Maybe there was hope for us.

Henry was more social the next couple of days than I'd ever known him to be. He had a constant stream of visitors in the few hours he was home. The rest of the time, he was visiting friends, and he even went out on Saturday night. Sunday, we barely made it out of church, there were so many people wanting to greet him, and he was out again that evening.

He was in high spirits at breakfast Monday morning and agreed to walk Rollo to school, much to Rollo's glee and Olive's dismay. "May I come with you?" she asked.

"Not today, I'm afraid," Henry said. "I have an appointment near Rollo's school, so I won't be coming back home until later, and you would find this appointment terribly dull."

"We will have more time for lessons," I said. Olive

was the rare child for whom that sounded like a treat, and Henry gave me a grateful smile.

He didn't come home again until late that afternoon, after I'd already retrieved Rollo from school and had turned all the children over to the music teacher. I was on the upstairs landing when he came bursting through the front door and ran up the stairs, taking the steps two at a time.

When he reached the landing, he grabbed me around the waist, picked me up, and spun me around. "We did it!" he exclaimed, keeping his voice too low to carry far, though his enthusiasm was still evident.

"Did what?" I inquired, a trifle dizzy either from the spin or from being in his arms like that.

He pulled me aside into the doorway of the nearest room, an unused bedroom. "It's not just the young people anymore. There's an earl who wants to form committees and create a colonial congress. That's the first step toward having our own government."

"An earl?"

"Yes! He's one of the baron's friends, and he was the one who asked to meet with me. Of course, there are details to be worked out, but this is proof that it's not just the dream of some crazy kids. If we do form a congress, I want to make sure everyone's represented. I wonder if there's anyone among the Mechanics who might be statesman material. Are they all students?"

"I don't really know. I'll have to ask next time I see them."

"Of course, that's if they're willing to throw in with us. They might still be leery of us and of any enterprise with an earl in charge." For a moment, his grin faded, but it was soon back again. "We did it, Verity! That article did exactly what we hoped it would. Now we can start taking definite steps. This may really happen!"

"So it was worth that hole in your shoulder?"

"What's a revolution without a little bloodshed?"

Only then did he appear to realize how closely he was still holding me, pressed against the door frame. He stepped away, sliding his hands off my waist, but he caught my left hand and held it a moment longer. Our eyes met, and he opened his mouth as though to say something, paused, shook his head slightly, and said, "I should let you get back to work."

"Yes, I should go check on the children." I moved to go, but he hadn't released my hand. I glanced down at it, then up at him.

"Oh, yes, right. Sorry." He blushed and let go, taking a step away.

I forced myself not to look back at him as I headed toward the stairs, but I could hear him whistling softly. I knew I had to be grinning like an idiot, but as there was no one to see me, I made no effort to school my features.

I was halfway down the stairs when the doorbell rang. Mr. Chastain opened the door and several police officers came rushing through the doorway.

"May I help you gentlemen?" Mr. Chastain boomed in his deep voice.

"We're here for Lord Henry Lyndon," one of the policemen said. "Where is he?"

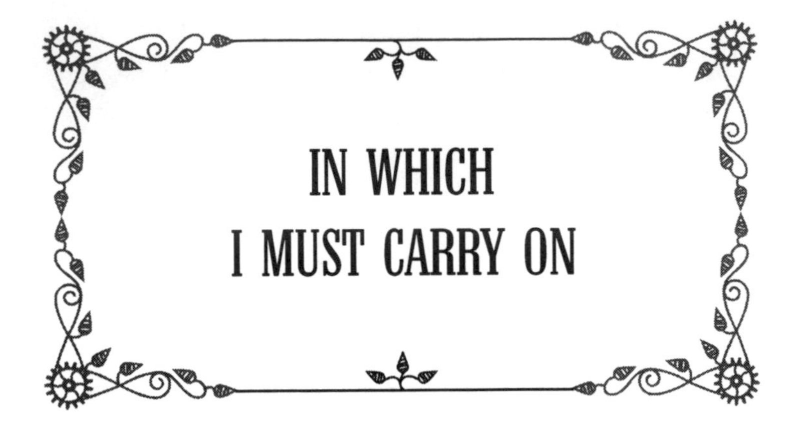

IN WHICH I MUST CARRY ON

Ever the consummate butler, Mr. Chastain said, "If you gentlemen would care to wait in the parlor, I will announce you."

They paid him no mind. Two of them rushed up the stairs, while the other two stood at the front door. I stood frozen to the spot on the stairs, even as they ran past me. I couldn't have moved if my life had depended on it. Not that I had anywhere to go. I couldn't escape past the men at the door, and I had no chance of warning Henry. One of the policemen at the door looked right at me. Our eyes met, and I thought his expression softened in something like sympathy, but if he felt sorry for me because I was about to be arrested, he made no move to take me into custody.

"Are you looking for me?" a surprisingly calm voice

said from above me, and I turned to see Henry standing on the upper landing. The policemen ran toward him.

By this time, everyone else in the household had come to see what all the commotion was about. Mrs. Talbot and several of the servants came into the hallway on the lower floor, and the children appeared from the upstairs parlor.

One of the policemen grabbed Henry by the arm. It was his injured one, and he gasped in pain as his arm was jerked backwards. "Lord Henry Lyndon, you are under arrest for conspiracy to commit treason," the policeman said. The other officer shackled Henry's hands behind his back. Henry remained surprisingly calm, but I could see the fear on his face. He looked so young and vulnerable.

"No! You can't take my uncle!" Olive screamed. She rushed toward him as they hustled him down the stairs, but Rollo caught her and held her back, even as she flailed at him with her little fists and tried to kick his shins to make him release her.

Henry met my eye as he passed me. I wanted to reach out to him, but I restrained myself. I felt so helpless when all I could do was watch him be taken out through the front door.

As soon as the door slammed shut, the household burst into chaos. Olive broke free of Rollo and ran to me. I rushed to meet her and caught her in my arms. "Miss Newton, what are they doing to Uncle?" she sobbed against me.

"I don't know, darling," I said, patting her back.

"I wonder what Uncle Henry did," Rollo said as he came toward us.

"It probably has something to do with his school friends," Flora said, also coming toward Olive and me. "He ran with a radical set. Someone must have said the wrong thing to the wrong person."

Rollo reached us and caught both Olive and me in a hug. He gave the appearance of trying to comfort us, but I got the impression from the way he clung to me that he was seeking comfort, himself. "What can we do?" he asked plaintively. "We should help him. And what will become of us?"

Those were very good questions, and I didn't have the answers at the moment. My first instinct was to run to my rebel friends to tell them and ask for help, but the more I thought about it, the more I knew that would be the wrong course of action. Getting in contact with known rebels at this time would only draw the wrong kind of attention, and it was likely that they would know soon, anyhow. That was what my network of informants was all about. We had scullery maids and laundresses in the barracks and prison, clerks at the police stations. One of these invisible people would surely learn about Henry's plight and alert the rebels.

Mrs. Talbot was the first to come up with a concrete action. "Mr. Chastain, you should contact Lord Henry's attorney," she said.

"Yes, very good idea," he replied, and he headed down to his office.

That gave me an idea. "Flora, perhaps you should send

a message to your grandfather. If anyone can help Lord Henry, he can." That was, if it hadn't been the governor who'd had him arrested in the first place.

"I will do so right away." She flounced off, her shoulders squared and her head held high.

I thought for a moment about suggesting that Flora pay calls on her friends so I could check on Henry's group, but I realized that paying social calls at a time like this would look decidedly odd. That meant that all I could do was wait and do my job of looking after the children. They'd had a terrible shock, and at the moment they needed a governess more than anyone needed a revolutionary.

Echoing my thoughts, Mrs. Talbot said, "I think we could all do with a cup of tea right now. I'll have some brought up to the parlor."

"Thank you," I said. I managed to herd Olive, who still clung to me, and Rollo into the family parlor. Shock seemed to have settled in on Rollo. He was stunned silent, none of his usual spirit in evidence. Olive wasn't sobbing quite so hard anymore, but she refused to let go of me. I had a feeling I'd be sleeping in her room that night—that was, if the governor didn't send for the children right away. He'd always wanted guardianship of them, and I doubted Henry would get them back, regardless of how this came out.

"He isn't in *serious* trouble, is he?" Rollo asked at last.

I couldn't answer that honestly and sound at all reassuring. The problem was that Henry was guilty of so very many things. "I don't know what the charges are or what evidence they have against him," I said, which was true enough. Which treasonous act had led to his arrest?

Flora swept into the room. "I sent a message to Grandfather, and I waited for a reply, but I got none. He may not be at his office." She sank onto a chair. "It's an outrage when someone from such a high-ranking family can be hauled out of his home, just like that. Did they even have a warrant? Henry should have asked for specifics of the charges rather than going meekly along with them."

I turned to stare at her. "My, you have been doing your reading."

"Of course I have. The fact that I don't like talking about boring things doesn't mean I don't know anything."

One of the footmen entered with a tea tray, Mrs. Talbot in his wake. "Mr. Chastain has reached Lord Henry's attorney, and he's looking into the situation," she reported. "I think in the meantime we should go about business as usual, as though Lord Henry is merely away on a trip. I'm sure arrangements for the guardianship of the children will be made, and we can adjust accordingly once we have those details. For tonight, we'll serve dinner at the usual time."

The sweet tea and cakes were wonderfully restorative. I was still shaken and afraid, but I was developing a mental plan. I knew I needed to stay at home the rest of the evening, but I could attempt to make contact with some members of my network the next day and see if anyone knew where Henry was.

It was encouraging that the police hadn't even tried to

search the house when they arrested Henry. That suggested to me that the arrest didn't have anything to do with the stolen letter and might just be about Henry's talk of revolution. That still wasn't good for Henry, but I thought it would go better for him if all they could convict him of was talk. He was doomed if the authorities knew about the banditry. I might be in danger, as well, if they learned about the letter and how its contents had become public. I took some comfort in the fact that I'd been right there and the policemen had paid me no notice. If they were going to arrest me, surely they'd have done so at that time.

All of us whirled when Mr. Chastain appeared in the doorway. "Miss Newton, there is someone who wishes to speak with you privately," he said, then hurried to add when he must have noticed the dismay on my face, "It is a friend of Lord Henry's."

I put down my teacup and told Olive, "I'll be back in just a moment." I knew how dire the situation was for the children when Rollo moved to sit by his little sister so she could cling to him in my absence.

I found Geoffrey waiting in the downstairs parlor. "I'm sorry if I put you in an awkward position by asking to meet with you alone," he said. "But I didn't think you'd want to discuss this in front of the children. Someone passing by saw Henry being hauled out of the house by police. What happened?"

"He was arrested for conspiracy to commit treason. I'm assuming they don't know much if you're still free."

"They didn't get you, either. I wonder what they know, or how they know it. Obviously, there's a traitor in our midst. Whoever it is, we'll find him and deal with him." His eyes were hard and his jaw set.

"I don't know that it will help. The damage has been done."

"It will keep the traitor from reporting on more of us. And I'd feel a lot better. Do you have a way to get word to the Mechanics?"

"I'm fairly certain they'll know soon enough, if they don't already. They may be the ones giving me information."

"Can you keep me posted? As well as you're able. Though I don't know how you'll manage that. There's not a good reason for a governess to send me messages."

"I may be able to persuade Flora to call on your sister."

"That might suffice. Otherwise, I believe I'm considered a close enough friend that it wouldn't seem amiss for me to check on Henry's family."

"The rest of you must be careful now until you know who the traitor is."

I went back upstairs, feeling somewhat better. At least Henry's magister friends would be sure to get the warning. Just outside the parlor, I noticed a bit of blue on the floor. I bent to find a key on a blue ribbon. Henry must have managed to drop it as he was being hauled away so the symbol would remain a secret. I picked it up and put it in my pocket, vowing to myself that I'd find a way to give it back to him.

I was rather surprised that we hadn't yet heard from the governor. I would have expected him to rush in to take control of the children as soon as he heard what had happened. He had to have heard by now. Even if he hadn't been informed through official channels, he would have received Flora's message. If he hadn't responded, did that mean he really was behind it? Was he even now interrogating Henry?

The governor finally arrived when we were at dinner. Mr. Chastain ushered him into the dining room and ordered a footman to set another place. "There's no need," the governor said brusquely. "I won't be staying to eat. But I thought I ought to see to the children."

Olive jumped out of her chair to go greet him. "Oh, Grandfather, please, won't you help Uncle Henry?"

"I'm afraid I can't show favoritism. He has to be treated just the same as anyone else."

Flora surprised me—and probably everyone else present—by giving an unladylike snort. "Come now, Grandfather," she said. "You can't pretend that to be the case. People are treated differently based on their rank all the time. I'm sure he's not being given the same treatment as one of the Rebel Mechanics might be."

"He is being treated with all fairness, but I can't use my power to free him. The charges against him are very serious."

"What did he do?" Rollo asked eagerly.

"That's nothing to be discussed here. Now, I suppose

it would be too much trouble to expect all of you to come to my house tonight, but Miss Newton, perhaps you could supervise the packing tomorrow."

"Packing for what?" Rollo asked.

"With your guardian in jail, you should come live with me."

Flora surprised us again. "No, we won't," she said firmly. "I think it best for Olive and Rollo that their lives are disrupted as little as possible. They need to be in their own home, with their own belongings, following their usual routine. The staff here can look after us, and Miss Newton can supervise the children. It will be no different than if Henry were away on business."

"This may not be resolved quickly. Your uncle may never come home."

"When it is resolved, we can make decisions."

I thought for a moment that the governor would argue with her, but he nodded and said, "You have a very good point. Miss Newton, I will leave them in your capable hands, but I will check in on the children frequently."

When he was gone, Olive said, "I don't want to go live with Grandfather. I want to live here, with Uncle." Tears trickled down her cheeks.

"We're not going anywhere," Flora assured her. "This home belongs to Rollo, and he has every right to stay here. The management of the estate may go to someone else if Henry is convicted, but there's no reason we should have to move. I won't go."

As I'd anticipated, Olive didn't want to sleep alone that night, so I stayed in her room with her. It was a sleepless night for me. The presence of that letter in my desk drawer seemed to call out, like a telltale heart beating its presence from its hiding place. I also found myself imagining Henry's plight, in varying degrees of horror. As relieved as I was not to have been arrested, I felt guilty for being free while he suffered when I'd committed nearly as many crimes as he had. Morning came as a great relief, for I no longer had to pretend to be asleep. I could get up and do something.

"Do you think we could visit Uncle in jail?" Olive asked as I helped her dress.

"I don't know. We'll have to see if his attorney has any news. I'm not sure Lord Henry would want you in the jail."

"But I want to see him."

"I do, too. But a jail isn't the sort of place little girls or young ladies should visit."

I tried to go about my normal routine, eating breakfast, getting Rollo to school. The news about Henry hadn't been in the newspaper, so I noticed no scandalized glances at our appearance there. Olive had no enthusiasm for her schoolwork, and I didn't push her. Flora joined us at lunch, though none of us were very hungry. We merely pushed food around on our plates. "I believe we could all use a turn in the park," Flora said as the plates were cleared. "It's a pleasant enough day, if we dress warmly."

I wanted to ask who this imposter was who was impersonating Lady Flora, but I'd always known that she was merely playing at being a brainless flibbertigibbet. That was why her uncle despaired of her. She was capable of being so much more than she allowed herself to be. Now she was rising to the occasion.

We put on coats, hats, and gloves and set out into the park. It was a crisp, cold day, and the wind was relatively gentle. Olive clung desperately to my hand, like she was afraid someone would take her away from me. Flora appeared to be on high alert, and I wondered if she was wary of the authorities or possibly hoping to encounter Colin. She hadn't said anything about him since we'd returned from our trip, but I didn't know if that meant she'd given up or if she was strategizing and hoping to lower my guard. All three of us flinched when we passed a policeman, but he merely nodded in passing.

A voice called out, "Why, it's Miss Newton!" and I turned to see a man and a woman sitting on a nearby bench. It was Lizzie and Colin, but their clothing was much more respectable than their usual Mechanics attire. No one would have thought twice about their presence in this part of town. Colin smiled at the sight of Flora, but his eyes were more serious than I'd ever seen them, and Lizzie's face was unusually grave. I got the distinct impression that they knew what had happened and had come looking for me.

Colin rose from the bench, doffed his hat, and bowed. "Lady Flora, Miss Newton. And who is this delightful young lady?"

"This is my sister, Lady Olive," Flora said. Seeing Colin

must have done her a world of good, for the color had returned to her cheeks, and she had a sparkle in her eye. "Olive, this is Mr. Flynn. He's a friend of Miss Newton's."

"And of yours, I would hope," he said. "May I present my sister, Lizzie?" Lizzie gave a slight curtsy.

Colin gestured to his left. "We just passed a cart selling roasted nuts that smelled absolutely delightful. Might I escort you two ladies over there to purchase some for you?"

"May we, Miss Newton?" Olive asked.

"Of course you may," I said. Under other circumstances, I wouldn't have left Flora alone with Colin, but I suspected he was arranging the situation so I could talk with Lizzie, and Olive probably made a better chaperone than anyone because she wouldn't hesitate to tell everything that happened. Olive released my hand and took Flora's, and Colin held his arm out gallantly to Flora.

When they were out of earshot, I said to Lizzie, "Obviously, you've heard."

"Yes. And I'm afraid I have even worse news. We've just had word from one of our people who's a clerk at the courthouse that they're going to transport him to England by the end of the week."

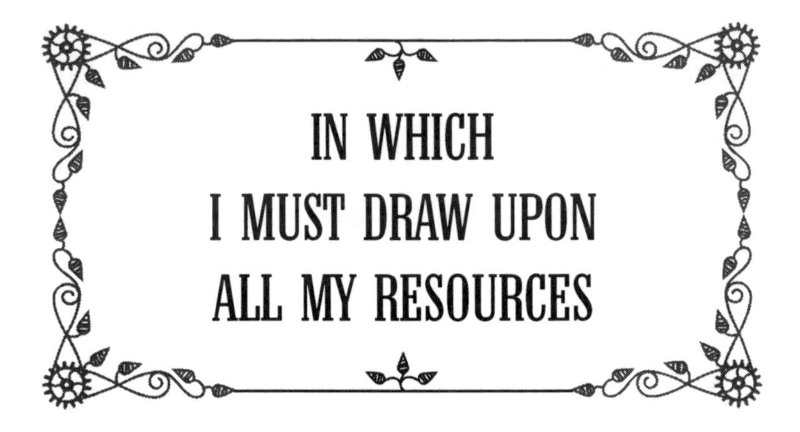

IN WHICH I MUST DRAW UPON ALL MY RESOURCES

"They're what?" I blurted, stammering in my shock. "But why? There hasn't been time for a trial. They only arrested him yesterday."

"I think that's the point. The governor is already facing scandal. It would be even worse if someone associated with his family were to be tried for treason. If they send him to England, it keeps things quieter here, and it doesn't make as much of a martyr out of Lord Henry. They're probably hoping the whole affair will be forgotten here."

"If they take him away, we'll never see him again," I said. My whole body suddenly felt heavy with despair.

"Probably not. Even if he's not executed, it would be nearly impossible for him to get back to the colonies."

"Executed?" I yelped.

"That is the standard penalty for treason."

"We can't let that happen! We have to save him."

"I'm not sure there's much we can do. They're holding him at the fort. That's not the sort of place where we can easily stage a jailbreak."

"But we have people on the inside who could help."

"And risk their positions? We need those resources."

"And we need Henry. Without him, we'll have a much harder time getting magister support."

"Even if you get him out, he won't be able to keep playing his regular role. You and the children won't be able to live with him. He'll be a fugitive."

"Just like the Rebel Mechanics he helped escape from the city," I reminded her. "You owe him. You'd all be in prison and your machines would be scrap metal if he hadn't helped you."

She sighed and glanced over to where Colin and the girls were returning with paper cones of roasted nuts. "I'll see what we can do. If you can find a way to get him out of the fort, we may be able get him out of the city and to safety. How likely is it that you'll be able to move freely?"

"For now, we're staying at the house. I only have to worry about the servants or the children noticing my movements."

"Then see what you can do and let me know. You'll have to act quickly. There's a government ship sailing for England on Friday, and odds are, he'll be on it."

Colin and the girls reached us, and we said our farewells to Lizzie and Colin before heading back toward home.

Flora was starry-eyed, and Olive was excited about the roasted nuts coated in cinnamon and sugar. "Colin is really nice, and he's funny," Olive said.

"He is nice, isn't he, Miss Newton?" Flora said. "I don't think he's the least bit insincere."

"He told me to get the cinnamon nuts because they're better," Olive added.

"Don't eat them all at once. You'll spoil your dinner," I said as I escorted them across the street.

My mind was already scrambling to create a plan. I knew so many people who had contacts or who were strategically placed. Surely I could use those contacts now. The difficult part would be finding a way to get Henry out of the fort. After that, I was certain the Mechanics could get him to safety, if they were willing to help.

When the music master arrived, I left the girls with their piano lessons and claimed Lizzie had informed me during our meeting in the park that one of our mutual friends was ill, so I needed to go look in on her. Mrs. Talbot offered to retrieve Rollo from school for me.

Lizzie hadn't wanted to risk any of our highly placed operatives, but what I had in mind was lower down the scale. The people no one ever noticed might be just the group to pull off something like this. I didn't personally know any of the laundresses or scullery maids at the fort, but I was sure that some of my shopgirls and laundresses would know someone.

The "sick friend" gave me the ideal excuse to visit the

florist shop, where I put out the word of who I needed to find. From there, I caught a ride on the secret subway heading downtown. I checked in at my usual shops, but I didn't have much luck in anyone knowing the sort of people I needed. My last stop was the laundry, where I was relieved to find my contact at the counter and no other customers.

I quickly explained my situation, and she smiled. "I have friends who work there. We may be able to get in and out, but not to the cells."

"Could they tell me more about how things work, who might be able to get to the cells?"

"They might. I will have to ask. I will see them tonight. Can you come back tomorrow?" Just then, the door opened and a customer entered. The counter girl wrote out a ticket, handed it to me, and said, "Ready tomorrow."

I wasn't sure how I would manage to get away again, but right now, I didn't care. Even if I had to vanish along with Henry, I had to get him to safety. I wasn't sure how long I'd manage to keep my position, anyway. The governor seemed pleased with my work, but I knew he wanted to send Flora and Rollo to England—her to find a husband, him to boarding school. Even if I risked it all, I wasn't really risking much.

Back home, I claimed that my friend was very ill and would surely need me to look in on her again the next day. I felt guilty for the sympathy the children and Mrs. Talbot expressed, but I knew my lies were for a good cause. And I did truly have a friend in distress who needed my help.

But apparently, my lies weren't quite as polished as I would have liked. Flora stopped me as we left the dining room after dinner and said, "What are you up to?"

"Whatever do you mean?" I asked, knowing my tone didn't sound as flippant as I would have liked.

"Do you have some sort of plan to help Henry?"

"What makes you think that I'm the kind of person who could do anything for him?"

"I think that there's more to your friends than you let on."

"Such as?"

"Colin—Mr. Flynn—looked very different this time, like he was in disguise, and he and his sister seemed to be in the park looking for you. I noticed that he came up with an excuse to get Olive and me away from you so that you could talk to Miss Flynn. If he'd only wanted to flirt with me, he wouldn't have included Olive. Then you let us go with him. You know he and I have a very improper attachment, so it would have been your job as chaperone to stay with us."

"I didn't think you'd do anything untoward in front of Olive."

"I wouldn't do anything untoward anyway. I know better. Are you doing something to help Henry? Because if you are, I want to help. What can I do?"

I studied her face for a long moment. Her eyes were steely and her jaw was firmly set. For once, I could see some family resemblance between her and her uncle. I decided that I had to trust her. She could prove quite useful. "I don't know yet. We'll have to act quickly because I hear they're sending him to England by the end of the week."

"He really is guilty, isn't he? I've always known he had radical views, but he's been doing things. He just *acts* like a silly amateur scientist, but I know that's not what he's really like. It's like his secret identity."

"Whatever gave you that idea?"

"You're not the only person in this house with a weakness for pulp novels, Miss Newton."

"Really?"

"Well, I can't let that sort of thing get out. I have a reputation to uphold."

"One way you can help me is by taking over Olive's lessons in the morning. I have to go meet with my contacts and see if the plan is shaping up."

"I'll have my maid get me up early. Then you can go visit your 'sick friend.'"

This surprising turn of events made my life easier. The next morning, Flora appeared at breakfast and took care of Olive, so after I dropped Rollo off at school I was able to head directly downtown. My friend intercepted me on the street corner nearest the laundry.

"Oh good, perfect timing!" she said. "I was hoping you would come this morning, and right when I go on break you appear. That is a good omen. Come, we must talk. There are people you should meet."

She guided me down a set of steps into a basement.

The air in there was so warm and damp that I struggled to breathe for a moment. It was a laundry room, where women stirred great vats of steaming water. They glanced at us as we entered, but went back to their work.

My friend took me through the laundry to a small room at the back, where several women waited. One was Chinese, like my friend. Another was a tall, heavyset woman with curling fair hair. The third was dark-skinned and wiry. As was usual in these circumstances, no introductions were made.

"They all work at the fort," my friend said. "Your friend is there."

The Chinese girl said something in her language, and my friend translated, "She says they can get you in and out through the laundry."

"I can get you close to the cells, if you don't mind pushing a broom," the dark-skinned woman said. "I'm on the night cleaning crew. No one ever looks at us, so that much should be easy. The trick will be getting the cell open. I don't know how to get keys."

I could pick an ordinary lock in a house, but I doubted the lock to a cell would be so easy. I thought for a moment that I might be able to use magic to open the lock, but then I realized that they would have to do something to keep magic from working in order to hold a magister prisoner.

"Do you know anything about the locks?" I asked.

"I haven't paid much attention. The day crew cleans inside the cells. They aren't opened for us."

"The locks are strong," the blond woman said in a thick

German accent. "You cannot break them. There is an iron plate behind them so the prisoners can't reach them from inside their cells." That might be what blocked the magic, I thought, which meant they might be opened magically from outside. Even so, I knew I'd better have a backup plan.

"Do you know where they keep the keys?" I asked.

"You will not be able to get to them. They are in the office, where there is always a jailer."

"So, you can get me in through the laundry, then get me to the cells as a charwoman," I summarized. "If we can get my friend out of the cell, do you have a way to get him back to the laundry?"

"How good does he look in a dress and apron?" the dark-skinned woman asked with a grin.

"He's rather tall, I'm afraid. People would notice a woman that tall. But perhaps he could crouch under a long skirt. Then how do we get him out through the laundry?"

The Chinese girl said something, and my friend, who'd been relaying the conversation to her all along, translated for us, "No one counts the number of laundresses who go in and out. We wait for a shift change. But we will not have very long before his absence is noticed."

"I might be able to do something to keep the escape from being noticed, and I have ways of getting him quickly out of the area," I said. At least, I hoped I did. "When will we be able to do this? Time is of the essence."

"How about tonight?" the German woman asked. "You will come in with us when we start work at eight. You should wait before going to the cells because there isn't another shift change until four."

"Tonight? That doesn't give me much time to have everything else in place, but I can do it." I had to do it.

We finalized the details about when and where I would meet them, and my mind was already racing ahead to everything else I needed to set up. I needed to get the Mechanics ready to get Henry out of the city, and I felt like I'd need some other help. The biggest gaps in the plan were how to get Henry out of his cell and how to get him to the subway that could take him almost to the edge of the city. There were far too many blocks between the fort at the lower tip of Manhattan and the lowest station.

I didn't actually know where Lizzie spent her days, but I headed to her boardinghouse to look for her. Her landlady directed me to the theater. "They're in rehearsals," she said with a wink.

Nat was watching the door at the theater and let me inside. The place was still set up as a theater, with no sign of Mechanics activity, but I heard Colin's voice coming from the balcony. I hurried up the stairs, remembering the night not so long ago when Henry and I had come to warn them about the raid. I hoped the Mechanics remembered that night as vividly as I did.

I found that Lizzie was also there, along with Alec and some of the others. "I'll be getting Henry out of the fort at four in the morning," I said without preamble. "I'll need help getting him out of the city soon afterward. Are you going to help me?"

"You sound very certain that you can get him out," Alec said, frowning.

"I am. I have a plan, and I have help."

"If you can get him out of the city to the airship hangar, we can get him to safety. But that's about all we can do."

"But what about the subway? Wouldn't that be safer?"

"I'm not sure the subway would be of much use because by the time you get him there, the alert may already have gone up and he won't make it across the bridge. That's a long way from the fort."

"I know," I said.

"And there will be a manhunt," he added. "They've been patrolling more heavily since we escaped."

"I *know*. Don't you think I know?" I snapped. "Do you think I shouldn't try?"

"I didn't say that," Alec said.

"But you're thinking it. What's one more magister to you? Even if I free him, he's *no use* to you anymore. He won't have access to his money or to his friends. But he's been there for me, and he's been there for you. He's the one who took the risk to get the information that may bring down the government and kick off your precious revolution. We all owe him, even if he's no good to us anymore."

"We'll help," Lizzie said, standing up and shooting the men a glare. "But there's not a lot we can do right now aside from moving him out of the city and giving him sanctuary."

"You can create a diversion," I said. "Perhaps another

midnight riot? Something big enough to draw troops away from the fort."

"We don't have our machines to really make a fuss, but I suppose we could come up with something. Did you have a particular place in mind?" Colin asked.

"The neighborhood near the fort would be good. And maybe somewhere else on the island, earlier in the evening."

"We're very good at making noise," he assured me, grinning in a way that told me plans were already brewing in his head.

"Is there anything else you want from us?" Alec asked. I thought I detected a trace of sarcasm in his voice, but I ignored it.

"Can you teach me to pick locks?" I asked, abruptly coming up with an idea.

"Pick locks?" Alec asked, raising an eyebrow.

"I have a plan for getting the cell open, but I want a backup plan. I know how to pick easy locks—I can open just about any door in a house with a hairpin—but I suspect a cell door might be an entirely different story and would require more specialized tools."

The other man who'd been sitting silently during this discussion grinned. "I can teach you," he said in a brogue heavier than Colin's. "I can't guarantee you'll be an expert with one lesson, but if you already know the basics, it could be possible." He rose from his seat and gestured for me to follow him.

We went down to a basement workroom, where he got

out a set of tools and some heavy padlocks. "These should be about the same size as you'll find in a cell door. They're a different kind of lock, but the principle is the same."

I spent the next hour working on my lock-picking skills. Real locks were trickier than the simple latch of a bedroom door. It took me several minutes to do what my teacher managed in seconds, but I thought that if I also used magic, that might help. He gave me the tools I'd need and a padlock to practice on.

By the time I returned home just after lunchtime, I'd fleshed out my plan. Flora met me on the stairs and gave me a pointed look before pulling me into the library. "So?" she demanded.

"I have something arranged for tonight, but I'll need your help."

"Anything."

"We need to pay some calls this afternoon."

"Pay calls at a time like this? Will we even be admitted?"

"Nothing has made the newspapers, so I don't know who knows about it. But the brothers of a couple of your friends are part of Henry's group, and I'll need their help. If you visit your friends, I'll have a chance to talk to these men."

"Then calls it is!" I was impressed with—and a little alarmed by—her enthusiasm.

Later that afternoon, we set out, first to Lady Charity's home. Flora gave me a meaningful glance as she pointedly left me alone in the foyer. Soon afterward, Philip appeared and gestured for me to join him under the stairs. "Is there news of Henry?" he asked.

"He's being held at the West Battery fort, and they're planning to transport him to England." Before he could get indignant, I hurried to add, "But I've got a plan to get him out tonight. I'll need your help. Your whole gang's help. Do you remember the night you robbed the payroll delivery at the fort?"

"You know about that?"

"I helped. We'll need a similar getaway. Can you get a boat near there? A fast one? I'm not sure we'll be able to rely on stealth or even subterfuge. The drunken party gambit won't work this time."

"I can arrange something, I'm sure. What time?"

"By four in the morning. That's when we're most likely to be able to slip away. You'll want to be west of the fort. Things are likely to be unpleasant to the east at that time."

"Unpleasant?"

"Diversion."

"I was going to suggest that."

"I have the Mechanics on that. I was worried that if the Masked Bandits were up to something while Henry was escaping, it might tie it all together, and so far, no one seems to be aware of the banditry. All they're accusing Henry of is organizing a rebel movement." I laughed at that, realizing how absurd it was that treason on that level was the least of Henry's crimes.

"I'll let the others know," he said, "but only the inner circle I'm sure I can trust. Mostly because we all have too much dirt on each other." He clapped me on the shoulder. "I say, you really are rather extraordinary for a governess. Have you considered banditry?"

"That's not nearly exciting enough for me," I said with a smile.

We arranged details for a meeting place, and he said Henry would know the right signals. I returned to my spot in the foyer, and Philip ran up the stairs. Flora and Charity came out of the parlor, and as soon as we were in the carriage, Flora whispered, "Well?"

"Everything is set."

"I want to help."

"You have."

"I want to do more than pay a call."

"You can cover for me when I go out. I'll need to leave before dinner."

"Your sick friend has taken a turn for the worse, and you're going to sit with her through the night?"

"Of course."

"What else can I do?"

"Do you have any money—any cash on hand? Or do you know if Lord Henry has any? He'll need money, and possibly some clothes and other things while he's on the run."

"I'll talk to Matthews. He'll get the things Henry is likely to need."

"Is there a way you could arrange to get those to Mr. Spencer or Viscount Hayes?"

"Leave it to me," she said confidently. Her eyes grew bright with tears and she reached across the carriage to take my hand. "You are going to save him, aren't you?"

"I'm doing everything I can. But you know, he won't be able to come home. He'll be a fugitive, probably for the rest of his life."

"Or until we overthrow the government."

I would have thought she was the least likely revolutionary, but she was full of surprises.

I spent the rest of the day working on the padlock until I could open it within a minute. A couple of times, I risked using magic, and that dropped my time to just a few seconds. I tried to get some rest because I knew it would be a long night, but it was futile. I couldn't shut off my mind as it rehashed every detail of a plan that was frighteningly lacking in detail. So many things would have to come together for this to work, but the alternative was unthinkable.

I finally gave up and forced myself to down some tea and a sandwich before heading out to visit my "sick friend."

It was time to see if my mad plan had a chance of working.

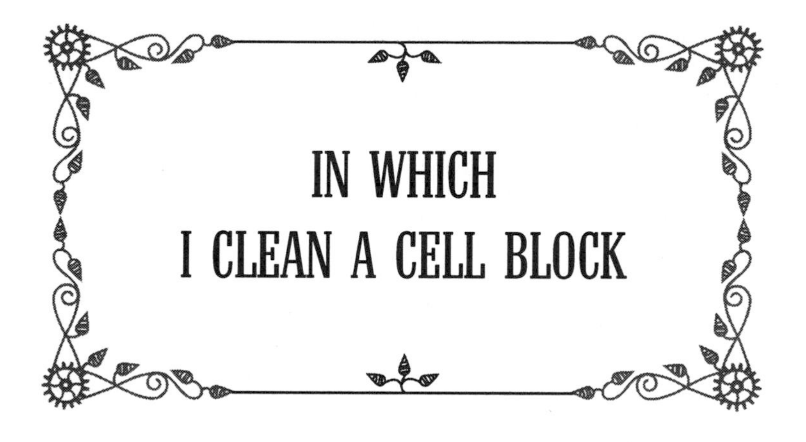

IN WHICH I CLEAN A CELL BLOCK

"So, it's all set?" Lizzie said when she ushered me inside her boardinghouse.

"I believe so, if the Mechanics are ready on their end."

"They'll be waiting at the hangar. The rest is up to you. We also have a couple of riots ready to go. I must say, you've put a bounce in Colin's step. He hasn't organized a good riot in far too long."

"I might also need an alibi for myself tonight. I'm supposedly visiting a sick friend here, one who might die tonight and leave me utterly distraught."

Lizzie smiled. "I believe we can manage that. If we need to, we'll even have a funeral. Everyone here at the house will be wearing black if any officials come by tomorrow. I'll arrange for a funeral wreath on the door."

I took a deep breath and let it all out in a sigh, trying

to release some of the tension that had built up within me. "Then I believe I'm as ready as I ever will be. Pray that this works. I can't believe I'm doing anything this audacious."

"I always knew you had it in you. You came to New York City on your own, with no support and no clear plans. That was as bold as anything else you've done."

"It was naive. And I suppose this plan is just as naive. But I can't leave him there."

She studied me for a moment, a look of realization spreading across her face. "You really love him, don't you?"

I felt my cheeks grow quite warm. "I—I owe him a great deal. And I care about him."

She smiled and nodded. "Yes, I thought so."

I sighed, conceding her point, and shook my head. "It's utterly hopeless."

"Well, he'll be a fugitive, so maybe who he is won't matter much anymore. Now, we'd better get you ready to go." We went up to her room, where she had a loose gray dress that fit over my clothes, with a dingy white apron and a kerchief that covered my hair. I left my coat behind, with a shawl over my shoulders instead.

I had just finished tying the kerchief when one of Lizzie's housemates rapped on her door. She was dressed much like my disguise. "Are you ready to go?" she asked.

"As ready as I'm likely to be," I said, my voice trembling. I gathered up the cloth bundle that held my supplies and joined her and one other girl from the house as we left and caught a bus heading farther downtown. There, they went off to their jobs and I went to the back of the laundry, where I was to meet my helpers from the fort.

I tried not to panic when I didn't see anyone there. I was early because I was so afraid I'd miss them. They were taking a huge risk for me, so I didn't want to inconvenience them further by making them wait. Even so, each minute that I waited seemed to drag. I closed my eyes and counted to fifty, telling myself that they'd be there when I opened my eyes again. It was a game I'd played as a child whenever I had to wait.

When I reached thirty, a voice said, "Good, you're on time." I opened my eyes to see the dark-skinned girl who worked on the nighttime cleaning crew. Soon, we were joined by the laundresses. "You won't be able to carry in that big a bundle," the German girl said. "It will look out of place."

"But these are things I need," I said. After thinking for a moment, I untied my apron, lifted my borrowed dress, and wrapped the cloth items around my waist. With the dress back in place, I used the apron to secure the bundle. I didn't think the result looked too obvious once I had my shawl pulled around me, and the extra padding helped disguise my body shape.

As a group, we caught a bus down to the lowermost tip of the island. My heart began pounding as I stepped off the bus in front of the fort. As much as I'd been sneaking around and covering my tracks until now, I hadn't actually been doing anything wrong, and no one was likely to have been watching me. Now, though, I was about to start breaking so many laws that if I were caught, I'd be in as much trouble as Henry, but without the noble title to protect me.

We joined a flock of other girls, all dressed more or less alike in loose dresses, aprons, shawls, and kerchiefs, coming from other buses or on foot. My helpers kept me in the middle of their group and moved us all to the center of the crowd as we passed through the gates of the fort. I held my breath when I crossed the threshold, but the guards didn't look twice at us.

The laundresses took me with them to the laundry shed at the back of the fort. "You'll have a few hours to wait," the tall German girl told me.

"How can I help until then?" I asked.

"Help?"

"Well, it would look suspicious if I just sat around, and I may as well earn my keep while I'm here. Give me a job to do so I'll fit in."

She put me to work moving carts of linens around. I was surprised by how much laundry the barracks generated. There were sheets and towels for all the men, as well as their shirts and undergarments. Apparently, only the officers who had money sent their clothes out to be cleaned. Everyone else had to take the service they got from the fort's laundry, where just about everything was thrown into a couple of huge copper tubs of boiling water.

The work was mind-numbing and made me grateful

that I was educated enough to work as a governess. That mind-numbing quality also helped pass the hours. I was startled when my German friend tapped me on the shoulder. "It's time," she said.

If my heart had been pounding before, now it felt like it would burst out of my chest. I could hear my own heartbeat. Before I left the laundry, I paused to pull the clothes out from under my borrowed dress and stuff them with rags from a pile I found. The result looked nothing like Henry, but I hoped this would help delay discovery of the escape. I put the pieces of the dummy in a laundry bag.

The dark-skinned girl met me at the entrance to the laundry. She pushed a dustbin on wheels and had a broom in her hand, which she gave to me. "I assume you know how to use this," she said.

"I've done my share of chores," I replied. We'd had a housemaid at home, but I'd had to help while my mother was ill, so I didn't think I'd be an obvious amateur. She hid my bag in her dustbin, and we set off, going deeper into the fort.

We had to work our way around the entire fort before we could get to the cells, and I was sure my hands would blister from all that sweeping. There was a great deal of chaos in the fort, with soldiers running to and fro, dressing and gathering weapons before assembling and then marching out. I took that to mean that the riots had started. I wondered if that had been the wisest plan, as it meant there were many more soldiers out and about rather than sleeping, but the chaos did seem to mean that they looked even less at the workers than they normally might have.

Finally, we reached the cells. A guard had to let us in, but he didn't seem to notice that I was new. He went back to his office while we got to work. "Won't he notice if there are more of us leaving?" I whispered to my partner.

"There's a shift change soon. The new one won't know how many of us there were if we're scattered and working when he arrives."

Every instinct I had told me to hurry and find Henry, but I knew we needed to do our job systematically and according to the usual routine. We started at the rear of the cell block and worked our way down, sweeping and mopping the floor. Most of the cells we passed were empty. The few that were occupied contained soldiers who seemed to be sleeping off bouts of drinking.

I was starting to panic that Henry might already have been taken away when I reached a cell whose occupant was sitting up on the narrow ledge that served as a cot, his back against the cell wall, and his knees drawn up to his chest. Even in the dim light, I knew it was Henry.

I tapped lightly on one of the cell bars to get his attention. He lifted his head, then slowly unfolded himself to stand and move to the bars. "Verity? Is that you?" he asked, his voice barely a whisper. "What are you doing here?"

"I'm here to rescue you, of course," I whispered in reply, hoping the quaver in my voice wasn't too obvious.

I slipped my hand between the bars, and he clasped it,

squeezing like he was holding onto a lifeline. "How?" he asked.

"I have a plan. First, we need to get you out of that cell." I reluctantly withdrew my hand from his grip and took the lockpicking tools out of my apron pocket. This lock was more similar than I'd expected to the padlock I'd used for practice. While the lock was resistant to magic and I was unable to unlock it with magic alone, I found that magic plus the tools worked.

"Hurry," my colleague hissed. "Shift change."

The last tumbler clicked, and the lock opened. Henry rushed back to his seat and I stood in front of the unlocked door, sweeping, as the guard came out of his office, unlocked the entrance for his replacement, and they switched places. The new guard barely glanced at us as he headed, yawning, into the office.

Once he was gone, I pulled the door open, and Henry rushed forward. My colleague took a bundle out of her dustbin. "Put these on," she ordered. I helped Henry pull a loose dress over his clothes and tied the apron around his waist. The kerchief was oversized, and we arranged it so that it hid his face.

Next, I took the laundry bag out of the bin and arranged the pieces of dummy on the bunk, covering them with a blanket. Henry shook his head, frowning. "I'm afraid they gave me something that makes it difficult for me to use magic, so I won't be able to make that look more authentic."

I glanced over my shoulder to see that my colleague was back outside the cell, pushing her broom. "Let's see what I can do," I whispered. I'd struggled with illusion and hadn't had much opportunity to practice lately, but with Henry unable to help, I had to make it work. I only needed to affect the dummy's head, making a lump of cloth look like it was covered in hair. I glanced at Henry, noting how his sandy hair was disheveled, and laid that mental image over the dummy, shaping the ether. Soon, it looked like Henry really was lying on his side, his back to the bars.

"I don't know how long it will last, but it should buy us some time," I whispered.

Henry and I left the cell, and I paused to gently push the door closed. My colleague eyed Henry up and down. "You're too tall, so you'll have to do something about that," she said. "Push the dustbin."

He crouched, bending his knees beneath the loose skirt, and stooped his shoulders over the dustbin as we headed for the exit. The cleaning woman knocked on the doorframe of the guard's office. "We're done out here. Need me to sweep up in there?"

"Just empty the rubbish," he said.

While she emptied a small waste can, he walked toward the exit to unlock it. The guard waited while we trooped out before locking up behind us and returning to his office.

I wanted to hold my breath the whole way back to the laundry room, but I knew that wouldn't decrease our chances of being detected, and if I passed out, we would be noticed. Now we were really in trouble if we were caught, and I doubted we'd get another chance to rescue Henry if this attempt failed.

One shift of cleaners and laundresses was getting ready to leave when we arrived in the laundry room, and the scullery maids were arriving for the morning. Henry and I blended into the group shuffling out at the end of their shift. His slouched, crouched posture fit in well with the weary women leaving after a hard night's work, though his head still stood above most of us.

I found myself holding my breath again as we approached the fort's gate. This was perhaps the last dangerous point of our escape attempt. If the guard there noticed anything odd, we were doomed. If the guard in the cell block noticed Henry's absence before we were through the gate, the gates would likely be closed on us.

We were so close. Twenty more feet. Ten. Then we were walking past the guard. "Good morning, ladies!" he called out. I tensed, waiting for him to tell us to stop. "There's been rioting all night, so it's not safe for you to go home your usual ways. We've got buses to take you away from here."

I forced myself not to look at Henry in dismay. We were more likely to be spotted on a bus, and we might still be under their supervision when Henry's disappearance was noticed. Where would they take us? But I was afraid we didn't have any choice but to get on a bus.

Henry and I found a seat together, with him closest to

the window. He sat with his head down and his shoulders slouched. I tried to look like I was tired rather than tense, but all I could think about was that we were getting farther and farther away from where we were supposed to meet Henry's friends.

I wanted to cry out for joy when the bus stopped a few blocks away to let off some of the women. Henry and I joined them. We moved slowly, letting both the bus and the other women get out of sight before we headed west. In a dark, narrow side street, Henry paused to pull off the dress and kerchief. "I think I'm more noticeable dressed like that than as myself," he said, "and I'm not sure how much longer I can walk so stooped over."

"You really made a terrible woman," I agreed, "but I didn't have time to come up with a better plan."

"It was a brilliant plan. It worked, didn't it?"

"We're not safe yet, and we're running late and in the wrong place to meet our transportation."

"Airship?"

"Not yet. Your friends are supposed to be coming back from a yachting excursion. Now we'll have to backtrack to meet them."

"I'd rather not go back toward the fort, if you don't mind." He shuddered, and I had to wonder what had happened to him while he was imprisoned.

The streets weren't entirely deserted, as people were coming home from late shifts and leaving for early shifts, but I still felt like we were conspicuous. Perhaps it was a guilty conscience that made me feel like it was very obvious that we weren't where we were supposed to be. In truth, no one gave us a second glance.

As we drew closer to the shore, we left the rows of tenement buildings behind and entered the commercial area around the docks. There was more activity here, but both of us were out of place. We were sure to be noticed.

And, soon enough, we were. A policeman walking his beat approached us. He'd changed his course, so it was clear he'd seen us. It was too late for us to duck away or hide. Thinking quickly, I slipped my arm around Henry's waist and leaned against him.

The policeman held his lantern up as he approached us. "May I ask what you're doing here?" he asked. His tone was brusque and professional, but I didn't think he sounded like he was desperately searching for a fugitive.

"I'm seeing my husband off to work," I said. "I work nights, and he works days, so this is our time together."

"You work at the docks?" the policeman asked, eyeing Henry skeptically. I winced inwardly. Henry's clothes were rumpled, but they were still obviously not something a dockworker would wear.

"I'm a bookkeeper for one of the shipping lines," Henry said.

The policeman nodded and lowered his lantern. "Very good, then. We're being careful tonight. There's rioting in the streets. Can't let them get to the docks, you know." He resumed his patrol, and we continued on our way.

"Rioting?" Henry asked softly. "I don't suppose you know anything about that?"

"We needed a diversion so they'd be more worried about that than looking for an escaped prisoner. Though it seems they might have been a bit overzealous about it. Now, how should we find your friends?"

We looked for an empty pier without any activity on either side. Tall ships blocked anyone on other piers from seeing us. Once we were at the end of the pier, I saw what I thought might be our boat out in the river.

"There they are," I said, "but how will they know where to meet us?"

"You'll need to signal them. I'm still magically useless."

"What do I do?"

"You know how to make a light, but cover it with your other hand."

It was difficult to do magic when I was so tense. I had to take a few long, deep breaths before I was able to form a steady light in my hand. I covered it with my other hand as he instructed, then followed his directions in briefly lifting my hand in a certain pattern. There was an answering flash from the boat. It began moving up the river.

"They're coming for us," he said.

It seemed like forever before I heard the splash of oars. We looked over the edge of the pier to find a small rowboat pulling up next to the ladder on one of the pilings. Philip pulled the oars into the boat, looped a rope around the piling to hold the boat steady, and gestured for us to come down.

Climbing down a ladder into a tiny boat that was moving with the water, in near-total darkness, was rather frightening, but I reminded myself that I'd climbed a rope ladder into an airship. When I neared the bottom, Philip caught me and eased me into the boat before turning to help Henry. Henry immediately released the mooring rope while Philip picked up the oars and began rowing out to the small racing yacht we'd signaled.

When we reached the yacht, other members of the gang helped us board and pulled up the rowboat. Soon, we were off, flying up the river.

Geoffrey greeted Henry with a big hug. "I wasn't sure I'd ever see you again," he said before releasing Henry. "In case you want to clean up, we have clothes and hot water below."

"Oh, you have no idea how good that sounds," Henry said. He was still wearing the clothes he'd been arrested in, and he was more disheveled and unkempt than I'd ever seen him before, with a couple of days of beard shadowing his jaw and his hair in total disarray. There were dark circles under his eyes and I thought there was a dark spot like a bruise on one cheek, but it was hard to tell in the darkness.

He went below, and Geoffrey wrapped me in a large overcoat. Philip handed me a mug of hot tea, and Geoffrey shoved a man's hat on my head. "No one will mistake you for a boy, but from a distance, they won't see the silhouette of a woman." He clapped me on the shoulder. "Good job in getting him this far. You can leave the rest to us."

I wasn't ready to relax yet, even if all I could contribute

to the effort now was willing the boat to move faster and watching anxiously for anyone who might be following us.

Henry emerged from the cabin wearing a tweed suit and an overcoat. Philip handed him a mug of tea. "Thank you. Thank all of you," Henry said, his voice a bit raspy with emotion. "They were talking about sending me to England, and I don't think I'd ever have returned."

"Why do you think we pulled this?" Philip said. "But it was all Miss Newton's plan. She's the one who managed the hard part. Believe it or not, she got the Mechanics and the magisters to work together."

Henry smiled at me. "I am so very glad I hired you. I shall have to add an ability to mastermind a jailbreak and unite rival factions to the job description the next time I hire a governess." The smile faded from his face. "Though I suppose it's unlikely I'll have occasion to hire a governess in the future."

Philip patted him on the back. "Nonsense. We just need to start a revolution, win it, and then you can return as a conquering hero and elder statesman. You'll need to hire an army of governesses for all the children you'll have."

I was glad it was dark and all the men were looking at Henry because I'm sure my face would have given away my emotions at that thought. Lizzie was right, I knew as I watched him. I did love him. This wasn't just about loyalty to my employer, concern for the cause, or even support for a friend. If he'd been sent to England, I might never see him again. This way, he could still be in my life. Now that he was an outcast, we were now both outside proper society. Maybe Lizzie was right and there really was hope for us.

I let myself follow the flight of fancy, imagining a life with him in exile in the wilderness, and I was startled when he came to sit next to me. "I can't thank you enough, Verity," he said. "It's incredible that you pulled this off with such short notice."

"I had the contacts already in place. I'm not sure anyone other than a governess could have done it, really. Or perhaps a maid or shopgirl. It only worked because no one notices people like us. They don't pay any attention to the women who do their laundry or clean their floors, so we were able to walk in and out without them even looking at us."

"I doubt it will remain that way after this."

"I'm not so sure. They may never know how we did it." I couldn't resist a grin. "We should probably have tied a rope to your cell window to make it look like you climbed out that way. But I'll bet that they give you the credit for a feat of daring cleverness without considering that their laundresses and charwomen were responsible."

His grin soon faded. "How are the children?" he asked.

"Worried about you. Olive is inconsolable."

"I'm sure they don't enjoy living with their grandfather."

"They aren't. Not yet. Flora put her foot down rather decisively and insisted that they stay in their own home."

"I'm impressed."

"Yes, she has really risen to the occasion."

"So, making her read actually paid off."

"It seems to have, though I suspect there's been more to her than we gave her credit for all along." I pulled up the hem of the coat and the skirt of my working attire so I could reach my pocket and take out the little key on its blue ribbon. "By the way, you seem to have dropped this," I said as I handed it to him.

He held it up to study it. "I don't know that it's necessary anymore. I doubt I'll have to prove my credentials in any clandestine meetings. But it will be a nice reminder of what I stand for."

We were nearing the northern tip of Manhattan, and I couldn't see any sign of pursuit. There also wasn't any indication of a great manhunt on land. I wasn't sure what signs I should look for, aside from perhaps clanging bells and great mobs of police. With any luck, they hadn't yet noticed Henry's absence from his cell. If they didn't notice until breakfast time, it would be all the better for us.

There was a flash of light from the shore, and then another. I jumped, alarmed. "What is it?" I asked. "Are they waiting for us?"

"There are patrols on the shore," Philip said, his face grim.

IN WHICH WE ARE DISCOVERED

"What do we do?" I asked. We were so close that it was frustrating to be thwarted.

"We'll put in somewhere else, and then you can meet up with the others."

"They must have noticed my absence," Henry said.

"Or it's an ordinary shore patrol," Geoffrey suggested. "They may be on heightened alert because of the riots."

I groaned. "Maybe that wasn't the best idea I've ever had."

"It helped us get out of the fort," Henry said, resting his hand on my shoulder.

We went farther up the river before they put the rowboat over the side and helped Henry and me down. Philip joined us to row to shore. He got the boat far enough up on the bank that we barely got our feet wet, then shoved off to row back to the yacht.

Henry and I made our way through the tall grass, pausing before we reached the road. Henry whistled in an impressive imitation of a bird's call. A few seconds later, we heard the same call from a distance. It was followed by a couple of urgent chirps. "That way, but there's someone between us and them," Henry whispered.

"You got that much from a few whistles?"

"We've got a system of signals. It comes in handy when setting up or escaping a heist."

The grass ahead of us rustled, and I grabbed Henry's arm in terror. There was no place to hide, nowhere to go other than back into the river. We remained perfectly still, hardly daring to breathe, as a soldier came into view. Henry began walking toward him, dragging me as I took a little longer to be able to force my feet to move. I barely stopped myself from crying out in dismay when Henry approached the soldier and held up his hands in a warding-off gesture.

I thought for a moment that he was using magic, but instead he said, "Shh, we just spotted what I think might be a pied-billed grebe. You don't want to disturb it."

"You're out here at this time of the morning watching birds?" the soldier asked, frowning skeptically. He couldn't have been much older than Henry, and he looked as tired as I felt.

"Of course," Henry said. "When else would one observe night birds? There's interesting activity just before dawn."

"Oh?"

"Well, yes. That's when the night birds settle down and the day birds become active. It's fascinating." Henry sounded like he did when he talked about insects as a way to make people want to ignore him.

The soldier then noticed me. "You're a birdwatcher, too?"

"Oh, yes," I said. "That was how my husband and I met."

"Huh. I suppose it takes all kinds. Now, you folks be careful. There's been rioting tonight."

"That's why we prefer to be out of the city," Henry said. "Come along, dear. I want to check on that roosting spot we saw last week. Good morning, officer."

The soldier waved us on, and I forced myself not to heave a great sigh of relief. "Birds? I thought it was bugs," I whispered to Henry.

"I didn't think he'd believe we were looking for something as small as bugs without a lantern."

Just then, the soldier called out, "Halt!" We turned to see him aiming his rifle at us. "I just got word about a fugitive, and you fit the description." He must have been alerted by the magical communication system.

Henry gave a loud whistle even as he raised his hands. I assumed he'd signaled the others, but whether to clear out or come to the rescue, I wasn't sure. I didn't want to take any chances, not when we were so close to freedom.

With a silent prayer for aid, I moved cautiously toward the soldier. "Do you know why he's a fugitive?" I asked.

"It's not my job to know. Now, step back, miss."

I held my hands up to show I meant no harm. "He's fighting for freedom. That's why he was a prisoner. He wants to create a better land for all of us. Do you like having to answer to magisters who hold all the power?"

It might have been my imagination, but I thought the tip of his rifle wavered slightly, so I pressed on. "He wants a land where all of us are equal, where we all share in power, where we don't pay taxes to some foreign government in which we have no say. What kind of land would you rather live in, one in which you're limited by your birth, or one where everyone stands a chance?"

"That's what he's doing?"

"Yes. Surely you've heard about the scandal in the government, the way they're misusing the money and raising taxes on us to cover it. That's what we're trying to stop. If you bring him in, you're helping your oppressors."

The rifle lowered slightly. "There are really people trying to change things?"

"There are," Henry said. "People at every level of society, even some magisters. That's why they feel threatened."

"What'll you do if I let you go?"

"Hide for a while, but keep working. Things are going to change. You can be a part of it."

"You won't tell anyone?"

"No one has to know you saw me."

The rifle raised again, then sagged, and I held my breath, waiting for his decision. "Go on now," he finally said.

"Thank you! I thought I could trust you to do the right thing," I said. Henry added his thanks as he took my hand and led me away.

I didn't relax at all until we found a large magical

carriage waiting beside the road. Several men in hunting attire stood around it.

One of them, a slightly built boy I didn't recognize, ran toward us and threw his arms around Henry. "Oh, I'm so glad you're safe," he said, except it wasn't a male voice.

At the same time, both Henry and I said, "Flora?"

"Did you think I'd let you go away without saying good-bye?" she asked.

He turned to me. "You brought her in on this?"

"I needed all the help I could get, and she figured out what I was doing on her own. But I did not arrange for her to be here."

"Oh, stop gabbing," Flora said. "We must go."

"Yes, the word has apparently gone out about my escape," Henry said.

We climbed into the carriage, and it took off down the road. Henry and I sat side by side, and he took my hand, clutching it. We were so close. Once we made it to the airship, he'd be on his way out of British territory. I didn't think the governor would risk the treaties with the native tribes to search for a fugitive. Henry out of the colonies would be almost as good as Henry in England. At least, I hoped that's what the governor would think. Did he have any idea of the full role Henry played in the rebel movement?

The small window onto the footman's roost opened, and the man there said, "There's a patrol carriage signaling for us to stop. Hang on. We're about to speed up."

I clutched Henry's hand tighter. Had the soldier had

second thoughts, or were there more patrols? I was surprised to see that Flora didn't look concerned at all. "Don't worry, we have plans," she said.

"I wasn't part of planning this," I said.

"My friends are very good at escapes," Henry assured me, but I was close enough to feel him trembling.

The carriage made an abrupt turn, throwing me against Henry. It continued at a rapid pace for a few minutes more, and then the window opened again. "They took the bait!" the rear lookout said. "They're going to be surprised when they find Lord Melton in the carriage they catch. Lucky for us, his is identical."

Henry laughed, leaning back against the seat. "Ah, yes, the ploy we used to escape after we robbed the excise house. Good old Melton."

Knowing that they already knew about Henry's escape made me worry what else we would face, but we reached the hangar without further incident. Everett, the airship's pilot, ran toward us as we got out of the carriage. "The *Liberty*'s ready to go when you are."

"Good, because we ought to hurry," Henry said. "I don't know how long our little ruse will throw them off."

As we approached the airship, Flora handed Henry a bag. "Matthews put together some things for you, and there's some money in there, too." We reached the ship, and she embraced her uncle. "Take good care of yourself, Henry. I know I'll see you again."

"And you take care of yourself and the other children. Keep up your reading."

She released him and turned away, wiping tears off her face. He looked at me, smiling at me in a way that made my heart melt. "And you, Verity. You've got to be more careful."

"I'm not the one who got arrested."

"You could have been. You still could be. Please look after the children as well as you can. I know they'll end up under their grandfather's control, but he likes you, so there's a chance he'll keep you on. I know the cause is important, but please, for me, make the children your priority for now. You've done so much already."

Tears stinging my eyes, I nodded.

"I'll try to send word to you through the Mechanics," he continued.

"Maybe we'll even be able to arrange a meeting," I said, my voice rough with the tears that threatened to spill at any second.

"Wait until things die down."

"Of course," I agreed.

"Well, then, I suppose this is good-bye for now. Thank you again." He turned to board the ship, then turned back, dropped his bag, pulled me into his arms and kissed me. His mouth against mine was hungry, desperate, saying without words all those things that it was too late to say. When at last both of us needed to come up for air, he held me a bit longer, cradling my head against his shoulder. "I will see you again, Verity. Count on it," he whispered.

I was so stunned I couldn't speak or move as he picked up his bag and jumped on board. Flora joined me, hooking her arm through mine and leaning against me while we watched the crew release the mooring lines. Henry leaned over the side of the gondola, waving to us, as the ship lifted off the ground and sailed away. When it was out of sight, the carriage driver called out, "Come on, ladies, we need to get you back into the city."

Henry was safe, but our night wasn't over yet. We climbed into the carriage, and it started off down the bumpy country road. Soon after we turned onto the main road, we stopped. I heard a harsh voice asking, "What are you doing out here?"

"Coming back from a hunting trip," was the reply.

"We need to check inside."

"Be my guest."

Flora was still in her boy's clothes, and I was wearing the oversized coat and hat, but I didn't think either of us would pass as boys under close inspection. However, I didn't know if they cared about anything odd, so long as they didn't find their fugitive. The carriage door opened, and a uniformed man held a lantern up as he peered inside. Apparently satisfied that we weren't harboring an escaped prisoner, he shut the door, and soon the carriage resumed its journey.

We weren't stopped again on our way back into the city. I had the driver drop Flora and me off at the northernmost subway station, as that seemed the safest way to get around while the police and soldiers were on high alert. "What is this place?" she asked, gazing around the station with awe.

"It's a small railroad that runs underground. There's a station near the house."

"We can't go back there."

"What do you mean?"

"I got an emergency message in the night from you that your sick friend was dying, and I went out to sit with you. At least, that's what the staff knows. If the authorities are searching for Henry, they'll wonder where we've been, so we should be seen leaving wherever your friend is and coming home from there."

That made sense, so I had the subway operator take us all the way down to the station nearest the boardinghouse. While we were still in the station, I took off the overcoat I was still wearing and had Flora put it on over her boy's clothes. Underneath, I still had on my working attire. Flora carried a bag she'd brought with her from the carriage that I presumed contained her usual clothes.

Once we emerged on the street, we trudged as though coming home from a long night of work, making our way to the boardinghouse. Lizzie opened the door for us. "I assume he made it," she said.

"Yes, he's away," I replied. "But I'm afraid my sick friend didn't make it. Lady Flora was kind enough to come sit with me through the night and comfort me in my friend's passing."

Lizzie raised an eyebrow at that. "Then it sounds like we'll be having a funeral this week."

Flora raised her bag. "Is there somewhere I can change?"

Lizzie sent her to the bathroom while we went to Lizzie's room. I peeled off my working clothes. While I adjusted my dress and tidied my hair, Lizzie gestured down the hall where Flora had gone. "So, that's the girl my brother's been swooning over."

"You met her in the park."

"Only briefly. This seems to be an entirely different side of her."

"One I only just discovered, myself."

Flora joined us, looking more like her normal self. She paused, staring at me. "Well, you do look like you've had a sleepless night," she said with a satisfied nod. "And your eyes are even red and puffy. I think you'll be very convincing."

I put on my coat and hat, feeling myself transform back into a governess as I did so. As we stepped out the front door, Flora hooked her arm through mine and whispered, "Lean on me."

The events of the night were catching up with me, and the relief of having made it through made me weak, so I didn't have to act like I needed to lean on her. I was grateful for her support as we made it to a busy street where she could hail a cab.

The city was waking up as we journeyed uptown, and the morning traffic made our journey slower. I wasn't at all surprised when we reached the Lyndon mansion and saw a police carriage parked in front. Henry would have had to be stupid or crazy to go home after escaping, but I supposed the authorities had to look there.

At least, I hoped they were only looking for him. Might they be looking for me? I must have tensed because Flora said, "Relax, Miss Newton, and leave the talking to me."

We waited for Mr. Chastain to come out and pay the driver and open the cab door for us. Flora lent me her arm again as we made it up the front steps.

"Why are the police here, Chastain?" she asked once we were inside the foyer.

Before he could answer, a police officer stepped out of the parlor and faced us. "Where have you ladies been?" he demanded.

"Miss Newton had a very ill friend facing her final hours last night," Flora said, now sounding very much like Lady Flora Lyndon, granddaughter of the royal governor. "I sat with her as we waited for her friend to pass. It's been quite a trying night for both of us, so I would appreciate it if you told us your business here and then left us alone."

"Do you know the whereabouts of Lord Henry Lyndon?"

"He was arrested a few days ago, but we haven't seen him since then. I would have thought you'd know that."

"He was missing from his cell this morning."

I gasped in shock and leaned more heavily on Flora, feigning a fainting spell. The truth was, I was so scared right now that I didn't have to fake much. I thought my legs would go right out from under me.

"Can't you tell that she's already been through a lot?" Flora said. "She needs to sit down. Mrs. Talbot, please bring Miss Newton some tea."

Not waiting for the policeman to respond, Flora helped me into the parlor and eased me onto a sofa. She sank onto the sofa to sit next to me with her arm around me. "How can Uncle Henry be missing?" she demanded of the police officer, who'd followed us. "What have you done to him?"

"We didn't do anything, my lady," the officer said. I thought he looked a little flustered. I could hardly blame him, given the ferocity of Flora's glare.

"The soldiers might have. He was in military custody, wasn't he?"

"I, er, um, well, we don't believe the soldiers did anything. They reported him missing."

"I don't think he would come here. He should know you'd look for him here first."

"Do you know where he might be, my lady?"

"Have you checked our country estate? It's up in Westchester, on the river. I know he goes hunting sometimes, but I'm not sure where. He's very good in the outdoors. He's an expert on bugs, you know. He might be able to survive in the wilderness for quite some time."

The officer jotted this down in his notebook. "Thank you, my lady, you've been very helpful. We will keep you informed."

"Do let us know if you find him. We're quite worried. And I think you should look into the soldiers. They might not be kindly disposed to traitors and may have taken matters into their own hands."

He frowned, as though actually considering that, and made another note in his book. "Then I will leave you ladies alone." He started to leave, paused, and turned back. "And my sympathies for your loss, miss."

I nodded a thanks, and Mr. Chastain opened the door to show him out. Mrs. Talbot arrived with a cup of tea for me. "You poor dear, I'm so sorry about your friend," she said. I took the tea and gratefully let its hot sweetness revive me somewhat. "Did they say that Lord Henry had escaped?"

"They don't know," Flora replied. "He's missing."

"Oh my! I hope nothing's happened to him."

"All we can do is wait and pray," Flora said piously. "Now, I think both Miss Newton and I could use some rest. We've had a long and difficult night."

She helped me up the stairs, and I wasn't sure I'd have made it without her assistance. Now that my mission was done, I felt drained of all strength. Once we were in my room, she surprised me by giving me a big hug. "We did it!" she whispered. Before I could respond, she was gone.

I wasn't sure how long I slept, but I woke up groggy and hungry in the middle of the afternoon. I dressed and had just come out of my room when Rollo came tearing down the hallway from his room. "Grandfather's carriage is outside," he said.

I had a sinking feeling in the pit of my stomach. I supposed it was inevitable that the governor would take charge of the children, and even more so now that Henry was gone. I'd just hoped he would have waited longer.

I didn't make it down the stairs as quickly as Rollo did,

but I was there in time to see Mr. Chastain open the front door. Instead of the governor entering, it was a pair of footmen bearing a sedan chair in which a veiled woman sat.

When the door had closed behind them and the footmen set the chair on the ground, the woman sprang nimbly from her seat. She was about my height, and there was something familiar about the way she moved. Before I could figure out what it was she reminded me of, she threw back her veil. It was Lady Elinor.

"Aunt Elinor!" Rollo cried out. "I didn't think you could get out of bed."

"Can't and don't want to are two different things," she said. "I do calisthenics in my room when no one is there."

"Aunt Elinor!" Flora echoed, coming down the stairs to join us, Olive trailing behind her. "What are you doing here?"

"Why, I'm to be your new guardian, of course. I persuaded Father that he was far too busy to take on the additional responsibilities, and it was better for you children to remain in your own home. So I will stay here with you. Is the Blue Room free? As I recall, it has a nice view of the park. That's where I always stayed when I visited Lily."

"But are you up to it?" Flora asked.

"Just as long as I don't have to host dinner parties." She turned to the footmen. "You can bring in my trunks."

They carried the sedan chair away, and Elinor addressed me. "I think we should stick with your usual routine, the way Henry did things. I don't anticipate there needing to be any changes around here, though you don't have to worry about me disappearing to go hunt bugs."

"And Flora and I won't have to travel to have tea with you and discuss books," I said, still feeling a little dazed by how much had happened.

"Of course not! And that means we can do it every day. Really, Miss Newton, you won't have to change a thing." There was something odd about the way she said that, looking directly at me and emphasizing the words as though they were significant. She turned to head up the stairs to her room, and as I watched her go, her veil still hanging behind her head and down her back, I realized who she reminded me of.

Lady Elinor was the veiled lady who appeared at the Rebel Mechanics' events. Which meant she'd known all along about my involvement with them. And I suspected that meant our household was going to remain a rebel stronghold.

I couldn't help but smile. Things were about to get very interesting.

SHANNA SWENDSON earned a journalism degree from the University of Texas and used to work in public relations but decided it was more fun to make up the people she wrote about, so now she's a full-time novelist. She's the author of *Rebel Mechanics* and the popular adult romantic-fantasy series Enchanted, Inc. She lives in Irving, Texas, with several hardy houseplants and too many books to fit on the shelves.

CPSIA information can be obtained
at www.ICGtesting.com
Printed in the USA
LVOW11s0501250517
535770LV00001B/155/P